MY HEART ACHED. "LET ME COME IN."

"No."

"Just for a minute."

"Not tonight." She reached out: with her fingertips she touched my cheek.

"Leave it at this. For tonight. It's enough. We're lovers." She turned and lightly ran into the house.

I sat out in the car awhile.

Our date had been like the phone calls: not much had happened, but I was left exhilarated. Sara was skilled at getting to the door, as skilled as, out on the tennis court, she was at parrying a hard serve. In a way, though, I think I was getting what I wanted, and what I wanted was breathlessly to be a chasing a girl who was out of my reach, and who never—as she eluded me—did what I expected. . . .

FOOTBALL DREAMS

The Latest Books from SIGNET VISTA

Football
Dreams

David Guy

A SIGNET VISTA BOOK
NEW AMERICAN LIBRARY
TIMES MIRROR

SIGNET VISTA TRADEMARK REG. U.S. PAT. OFF. AND FOREIGN COUNTRIES
REGISTERED TRADEMARK—MARCA REGISTRADA
HECHO EN CHICAGO, IL., U.S.A.

SIGNET, SIGNET CLASSICS, MENTOR, PLUME, MERIDIAN AND NAL BOOKS are published by The New American Library, Inc., 1633 Broadway, New York, New York 10019

First Signet Printing, January, 1982

1   2   3   4   5   6   7   8   9

PRINTED IN THE UNITED STATES OF AMERICA

For Beth and Billy

The Past

Every gain has its loss, not every loss
       its gain but sinks into the waste
the primal pain unplastic the chaos
       without a future the astounding past

O monument of agony! if I could
       carve you a few hacking strokes
unfinished, you'd be worthy to be stood
       in Florence among the other rocks.

Paul Goodman

Football
Dreams

WHEN I WAS a kid I always had dreams of playing football. Those were the days of the fabulous pulling guards, short squat men, heavy of torso and thigh, remarkably fast for all their bulk, who would lead the sweeps for the fullback or halfback. You would see the defense rushing desperately for the sidelines while those three attackers swept wide, the guards chugging, pumping, for all they were worth, then abruptly, one after the other, ducking their heads and blowing a couple of defenders off their feet.

There were stories in sports magazines of guards who had taken out two men, three, with one block, of guards who had thrown one block and then gotten up to throw another. There were guards only a couple of steps slower than the fleetest halfback, who could nevertheless handle the most massive tackles, butting and digging against those fearsome giants who charged like bears, swung their arms like clubs.

Often fullbacks sang the praises of the skillful guards who had led them to paydirt. They were said to be jolly men, practical jokers, ukulele strummers, who liked nothing better than driving their heads into a linebacker's gut. They bowed in the huddle while the fullback got all the cheers. They were the cornerstones of any successful team.

Those were the days also of the fabled middle linebacker. An intense man, fierce, he was thirty pounds short of a tackle and a step or two shy of a halfback.

He keyed the defense. Ranging the entire field, he stopped the dive cold, was quick in lateral pursuit of a sweep, batted down middle-length passes, got a piece of every gang tackle. Sometimes on a pass he blitzed the quarterback, whipped him to the earth with a sickening thud. Occasionally he keyed for the entire game on a particularly dangerous back. He engaged with opposing players in verbal byplay that sometimes erupted into open brawls.

A difficult man even for his own teammates, he would take nothing short of a hundred percent. For days before a game he brooded, working himself into an implacable frenzy. Afterwards he could not be calmed, would carry a grudge from game to game and season to season. There was something inside him that no one, not even his family, could fully understand. He was the most vital and visible part of the defense.

The days of the fabulous pulling guards, the fabled middle linebacker: those were the days when I dreamed of football.

Part One

Chapter 1

EVENINGS WERE PRETTY dismal around the house my senior year. I hardly knew it at the time. It was just my mother and me, of course, which seemed a little strange. Probably I was only about half there. I would come in by the back door, the heat of the oven rising up to greet me, and I would give her a kiss as I passed through the kitchen, then drop my cloth bag of books—at least fifteen pounds' worth—in the hall, and walk in to collapse on a living room chair, slumped down against the back of it, my legs stretched out in front of me. I would still be wearing my sports jacket—a sturdy tan corduroy that year—easier to wear than carry, my tie stuffed into a side pocket. My shirt and slacks would be rumpled, the shirt still damp down the back. I would sit there and stare at the ceiling awhile, still, unbelievably, sweating a little.

It wasn't so much the practices as what happened after. Practice I was used to: calisthenics in the heavy awkward pads while the afternoon sun was still hot, muscles still sluggish and stiff; the quick rhythmic pounding feet, sudden falls, of the grass drill; fifteen minutes pushing the heavy sleds over the thick turf while the coaches stood obnoxiously on top of them and barked out commands; blocking and tackling drills, shouts at the shock of contact, pads clapping together like gunshots; long scrimmages half-speed and once a week full-speed; the endless series of fifty-yard sprints, searing our lungs, at the end.

But by the time we'd staggered up to the gym, stripped of our jerseys and shoulder pads and dragging them along, the late bus would already be waiting in the driveway, its motor running, so that while the boarders had a half-hour, could dally over their toilettes to impress the faculty wives, I had to rush through a steaming shower, throw my clothes on while I was still half-wet—shouts of "Late bus, late bus" echoing down the long dark hall—and carry most of my things, stumbling along in shoes but no socks, my hair still wet and uncombed, to finish dressing on the bus. The soccer and cross-country guys would have been sitting there for fifteen minutes. I really hated to have inconvenienced them. It was a walk of about a half-mile from the bus stop to my house, four lanes of Penn Avenue traffic hurtling by, that load of books growing heavier and heavier. There was a steep little hill up to our street. My thighs would still be quivering as I got to the door.

It was perhaps *this* aspect of football that coaches felt was valuable for building character.

My mother would step into the living room quietly, as if expecting to find me already asleep. "Do you want to take a nap before we eat?" she'd say.

"No. I'm really not tired."

That was known as saving your mother from the hard truth.

"It'd be easy to keep dinner warm."

"It's all right. I'm ready anytime."

My mother was a small woman, and petite. She wore her hair short, in a pixie, and for a few years it had been graying some from its dark brown; for a while we had kidded her about touching it up, though I didn't talk about it that year. She had a small thin face, small hands, would be wearing a house dress with a bright apron covering the front of it. She didn't eat much, and ate very quietly, with impeccable manners.

She might as well have been sitting down to dinner with a prehistoric beast. She would carry out the plates, hers with its little helpings, mine piled high and practically overflowing with whatever we were having, a haystack of spaghetti, say, that looked like the platter

6

for two that comes with a half-bottle of cheap Chianti, and I would lay into it. There wouldn't be much talk. My mother didn't want to disturb me, the way you don't bother a large dog that is wrestling with a slab of meat, tearing at it with its teeth. Whatever we were having—it was a conditioned reflex—I always went out for more.

I couldn't have been much company. It wasn't just that I was tired, or that I wanted to be rude. It was, I think, that a part of me wasn't there, was numbed, and quiet, and hiding in my silence.

The night before Hargrove, though, she did speak. She had a lot on her mind.

"Are you boys ready for the game?" she said.

All my mother's words about football were marked by a certain vagueness. She was the kind of mother who, when she went down to the field, had to be pointed in the right direction so she'd know where the game was.

"I guess," I said. "Ready as we're going to be."

"I talked to Anne Malcolm today. She was saying Hargrove has quite a big team."

"They have a few more to choose from." It was a public school, had 1200 students to our 240.

"I guess that's kind of a problem for you."

"It's the same every year."

She took a small piece of food, chewed it slowly and carefully, trying to be as casual as possible. She put down her fork, touched her mouth with a napkin. As if it had just occurred to her, was totally incidental to what she was thinking, she said, "Do you think you'll try the contacts?"

God. "Mother." I put down my fork. "Not the contacts again."

"I saw Dr. Saltz in Oakland just the other day. He still says you're a good wearer."

"I know that's what he says. That's what he says to me every time I go in there. I can hear the words. I can't see him, though, because my eyes are so full of tears from having the contacts in."

"I can't understand it. He says your eyes have made the adjustment."

7

"He wants my eyes to make the adjustment. He wants to rake in all that money."

"Dan. He's an old friend of the family."

"He ought to have *his* eyes examined. I walk around school all day feeling my way along the walls, crying like a baby. Tim Deitz came up to me the other day and handed me a yardstick to use as a cane. I step out into the sunlight and react like Count Dracula. It's been two months now. It's no use."

"I just want you to be able to see out there."

"I can see okay."

"You can*not* see. I know what the charts say."

"I don't need to be able to see. The players I have to worry about are inches away. They're coming right at me."

"It's just I'm afraid some enormous thug's going to sneak up and clobber you."

Apparently she thought there were places to hide out there. That the players all sneaked around quietly and suddenly leaped forth to dismember somebody. About like a dark alley in the ghetto late at night.

"I can see them before they sneak up on me. I can hear them before that. Hell, half those guys, I can smell them."

"It doesn't do any good to joke about it."

"Mom. I'm a senior. I've been playing football for three years now. I know what I'm doing. I'm ready for this. I'll be all right."

"I know you'll be all right." It was the way she would have spoken if I'd been flying off on a bombing mission. Oh, he'll be all right. "I just wish the contacts had worked out."

Since the beginning of the summer, all her anxieties had been soothed by the thought of those contacts. You'd have thought they held some kind of magic. The problem wasn't that she wanted me to wear contacts while I was playing football. It was that she didn't want me to play football.

We ate in silence for a while. Relative silence. No room where a first-string tackle was eating could be entirely silent.

"I think I'll go over to the Malcolms' after dinner," I

8

said. "I don't have much work." I had plenty, but I wasn't going to do it.

"It's nice they don't give you much before the game." Fat chance. "Anne said Hargrove is known for having a good team. They're in some other league."

In another league was right. "They were good last year. They don't have a whole lot coming back."

I could tell she had no idea what that meant—I was getting a little idiomatic—but she wasn't about to ask.

"I mean they have a lot of new players," I said. "The old ones graduated."

"This is probably a stupid question. I know you have high hopes. But do you boys expect to win?"

That was the kind of question a football player was supposed to spit on. Hell yes, we're gonna win. Naw, I ain't tired. But I wasn't going to string my mother along.

"Not really," I said. Knute Rockne was turning in his grave. "We're all saying we're going to win. We really believe we can play well. But they're a much bigger school. You wouldn't say we were favored."

We were expected to get slaughtered.

"You won't be disappointed?"

Lord. She was worried about how I'd feel.

"No. I won't be disappointed."

It was early September, still a light and balmy evening even after we finished our dinner. I stepped out front for a while. We lived on a small narrow private street, solid two-story brick houses, white-shuttered, facing each other from behind little lawns. Three towering massive oaks across from us shaded practically the whole street. Things were quiet that evening except for the dull rumble of traffic from Penn, a short block away. A sprinkler was waving lightly back and forth across the corner lawn. An old couple, the Bollingers, sat out on their porch across the street. Round, bald, his face like a death mask, Mr. Bollinger sat motionless for a while, then leaned sideways in his chair and yelled at me across the street. "Pitt and Miami."

I stood there a moment, considering. "Pitt by three."

"Go on." He waved a hand dismissively at me. "Dreamer."

9

I grinned. He never picked Pitt against anybody.

To the left of our house was a cyclone fence around a big yard that led to the next street. I didn't know how it looked for a 200-pound tackle to be climbing that fence—probably as if it were about to buckle and collapse—but I didn't want to go around. I had never been much of a climber. I managed to clamber up one side, hoist myself over the little spikes on the top, and fall off the other. I was always just glad to have avoided serious injury. At least the Bollingers got a good laugh out of it.

That was the yard where we had always played as kids, gently sloped, so one team was going downhill. You know what goal to defend if you won the toss. Four- or five-man teams, little leather helmets like you saw in the old pictures of Red Granger, pads that must have been made out of layers of cardboard, those tight little huddles where we all put our arms around each other's shoulders and cooked up some crazy play. Huddle, huddle, piss in a puddle. The intent, serious faces of children. We couldn't have been more involved if it had been the Orange Bowl, on those long autumn weekend afternoons when parents would finally start calling us for dinner, and we still wouldn't want to leave, shifting the teams around to get in another play or two. "First team to score wins," as if the fifty-odd (and I do mean odd) touchdowns already scored that afternoon didn't mean a thing. Sometimes I thought that was the real football, that anything you did after that paled in comparison.

I came out from between a couple of houses onto the street. Across the way the Hardys were sitting on their front porch. They did that most evenings, Mr. Hardy staring at the paper with a big cigar in his mouth, Mrs. Hardy doing some sewing or needlepoint, Rachel sitting there with a book. She was one of the few girls of her age in the world who could stand being in the presence of her parents for more than a few minutes, much less sit out on the front porch in full view of everyone. She was always, always, reading a book, usually a fat novel by an author I had barely heard of. Maybe she just didn't notice her parents were there. She must have been a little embarrassed about them; it was said she was the smartest girl at Ellsworth, the local girls' school, and I doubt that either of her parents had finished high school. Mr. Hardy had a booming car dealership, and was a quiet unpretentious man, strong and solid, the kind who seemed to have fought his way to the top with a monkey wrench. I had always thought there was something pretty about Rachel, except that she was always wearing thick glasses and what looked like a frown. Maybe she was just deep in thought.

As I walked by, Mrs. Hardy came to the edge of the porch. "Dan," she said. "Danny." She was a small plump energetic woman, who was always doing something with her hands. "We seen your picture in the paper. You and Bobby Malcolm."

"Oh," I said, as if I were embarrassed, or had forgotten it was in. "Yeah."

"I didn't see it," Rachel said. "What was your picture in the paper for?"

"They're on the Arnold football team," Mrs. Hardy said. "John seen it in the sports section. I said, see that? They used to play right over in that yard. We seen them get their start."

"You're on the football team?" Rachel said.

"It was right in the paper," Mrs. Hardy snapped, as if my words wouldn't have been enough. "They got a game tomorrow night."

I couldn't believe Rachel didn't know. It had been my impression, from God knows where, that the girls over at Ellsworth sat around drooling over the roster. Maybe Rachel was too busy with her books. Anyway, *now* she knew. Time enough. Now she could swoon at my feet.

"How awful," Rachel said, looking back at her book.

"We're all so proud of you boys," Mrs. Hardy said. "Aren't we, John?"

"We're proud of them boys," Mr. Hardy said. He had not looked at me, or stopped reading the paper, but he did remove the cigar from his mouth, as if that

11

acknowledged my presence. "But they won't be beating no Hargrove."

Mrs. Hardy raised her eyebrows, smiled, shrugged. At least she liked me.

"Good luck to you, Danny," she said. "You and little Bobby too."

"Little?" Rachel said.

"They'll be needing it," Mr. Hardy said.

I walked the three blocks over to the Malcolms' house, but didn't ring the bell when I got there. I had told Rosy I'd be coming over, and I knew that after a while he'd see me and come out. I sat on the steps at the edge of his lawn and watched a couple of skinny little girls across the street who were learning to skate, wobbling, balancing as if on a tightrope, giggling uncontrollably, holding each other up.

We called him the Rose because he had a terrific reputation for farting. I don't think he really farted much more than the next man; he just got careless at unfortunate moments, during a school dance, maybe, when the band had settled into a quiet number, or at the lunch table when he had the place beside the teacher. When beans were served everyone looked at him and laughed. He was one of those guys that things just happened to: he had a way of saying "Oh shit" just when he stepped in it, so we'd all say, "That's right" or "At least he knows what he's stepping in." But I'd known him since we were four years old, and we'd spent all kinds of time together, playing ball in that long sloping yard, sneaking a smoke in his attic, exploring the bowling alleys and pool halls downtown. We'd started at Arnold together in ninth grade, and I'd always thought it funny that from Point Breeze they should get two of the—what should I say?—stoutest kids in the class.

After a few minutes he came out. The Rose was big, no question about it, a little taller than I, and probably heavier; he had a funny way of walking, up on his toes, with his belly stuck out and preceding him, arms swaying back and forth. It was a little strut, though he didn't mean it that way. He walked down and sat beside me on the steps. We didn't go for elaborate greetings. What the hell, we'd been together almost constantly for years.

"How'd you like Grupp's performance this afternoon?" I said.

"Magnificent. Give him an Oscar."

"I know it made you feel all warm inside."

"The man couldn't be more full of shit."

That afternoon, in our last practice before the big game, our coach had become enraged at some trivial mistake, slammed his clipboard to the ground, and shouted so they could probably hear at Hargrove that we were the worst team he'd ever coached. He was short and round, and stomped on the clipboard a few times for emphasis. Probably that evening, puffing on a long black cigar, he had decided that moment was a masterpiece of psychological motivation.

"God, I'm tired," I said. "I ache. I can't believe how tired I am, with that game tomorrow night."

"You getting nervous?"

"Not that I've noticed. Probably I'm just numb."

"I am. God. I could shit."

Anytime in my life I have been about to make a change, some major change, I have always been ready for it a little early, the way people feel ready for a vacation a couple of weeks before it comes. I would be leaving home the next year—at that point I didn't know for where—and that evening I felt ready to go, or already gone, as if I were coming back to visit a place where I'd lived once and spent many happy hours.

It seemed touching to me, I was almost getting sentimental, sitting there with the Rose and thinking of all the things we'd done together, the pickup games of baseball in the narrow street that ended half the time in a hurried flight from a broken window, the nights we'd put on boxing gloves and slugged it out in his basement laundry room, the evening before his Mongoloid brother had been put in a special boarding school and would come out in the street with us, slobbering and crazy-eyed and saying all kinds of weird things, and I was all choked up trying not to laugh, too young to understand, and the Rose was getting redder

13

and redder, trying not to cry. When something big was coming up, something a little frightening, I always got sentimental that way. Maybe I was just trying to avoid the fear.

"You know, Dan," Rosy said. He turned to me with a pained, embarrassed expression; it was strong emotion on his face, that always looks awkward. "Tomorrow's the night we've been waiting three years for."

I nodded, swallowed. I was starting to feel a few butterflies myself. I pictured those kids in the leather helmets, the stark serious faces, fat little bodies.

It was the night we'd been waiting three years for, or more years than that, and already I was moving a little beyond it.

II

It was hot the next night like the worst nights in August, the air soupy and thick, a fog hovering low in patches of mist. You just had to step outside to start sweating. A perfect night for football. On the way over, the team bus was dead silent, all of us sitting still and staring straight ahead, little rodents gnawing at our guts. We got caught in the traffic jam for the game, so that off in the haze we could see the stadium lights, while all around us people in cars were shouting things at the bus, leaning out to bang on the sides. "Just ignore it, fellas," Grupp said calmly. "Don't stoop to their level." But two minutes later he had bolted out the door, shouting at the top of his lungs, "Shut the hell up! And keep your filthy hands off this bus!" He climbed back to his seat, muttering darkly. A tin can hit the side of the bus. The man was an example to us all.

Finally we made it up to the team entrance of the stadium, where the usual vagrants and perverts were hanging around, trash on the ground; you could see through the gate the bright field and all the color in the stands. Grupp had us take a lap before our drills, out on the field where the lights were glaring down. You could hear the noise beyond them, booing and screaming, a low steady roar, but you couldn't see anything for the glare, just blackness. I was tight and stiff from the bus ride anyway and could hardly move, stumbling on the chewed-up turf of the sidelines, and it seemed weird, lights blasting down, the fog drifting around, and all that noise, when all you could see was the players on the field. We did our calisthenics and went through some drills, cracking a little and loosening up. Apparently this was the big time. It seemed more like playing football at a carnival.

I wasn't in on the kickoff, not having much speed in the open field, and that play from the sidelines is always a blur, bodies flying by and hurdling blocks or getting cut down, the roar of the crowd hopeful and growing louder as the blockers converge, tacklers give chase, until the whole thing ends in a crash. But the roar started to build immediately again, and the Rose and I trotted out for the line of scrimmage, our gold uniforms almost luminescent under the lights. The guy over me that night was tall and rangy, looked strong, like a lean old farm boy, and was some kind of offensive captain; all night he was screaming signals to the rest of the line. "Strong right!" the quarterback would shout, and "Blue!" he would answer. "Blue!" the quarterback would shout, and he would yell "Fourteen!" Made lots of sense.

He kept watching me that first play, wouldn't take his eyes away, his face alert and eager. But I was solid and taut in a three-point stance, and when he charged with the snap, I was on him, standing him straight with a forearm to the chest, and he was digging away but I was holding, holding. I could feel the hitting against his back, hear the shouts; my legs went out from under me and I hit with my shoulder on the kid with the ball. Gain of a half a yard.

That was the way it went, that first half we'd waited all those years to play. I didn't have time to think about the big things because I had too many little things to worry about, like where the wide back was lining up, or whether the inside tackle was edging my way. The kid over me on offense was more along my lines, wide and hard and low to the ground. He never looked at me once that night, as if he were timid. Hitting him was like running into a load of sandbags.

But blocking was my strong suit, Coach Wiggins had taught me, to stick my head in a good spot and keep my feet moving. Tough as that kid was, I handled him. Late in the first quarter we nearly scored, drove sixty yards before they stacked us up around the twenty, and about half the plays went right up the middle. We took it to them. Near the end of that drive, though, the Rose came up from a pile hissing and wincing and shaking his head, holding his hand. We knew there wasn't a thing on the bench, and didn't look over that way. We didn't even ask him how he was, for fear of what he might say.

It wasn't until halftime that I realized how beat I was, the first chance I'd had to think about it, walking to the locker room over the slick floor of their gym, our footsteps clattering in echoes down the long dark hallway. As soon as I sat down I knew it was no sure thing I'd be getting up again. My jersey was soaked a dark gold, one side of my face scraped, my knuckles skinned and bleeding, leg muscles twitching as if in their death throes. Everyone who had played looked the same, flushed and wet and dirty. The back of Rosy's hand was all puffed up and blood red. I didn't know what had happened over on the sidelines—I hadn't had a chance to get over there—but the scrubs were suddenly all worked up about the game. The kid next to me was talking a blue streak, running over plays as if he wished I could have been there to see them, and when I didn't have much to say, he finally grabbed my arm. "Listen," he said. "You aren't tired, are you?" I just looked at him.

Suddenly Grupp burst into the room, all five feet six of him, his round little face beaming as if we'd just gotten a Rose Bowl bid, or, better yet, as if his team from three years before had rematerialized. He started screaming about how he didn't care what he'd ever said, in the first half we'd played a superb ball game, we looked like champions out there. While he was going on, Coach Wiggins came through and looked over his linemen one by one, leaning down to shake my knee when he came to me, which was worth all the words Grupp ever said in his life. Nobody thought we'd even be in that game, a bunch of seniors who were starting for the first time against an enormous high school which only scheduled us every year as a warm-up, and here it was halftime with no score. Quite a surprise. I chewed on an orange and watched my legs twitch.

But it was something to hear Grupp eat his words like that; he never admitted anything was right. While I was loosening up out on the field for the second half, who should appear in my path but the man himself, his chest butting mine and his face shining up just inches away, a look in his eyes as if he'd just tripped over the Hope Diamond. He asked if my man was big—he always wanted to know if a kid was big; it was everything to him—and if I could handle him, which made me want to ask if by chance he'd seen the first half. Then he went into a long lecture about staying low and penetrating, banging away at my chest with his little fat fist. This truly was a great coach.

But I'd even begun to believe it all myself, that we might have a shot at winning that game. After we received the second-half kickoff we went on a rampage again, moving down the field like a plague. Everything went, end runs, off tackles, dives up the middle, short passes. Grunfeld in particular ran like a dervish, bouncing off tacklers as if he were in a pinball machine. Off in a corner of the stands our little cluster of fans was screaming, and everyone in the huddle wore that hurried anxious look—the same one you wear when you've got her in the back seat and everything's coming off, blouse, bra, panties: you can't believe it. Shealy would spit out a play and we'd burst out of there like a bomb going off, as if it didn't matter what we ran as long as we got it off fast enough, while our luck lasted. It was like a kid fighter who's just caught his man with a lucky right and has him on the ropes; he's flailing away with things he never learned anywhere, going back to the way he fought when he was twelve years old—hand him a chair and he'll bash the guy's brains out.

17

But something happened again near the goal line—right down where we could see that huge stand of trees beyond the end zone—even though nothing we did changed: the linemen were firing out like torpedoes, the backs bouncing and twisting and clawing for the extra yard. We couldn't get it over, like the old man brought finally to the beautiful maiden and he's got it up like a poker but can't come off.

Finally Menhardt tried a field goal and it was the same thing: he told me later if he'd hit that ball squarely it would have carried fifty yards, knocked down one of those trees, but it just squiggled off the side of his foot the way it used to in the backyard games, when the kid holding pulled his hand away because he was afraid he'd get kicked. All that uproar and there still wasn't any score.

We never got a scoring drive going again. It was finally just two plays they beat us on, two long passes when somebody made a mistake, the second one way into the fourth quarter. It wasn't until the last few seconds that I finally got taken out, so some JV—junior varsity player—could get a thrill, the score 12–0 and Hargrove with the ball. Platt, the captain from Arnold's famous team three years before, was standing beside our bench looking very collegiate, and he said we looked tough out there but just didn't have it when it counted. "Yeah," I remarked.

Finally the gun went off and we straggled back to the bus. A bunch of guys were standing there under the high lights of the parking lot, and some girls too, trying to look as if somebody had just died. Sara Warren was there, in a little green cheerleading suit. The girls' school sent over a couple of cheerleaders for our games. You never knew who they were going to be until the beginning of the season, but you might have made a good guess that year. She was faintly smiling, as she always did, not a trace of that fake sadness in it. It was like at a party or dance, when she was looking my way: I could never tell if she meant it for me or not. But then she walked over toward me through the crowd.

"We lost," I said.

"Yes."

"We weren't too hot."

"Don't be stupid."

I had just been saying what I was supposed to, and she knew it. I grinned.

"We were okay," I said.

"You got what you wanted," she said.

Sara always knew the score. I never quite knew how.

"Yes," I said.

"Enjoy it," she said.

We all started climbing in the bus. Tim Deitz, who had played beside me both ways, fell flat on his face trying to take the first step. The Rose told me when we sat down that he thought his hand was broken; he found out the next day it was. Some kid in the back kept coughing the whole way home, and everybody else was dead quiet. All in all it was a pretty gruesome ride back.

But it was peaceful later, still and dark, just the gym lights on, when I'd had my shower and was all cleaned up and walked out to the car. Nearly everybody was gone. One knee was stiff and that scrape on my face was pretty sore, but I thought I would live. Finally it had cooled off a little, a light breeze blowing, as if I needed it then. Up on the hill just the bell tower of the chapel showed, bright with its spotlights, and down below me in shadows was the field, the blocking sleds covered, where we had spent all those days getting ready. I took my time, nursing some bruises, and after I put the top down I just sat in the car awhile, that beat-up old Nova that had belonged to my father. He had loved that little car.

So finally I had played in the Hargrove game.

Looking back on it all, the way you can from a distance of years, I think that moment out in the car, in the darkness, the cool breeze, was the closest I came to being content in all my four years at Arnold Academy.

Part Two

Chapter 2

ON FRIDAY EVENINGS, regularly, when I was ten years old, eleven, my mother and I took a streetcar downtown. I loved it there, the towering buildings, the rush and the lights. People seemed different downtown, dressed smartly and looking healthy and all in a hurry, women taking short quick steps in their tight skirts and high heels. We got off the streetcar at the end of the line and walked to the Jenkins Arcade, that interior of white stone and marble, high bright ceilings, shops with display windows on either side. At the elevator the uniformed operator nodded, "Hello, Mrs. Keith," took us up to the seventh floor, where the halls were narrow and the walls a drab green, the doors of heavy brown wood with frosted glass. It was the kind of old hallway that inspired dread of the offices it housed. We entered the waiting room, among patients sitting stiffly in the hard heavy wooden chairs, and after a while the door to one of the offices opened, the doctor in his long white coat stepped out, holding a card, and the patients turned expectantly, beaming at the sight of him. There was a warmth in the room. They all, it seemed, wanted him to recognize them.

But he would notice me, forget about the card for a moment, and smile. "Hello, Danny," he'd say. The patients all looked my way, smiled as they noticed the resemblance. He was my father.

He was a big man, burly, with broad shoulders, a thick chest, a heavy gut. You wouldn't have thought to call him soft, and he wasn't. That was the way fathers were supposed to look in the fifties. He had a heavy growth of dark curly hair on his chest, graying a little, and down onto his belly, and on his heavy forearms. Along his right forearm was a broad flat scar, and on the underside a little dimple, from a bad break he had sustained as a kid. It was a heavy warm tough body he had; when he hugged me I felt lost in its size, its huge strength. His legs were lean, well formed, the limbs of a sprinter, they did not seem to go with the torso he carried, though for the hard trim muscular body he had had in pictures of his youth, they were just about right. The hair on his head was brown, graying and thinning. He always wore glasses; without them he could barely see.

When the last patient had left we walked back into the office, with its strong antiseptic smell, everything starchy and white.

"How was the streetcar?" my father said, hearing us come in.

"Great," I said.

"Awful as usual," my mother said. "Those drunks in East Liberty. It used to be so nice."

"It's colorful," my father said. "You're squeamish." We had walked into the little room where he was taking off his examining coat. "You're supposed to enjoy the spectacle of the city."

My father never shied away from the seedy and peculiar.

"The winos of East Liberty are not my idea of a pleasant spectacle," my mother said.

He hugged her—my father was a great hugger— pulling her up a little off her feet. "Ben," she said, looking down, embarrassed at the thought of the receptionist still in the office, but he laughed, and kissed her, a long kiss on the mouth.

"Ben," she said again.

"All right." He let her down. "Let's go to dinner."

He knew better than to try to hug me.

He liked to take us out to the restaurant where he had lunch, mostly just a bar, specializing in seafood. It was dark, and loud, smelled of lobster, and broiled fish,

24

and the heavy scents of liquor. A huge blue marlin hung over the long mirror behind the bar. "Did somebody catch that, Tony?" my father once asked our waiter. "Oh hell, Doc," he said. "Paper-mâché." The waiters walked around quickly, straining under heavy trays, and shouted insults at each other, like cab drivers. They all knew Dr. Keith. My father loved the food there, especially the soups at lunch, fish and clam chowder, mulligatawny, Philadelphia pepper pot. He loved broiled red snapper, and bluefish, tender cuts of lamb and roast beef, all fresh vegetables.

He didn't eat quickly, but with huge enjoyment, taking large bites, his jaw cracking as he chewed. He always took the first strand of asparagus in his fingers, held it high in the air, and lowered it slowly into his mouth. His face lit up at the sight of brussels sprouts. "Little cabbages, Dan." He liked a big mug of beer with his dinner, and drank it in large swallows; as he took the mug away from his mouth there was a perceptible smack from his lips, and a light sigh, "Ah!"

After dinner we would take in a movie, then walk back to the parking garage where he kept the car.

"Why do you always cry at the movies?" I would say to my mother. We would usually have gone to one of the heavy melodramas of the late fifties.

"She likes to cry," my father said. "She enjoys it more that way. How come you never cry?"

"*You* never cry," I said.

"True." He could not get worked up about the play-acting of Doris Day and Frank Sinatra.

"Anyway," I said, "I don't cry anymore. I'm too tough."

II

There is a picture of my father with his father—who had also been a doctor, and died when I was young—at an early medical convention. My father's face is still boyish, and, as in the pictures of almost everyone in those days, he holds a little cigarette between his fingertips. But they are serious men, imposing—my father was just starting to acquire the heft he would carry later—and wearing dark double-breasted suits. They stare at the camera and do not smile.

Our church was a massive building of black stone, shaggy with green leaves, or jagged, in the winter, with brown dead clinging vines. On the mornings of communion the atmosphere was especially heavy, the organ playing a quiet, mournful, slightly brassy melody, and as it finally paused the elders entered from either side at the front with a heavy tread, in unison, that sounded almost menacing. Their faces were grave, and they took their seats in the front pew—a loud crack from the aging wood—with a kind of ultimate finality. From as early as I can remember my father was one of those elders. A couple of times in my memory, an older person—and we had a slew of them in that church—would collapse during the service, with a groan or a gasp from the folks around him, and the fearful eyes of everyone would turn to our pew, where my father would already be starting to stand. A certain awe attached to him in that setting. He was the man people turned to.

But that is not the man I remember. I remember the man who, getting home from work, would change into some old khaki slacks and a pair of slippers, and come downstairs in his shirtsleeves to read the paper. He drank a highball before dinner, and as much as drinking it, he seemed to enjoy spreading out in the kitchen and intricately mixing it, with ice, and orange juice, and a heavy slug of bourbon. He smoked a few cigarettes through the evening—he didn't think a doctor should smoke at work—and leaned back in his chair to expel the smoke, blowing it gently in billows toward the ceiling. As a child I loved to sit in the chair with him, feeling his warm breath on the top of my head, and catching the slight antiseptic odor he had, and the light smell of sweat. Even as I grew older, and sat on the nearby couch, his presence was soothing. The click of ice in his glass, and the rustle of the newspaper, and the soft sound of his breathing nearly put me to sleep.

In the evening he sat in the same chair with a book,

sipping a beer. He was a serious reader, of good literature—mostly American authors from the first half of the century—but he read with the same gusto that he had for everything else, so that often he would come upstairs to read a passage to me or to my mother, and when he hit a comic passage his shouts of laughter, in a loud baritone, echoed throughout the house and, if the windows were open, all up and down our little street.

It is that man I remember, who loved to drive, who on a long trip could drive ten or twelve hours without so much as yawning, his left arm resting out the window, his right steering easily; now and then, pounding the top of the car, he broke into a song. On our fishing trips to the seashore he sat in the stern of the little outboard we rented, back by the boiling wake, letting her rip—I was high in the bow, bouncing over the waves—and he grinned, shouted a greeting at the other boats, took us out of the bay and into the Atlantic if he felt like it.

When we stopped he dangled a hand in the water, scooped some onto his neck against the heat, holding the heavy gear in his right hand. When he got a hit he gave a hit back, wincing and biting his lip. He ate thick meat sandwiches, putting away a third with one bite, leaned back to guzzle a Coke, sat munching Fig Newtons the way another man munches on peanuts. He said he didn't care if we caught a thing, and often we didn't, but he loved to get out on the water, and navigate that little boat, feel the sun and the wind, and get a line down.

It was he who took me to the ball games at Forbes Field, shouting at a hit or a good catch, and he picked me up in Oakland after the games at Pitt Stadium, because he couldn't get out of work on Saturday. He would come out on the street to throw the ball around with me, or hit some out—sometimes to half the kids in the neighborhood—taking a quick stutter step and cutting down at the ball, so it would skitter along the cement, or sail gently into the air. In front of him kids jumped for the ball, lunged for it, gathered in packs under a pop fly, while he stood with the bat on his shoulder, grinning.

From the time I was twelve, though, I seldom had him out on the street playing anything but football.

Rosy and I would show up regularly on autumn afternoons when he was getting home from the office, tossing his gray felt hat onto the rack in the hall closet, or on Sunday afternoons, when he was sitting around looking through *The New York Times*.

"Dad," I'd say. "Could we go out for a few?"

"What's the matter with you kids? Can't you throw the ball to each other?"

"It's not the same," I said. "We can't get it as far."

"So don't go out as far."

"That's not like football," Rosy said. "The little passes we can throw." Rosy was picturing the long high spirals we used to see at the stadium.

My father's shoulders slumped—he was thinking of the highball he was about to make, or a long Sunday afternoon with the *Times* magazine section—and sometimes he said no, not that day, but often as not he pulled out his old windbreaker and came with us.

"What's the big thing about football?" he said one day. "You used to play baseball all afternoon. Or you could take up basketball. Something you can do yourselves."

"It's the season," I said. "It's exciting. We want to play it when we get older."

"We got the build for it," Rosy said. He was perfectly serious. Every fat kid in America thought he was shaped expressly for football. He thought all the chocolate creamfilled cupcakes had nothing to do with it.

"I can't wait till you can throw your own passes," my father said.

Did we detect a note of sarcasm?

The whole thing was perfectly understandable. Since third grade, on a day when the school doctor had been making the rounds and we had both tipped the scales at eighty-three pounds, Rosy and I had been known as the fattest kids in the class. We never won any foot races. We couldn't get the rebounds in basketball. We could catch a baseball if we could get to it: *if* we could get to it. In gym class we couldn't do the forward roll (if it had been the sideways roll we would have been in business). In a fight the other kid could dance out of our way, catch us off balance and give us a shove, and we would awkwardly fall on our butts (a loud boom from the bass drum). But in football uniforms, our pudgy bodies resembled the burly figures we saw week after week at the stadium. Our fat faces in helmets looked like the grim meaty visages the pros had. Football was to be the means we would use to turn what we had into something with dignity, that inspired respect, even awe.

I had stacks of tattered football magazines that I pored over endlessly.

"Doesn't it ever get boring?" my father said. "It's all pretty much alike." As a lover of literature, he was bothered most of all by my taste in magazines. "At least *read* something else."

"I want to read this," I said. "It's never boring."

Like a believer with his prayer book, I was poring again and again over the same words, but the spirit in me was ever new.

Out on the street, my father faded back with his quick little stutter steps, pumping the ball. He really wasn't much of a passer. Maybe that was why he didn't like to come out. He had the light easy motions of an athlete, like memories of his boyhood, but he cocked the ball up around his ear, threw with a quick snap that always floated the ball too much, in a wobbly spiral. It was just as well he was throwing to a pair of twelve-year-old kids who couldn't have caught a hard pass anyway. The day would be crisp, or cold, and he wore that light beige windbreaker, standing back by the hedge—later replaced by a cyclone fence—at the end of the street. In our dime-store equipment, the Rose and I were chugging down the street, flatfooted, our feet slapping the pavement. The Rose always made a tremendous amount of noise when he was going out, huffing and groaning and snorting, as if he were dragging a load up a hill, or as if somebody were beating him with a stick. The ball came wobbling out, floating, and since our hands were still too small we tried to bounce it off our forearms, or chests, clutching at the bounce and trying to hold on.

29

"Aww!" Rosy would shout, or "Oh!" or "Oof!" snatching at the ball as if it were greased.

"Oh!" we would shout, dropping the ball, or "Hey!" if we caught it.

"Lord," my father would say at the end of the street, shaking his head. "You two are a pair."

One evening that autumn—the Rose and I were in seventh grade at Point Breeze, the local grade school—I sat down with my father in the living room. For the past couple of weeks we had taken it easy on him about throwing the football, since we had a bigger favor to ask.

"We need a referee for a football game," I said. Might as well get right to the point.

"You kids can referee yourselves," my father said. "The team that punches hardest wins."

"This isn't a regular game. This is special. Us and St. Stevens."

"Who and St. Stevens?"

"Point Breeze. Me, Rosy, and some other guys."

Briefly, he closed his eyes. "Oh Lord, Dan."

"We can take them. I know it. I got all kinds of eighth-graders lined up."

"Where'd you get this idea?"

"The games we have are never any good. Three- or four-man teams. We want to have full teams. Or at least nine guys on a side."

"Those St. Stevens kids are tough. The nuns see to it."

"The nuns are no worse than our teachers." We had an eighth-grade teacher who, in my opinion, could have played linebacker for any major college in the country. Her name was Miss Frimbo.

"It'll be like playing Notre Dame."

"We'll be like Ohio State."

"Can't you get a priest or somebody to referee?"

"There's going to be somebody from their side too. But we've got to get somebody for us. Nobody else will do it." That wasn't exactly true. No one else had been asked. But I wanted my father to be there.

"All right." He shrugged, leaned back in his chair. "You'll probably need a doctor in attendance anyway."

30

We walked over to the school field together on the day of the game, Rosy, and me, and my father. The Rose and I were all done up in our equipment, the jerseys too tight, so our shoulder pads were sticking out crazily, our bellies bulging at the bottom. The weather had been bitter cold, and wet, but it was bright that day, so it wasn't too bad. It was the kind of autumn air that aches in your lungs when you've run too hard. The trees were nearly bare, and the dry leaves lay around in piles; we kicked our way through them along the sidewalk.

"I guess I was just about your age when I gave up football for good," my father said.

"How come?" Rosy said.

I knew, of course. But I wanted to hear the story again. I loved hearing the stories of my father's childhood. Things seemed real in his stories, and funny, and adventurous. Kids had known how to live in those days.

"It was pretty stupid. We called them football games, but they were more like free-for-alls. We had a ball, but no equipment or anything. Out there in our street clothes. The yard was all bumpy, with some rocks scattered around. But we tackled just the same. On some kind of crazy play, we didn't even really have plays, but the ball went skittering away and we were all charging after it. I don't think I got there first, but I can remember diving for it about the same time as some other kids. Somehow my arm got twisted as I was coming down. Johnny Kessler fell on it." He showed Rosy the dimple on his arm. It looked like a little belly button. "The bone came out there."

I'm not sure that was the perfect time to be telling that story to the Rose. He had been looking a little peaked anyway, with the game coming up, but he just stared at the arm, and looked solemnly up at my father, as though if he opened his mouth he would throw up.

"You should have seen the look on Johnny Kessler's face." Nothing compared to the look on Rosy Malcolm's. "He went running off after his grandfather. The old man was a doctor. Fixed it up good as new. Or almost." He held up his hand, the last two fingers cramped up like a claw. "I've never been able to open these fingers since."

"And you never wanted to play again?" Rosy said.

"Oh no. No. I wanted to play. But my mother wouldn't let me. Then my father. They said it was too dangerous. Something really serious might happen."

"That's what my mother keeps telling me," Rosy said, swallowing hard.

"It was an accident. Could have happened playing anything. They shouldn't have gotten so worked up. I missed out on a lot."

We were nearing the field by then. Point Breeze was less like a school than a fortress, a huge blocky stone structure. It had marble floors, and black iron stairways—just the things for kids to frolic on—and heavy black metal gates at all the entrances. They were supposedly to keep vandals out after hours, but they looked like prison bars to keep the students in. The field, also with a black fence around it, was just dirt, with oil spread on it to keep the dust down. Apparently oil was cheaper than grass seed.

Some of our kids were off throwing the ball around, but the St. Stevens kids were standing together in a group, watching us come in, as if they didn't need to practice. They stood holding their helmets at their sides, sneering. They always looked dirty to me, but of course it was just that with names like Joey, and Dominic, and Anthony, they were darker. Their candidate for referee wore tight jeans and a leather jacket, and looked as if his hair had been done at the grease rack of an auto garage. His sneer was the worst of all—one more penalty, kid, and I'll fuck you up good—but when he saw my father it softened.

"Hey Doc. Nobody said you was coming. It's John Natali. You remember. Them warts on my hand."

"Sure, John," my father said. "I remember." Each of his patients thought his warts were unique in all the world.

"Hey." He slapped the kid beside him on the side of the helmet, glancing to see if this gesture impressed my father. "You dint tell me Dr. Keith was coming."

32

"Aw." The kid looked crestfallen. "I dint know."

"Look at that." John showed the kid his hand, as if to make matters worse. "Not even a scar. You remember them warts."

"Yeah." The kid was obviously deeply ashamed.

"Not even a scar." John was beaming, a new man. "The big game. Hey, don't worry, Doc. We'll keep these kids in line."

The big game turned out to be a fiasco. Nobody on either side knew anything about football. We thought it was like cowboys: you watched it on TV and then you could play it. The blockers on the line just stood up bumping their chests against the defense, about like trying to get out of a crowded movie theater. The tacklers grabbed a kid with their hands and dragged him down, like bronco-busting. St. Stevens hadn't heard of forward progress, and thought it was nifty to drag a kid back twenty yards before they threw him to the ground. Then they piled on methodically, one by one. There was a lot of biting and scratching in the piles. The referees didn't call anything, just stood around shaking their heads. "Hey Doc. These kids. Jesus." But St. Stevens had a skinny little kid who could outrun any Protestant in the world, and anytime they gave him the ball around end he scored.

After the game John Natali came over to us. "Hey, don't take it so hard. You played good. Real tough out there."

"Yeah," I said.

He was trying to think of something to cheer me up. He racked his brains. Finally he held out his hand. "Look at that. See?" He grinned. "Your old man did that. Not even a scar."

I nodded, tried to smile. My father seemed as embarrassed as I was. Probably he understood. Sometimes it wasn't enough just to be Dr. Keith's son. Sometimes you wanted to win the game.

One afternoon on a walk—my father loved to take walks, was always dragging me along—we wound up on a narrow shady street, rough and pot-holed, lined with little brick houses packed tightly together. It was like many of the funny little streets around our neighborhood, but I didn't remember ever seeing that one.

"Gene Kelly once lived here," my father said.

"Who?"

"The dancer. Gene Kelly. From the movies." He started an impromptu soft shoe, shuffling from side to side in the middle of the street. I tried to find someplace else to look. There was no one else around, but he wouldn't have cared if the street had been jammed with spectators. The man was out of his mind sometimes. "I used to show him a step or two."

"Yeah."

"But he did live here. He was born on this street. You can look it up."

By that time we had reached a dead end. It looked out on a large field, a hill on one side; past the field were two buildings, one high and long, the other like a large comfortable brick residence.

"This is where I used to go to school," he said.

I looked again. "This is a school?"

"Garfield Academy. Or it used to be. It merged with Arnold years ago. Now it's their elementary school. But this is where I went for three years."

"Really."

"Yeah. I hated it here."

I had not heard him use quite that tone before. Often he had talked of his boyhood, bad times with the good, but always before in his mock-epic style that pictured everything as an adventure; you never knew how much of it was true.

"How come?"

"I'm not sure. I'd been at public school awhile. You always want to stay where you've been. It seemed a little stifling here at first. But I always thought it had something to do . . . I don't know. It was just before I changed schools that I found out I was adopted."

I knew he had been adopted—he had told me years before—but it had always seemed perfectly natural to me, I'd known so long. It had never occurred to me that it had been a trauma.

"I used to brood for hours about that. Who my father really was. Why he had left me. What my mother looked like. Where they were now. Texas, I'd been born in. I didn't even know what the place looked like. All of a sudden I'm in this little school for rich kids. I felt enough like a stranger already."

"So you were bad." He had often told me he was a problem in school.

"I don't think on purpose. I didn't make the connection. But I spent all those hours brooding. And at school I was a terror. Never studied. Gave the teachers fits. I would *not* do what I was told. Finally they sent me to that military school down in Virginia. And there I was okay. Off in the middle of nowhere, which was the way I felt anyhow. They gave you a rank at military school, so I didn't have to worry who I was. And I was my own man, that above all. What I did, I did. Nobody down there cared where I came from."

I was still staring at that building across the field, as if it concealed some mystery about my father that I'd never had an inkling of before, like those blurred faded photographs of his Garfield class; their hair slicked down, bodies jammed into tight clothes, the boys still somehow looked sloppy, and faced the camera with eyes that seemed desperate. For a moment I thought of that one boy, his owlish stare through wire-framed spectacles.

"Parents make the same mistakes with their children that were made with them," my father said. "You'd think it were fated. I don't want to do that with you. But I've thought about it a lot, looked at all the angles." He had raised his eyebrows, heaved a little sigh. "I think I'd like to send you to Arnold."

I blinked. "Here?"

"Not at this age. I think that's a bit much. But when you get older. High school, when you need some brainy teachers. I'm not wild about the idea. I think there's good and bad in it. But all in all." He shrugged. "I think it's the thing to do. If it's okay with you."

"I guess. Sure." I didn't know. I was surprised—touched, a little—that he would ask, touched by all he had told me. I hadn't often seen my father unsure of himself.

"I wouldn't want you cursing me the way I cursed my old man," he said.

I suppose it was that little school of his that my father was picturing when he decided to send me off to Arnold. I don't know if he was surprised—I know I was, when I finally saw it—by all it had become, the rolling green campus in a suburb fifteen minutes out of the city, the high chapel, four dormitories, separate library, huge complex of athletic fields.

We had a football along with us that day—I carried a ball everywhere, as if I never knew when I might run into enough kids for a pickup game—and we threw it around awhile. As usual, we didn't do too well. He kept failing to lead me, and I couldn't recover.

"You'll never make an end," he shouted.

"You'll never make a quarterback," I yelled back.

"A good pair of hands would have had that."

"You go out. Let me throw."

"No." He didn't want to run. "You'll never make a quarterback either."

I pegged the ball at him, a bullet, and he slapped it, batted it around awhile, before he finally dropped it. "Aw." He swiped at the ball, grunting. "You got the arm. But you got to be quick."

"I'll be quick. I'll do sprints." I was always planning some elaborate training program.

"No." He shook his head, wearing a big grin. "You'll be a guard."

Chapter 3

BEFORE OUR FIRST year at Arnold—we were fourteen, entering as freshmen—I asked Rosy if his father had given him any special reasons for sending him there.

"No," Rosy said. "He went there himself. He's had me signed up for years. You're going, period, is what he said."

They obviously had a close understanding. At least the Rose and I would be starting out together.

I hadn't been so nervous about a day at school since kindergarten. When the alarm went off, I bolted from bed as if it were an air raid siren. My face stared back at me from the mirror like a dead man's. My hands were actually trembling as I put on my shirt and tie, and I got a foot caught pulling on my slacks and fell heavily to the floor. It felt strange wearing all those clothes on a weekday, as if I had just become a business executive at the age of fourteen, and to make matters worse my mother had bought all new clothes, so I had to deal with pins and cardboard and pieces of plastic, and everything was stiff and scratchy when I got it on. I would have felt as comfortable being laced into a straitjacket.

"Who died?" my father said when I got down to the table.

"Very funny."

"Let me fix your tie." He had always, ever since I was a child, made the final adjustments in the knot of my tie. "What was that loud sound I heard a few minutes ago?"

"I knocked something over." Myself, to be exact.

"I was always a little jumpy on the first day of school." He took a big scoop out of a half-cantaloupe. He loved fresh fruits at breakfast.

"What for?" I said. I tried a piece of cantaloupe, but gave up on it. Couldn't swallow.

"Dan," my mother said, carrying in a large stack of pancakes. "You look so nice."

It was the way you speak to a man on one of the grand fateful days of his life, like the day he is going off to war, or the day he is getting married. At least you look nice, you poor bastard.

"Oh great," I said, trying again to swallow. "Pancakes."

The dirty old basement locker room at Point Breeze School would have smelled like a flowery meadow that day.

When I got down to the bus stop, Rosy looked the same as I felt, as if beneath all those clothes he were laced into a tight corset. He wore his hair short in those days, and sticking up in straight little spikes. The bus stop was down on Penn, so the four lanes of morning traffic were rushing by, filling the air with the sweet scent of exhaust. A couple of commuters were standing there reading their papers, and a tall beautiful nurse, with long ash blond hair, was watching us and smiling. The Rose and I weren't saying much. At one point I noticed we were walking around in a little circle, like a couple of flamingos in a mating dance.

When it finally arrived, the Arnold Academy bus was squeaking and rumbling, all kinds of chatter echoing around inside. "Whoa!" somebody shouted from the back. The door flew open and the driver stared. He wore gray grease-stained work pants with matching suspenders. His thick hair was combed straight back on his head. He had a two-day growth of beard, a long beak of a nose that had been broken in at least two places, and a huge soft possum belly. As he yawned, glancing up in the mirror, I noticed a gaping black hole: no teeth. In a small declivity in the dashboard he had parked a burnt-out cigar butt.

"Get on, damnit," he said. "I ain't got all day."

The Rose and I had just been standing there, staring at him.

Obviously he was a member of the competent and understanding staff the school advertised in its brochure.

The chatter ceased as we climbed on. The front seemed packed, hardly room to walk down the aisle. There was room in the back, but you could tell at a glance—smiling faces offering a challenge—not to go back there. "Sit down, goddammit," the driver said. "I can't go till you're down." We managed to squat down and wedge our butts in among the teeming masses up front. Things were so tight we were practically in each other's arms.

Nothing but the best in modern facilities, as the brochure put it.

"Make plenty of room," a kid at the back shouted.

"Coupla first-rate porkers."

Somebody snuffled, like a hog in a pen.

The Rose and I were avoiding each other's eyes. That wasn't easy, since we were only about six inches apart. Some of the kids up front, though they were obviously sympathetic, couldn't help themselves, and started to laugh.

"Roll it, you Bolshevik," somebody shouted from the back.

The driver looked in the mirror and held up his middle finger, as big around as a broomstick.

Eventually those bus rides were among the most exciting events of the day. The older kids, sophomores and juniors, sat toward the back, as if it were some kind of privilege to sit among the really strong fumes of exhaust. Now and then a couple of them would step up front, haul a freshman to the back, hold him in the aisle while they removed his trousers. De-pantsing, that was called. Once they had his pants, he was allowed to return to his seat, to sit there in his underwear, and his jacket and tie. Usually they gave them back when it was time to get off; once, though, they made one kid—who was very studious-looking and always carried a briefcase—walk off the bus that way. "Hey kid," somebody yelled from across the campus. "Feel a draft?"

They also had an arrangement whereby they guaranteed immunity from such treatment to any freshman who, while the bus was in motion, could touch the back door. Now and then one tried it, streaking down the aisle when it seemed nobody was looking, but always he got hit, as if by a middle linebacker, about four seats from the back. There would be a brief moment while he was still in flight, struggling, then he would disappear with a scream among bodies that descended on him from all sides.

"You got guts, kid," they would say, as they finally let him up.

It hardly seemed worth the trouble.

The bus unloaded into the basement of the academic building, where the lockers were. That wouldn't have been a bad place to linger—there was a little shop where you could buy candy and soft drinks—but almost immediately a bell would ring, and everybody, grumbling, would make their way to chapel.

That didn't have to be a dreary room, high-ceilinged and with pale blue walls, sunlight drifting in through high windows onto pews with a light finish. But the school music teacher, Mrs. McElderry, would be playing the organ as we entered. Her dress always looked as if somebody had rolled it into a ball and jumped up and down on it for a while. Her face was as wrinkled as the dress, except with deeper wrinkles, her eyes deeply hollowed and blinking wearily with fatigue. She played an introit of long mournful chords. After a few verses of "A Mighty Fortress Is Our God," apparently the only hymn she was entirely sure of, Mr. Bates, the headmaster, led us in prayer, everybody throwing himself suddenly forward in the pew as if a sniper had just appeared on stage. He was an extremely short, portly man, his eyes, as he stood before us, just slits.

After the prayer he gave a talk. It was like a sermon, long, dreary, punctuated—while Mr. Bates flexed his jowls—by significant pauses for effect, and an odd mixture of remarks about God, our parents, studying hard, his own experiences as a five-foot-two-inch student at the same school, and his feeling that we should all go out for some JV sport even if we were crummy. Really it was the same endless talk all year long, and from year to year: you could hack it off by the yard. Every morning we got a random twenty-minute sampling.

You ran the rest of the day like a four-forty, taking off in a sprint and holding that speed as long as you could. There were four minutes between classes, and often enough—*he* wasn't going anywhere—the teacher lectured overtime, so the freshmen, who still took such things seriously, made a dash between rooms, hurtling down stairs, banging through doors, clutching at books that wiggled from their grasp. No one discouraged such behavior. The school *liked* to see its students running around like loonies.

You could hardly call study hall a rest: crammed into desks bolted to each other like elephants in a row, students scratched out assignments, crammed for quizzes, while a teacher on a platform at the back of the room sat ready to bark at the first move. Even in the dining hall—where the teachers frowned in distaste as they ladled some steaming murky concoction from a huge tureen—student waiters bolted for the kitchen when the bell rang for seconds, and afterwards, bearing massive stacked trays to clear, took the short quick steps of a tightrope walker on their precarious trips to the kitchen.

On the second day I was a waiter, when I was trying to raise the serving tray above the fat heads at tables on either side, I made the mistake of tilting it, and watched the lidded tureen slowly slide toward me, hit the edge of the tray, tilt, flip open, and—I lowered the tray, too late—spill, to the cheers of the entire dining hall, all over my new plaid jacket. Chop suey for lunch. I didn't even like chop suey. The rest of the year, as I sat in study hall, that odor wafted around me; it never entirely left my jacket.

The classrooms in the academic building were bright and airy, with high ceilings, tall windows that in hot weather were flung open with a rush, fluorescent lights, battered heavy wooden desks, radiators that hissed and clanged in the cold. We hurried in, a little breathless, at the beginning of class, carrying heavy stacks of books, and sat stiffly in the hard wooden seats. The teachers were mostly older men—the school wanted to get the freshmen started off right—who frowned, glancing at their watches, as we entered. When the bell rang they immediately closed the door and began to talk. Our hands would already be tired from note-taking in other classes, but we would have to write down these words too. They never meant much to us as we hurried them onto the page. The lights above our heads blinked and buzzed, flies sailed lazily from desk to desk, and from the front of the room, endlessly, the voice droned on and on.

II

We did have one young teacher, a man named Sickert, who taught freshman math. He did not exactly look young—his hair was rapidly thinning, and he had laid the foundation for a paunch that would have done justice to middle age. He told us he had come to Arnold straight out of a graduate program in organic chemistry. How he wound up teaching fourteen-year-olds in a prep school was not entirely clear.

"Oh, I probably coulda had another job," he said to us the first day, as he filled us in on his background. "Paid a lot more money. But I love teachin', men. I love teachin'."

How did he know he loved teaching, when he had never done it before?

"Take seat!" he would shout as he strode into the room. He seemed not to want to clutter his speech with too many articles or prepositions. "Let's take seat here!"

We had his class after lunch, and he always seemed a little foggy at that point. That was understandable, because at lunch he had just eaten like a starving man, hovering warily over his plate and shoveling the food into his mouth. When he was handed a bowl of mashed potatoes, he stuck a serving spoon directly into the center of it and shuttled the near half onto his plate. His clothes seemed mismatched: his jacket was at least a couple of sizes too small, though he never took it off and always kept it buttoned, straining, at his paunch; his slacks, on the other hand, looked like the baggy pants of a clown. One corner of his jacket was always smudged white, because he kept wiping chalk dust there. He wore thick black-framed spectacles that were constantly slipping down his nose; with the heel of his hand, or at least a piece of it that wasn't thick with chalk dust, he would push them back up.

He was not hard to follow in class, particularly if you had read just one section ahead in the book. His own book was propped open on his desk, and he would stand at the board just behind it, lecturing apparently at random.

"All right, men. Let's see here. Let's pick an unknown. We can call it anything. Remember, men, it doesn't matter what we call it. So why don't we call it, let's see here, why don't we call it"—a frown of concentration, a glance at the book—"X." And so on.

The constant motion of his glasses seemed to have something to do with the fact that his eyebrows were flipping up and down at an incredible rate. It was as if he had a blinking sign on his head. As he lectured, he winced, frowned, grimaced, twisting his mouth into incredible shapes. At times, overcome by his lunch, he belched, or yawned at length. Despite the fact that he was reading straight out of the book, and in fact reading the same thing four times a day, he got quite involved in his lectures, his voice rising and falling dramatically, the chalk racing across the board. If he made a slip at a crucial moment, he was so impatient that he skipped the eraser and wiped it off with his hand. Sometimes, when he reached the final answer, he put it up on the board so triumphantly that he smashed his chalk to smithereens.

When he asked someone the solution to the problem, his voice booming across the room—"So we can plainly see, here, that X must equal, all right . . .

Keith?"—and got the wrong number, he was as shattered as the chalk.

"Oh no, Keith. No no no, Keith. God no. No."

You felt as if you had done something absolutely despicable. At the same time, of course, it was all you could do to keep from shouting with laughter.

As deliberate as the man was, I couldn't make head or tail of the subject. That was hardly a successful year for me academically. I spent countless evening hours at our dining room table, wading through page after page of ancient history, laboring over themes for English, conjugating irregular French verbs. But the subject that really gave me fits was algebra. Sometimes I asked my parents for help.

"I remember algebra from school," my mother said. "I was pretty good. But this isn't anything like what we did."

We were being taught the new math.

Sitting at the table with me and poring over the book, frowning, my father was more blunt. "They got the whole thing ass backwards," he said.

He promised to talk to Mr. Sickert about my difficulties at the first parents meeting, but when he got home after the meeting he looked dejected. "I'm sorry, Dan," he said. "I couldn't get anywhere with the man. I don't think he ever really heard what I was saying. You'll just have to do the best you can."

I shrugged. "What the hell."

"Lord," my father said. "My teachers in Virginia. Even at Garfield. They were geniuses beside that man."

On the third day of class Mr. Sickert had said, "How many you men playin' ball this year?"

At first we didn't know what he meant. It turned out that was his way of telling us he was the freshman football coach.

44

III

That first year at Arnold you *had* to go to the Hargrove game. It was all anybody talked about the first week. Nobody mentioned where the various classrooms were, or where you got a locker, or how you were going to do the impossible amount of work that was being assigned. All anybody talked about was the Hargrove game.

In chapel, for instance, when Mr. Bates was bringing his talk to a close, his eyes getting narrower and narrower until they weren't even there, his pauses growing lengthier and weightier; just about when you might have expected some chimes or light chords from the organ or a heavenly chorus with a sevenfold amen, some hoarse-voiced senior down front would scream "Beat Hargrove!" and the whole place would erupt, everybody jumping to their feet and screaming, stomping, whacking the pew backs with their hymnals. It was probably the most sacrilegious display I'd ever seen, enough, you would think, to cause any normal speaker to faint dead away, except that Mr. Bates, a round benign man with huge jowls, would be beaming up there at the podium as if we had just broken into the doxology.

It was the same elsewhere. At lunch, just about when everyone was settling down to the butterscotch pudding, a low haunting chant would start up, keep building, for minutes at a time, "Go Arnold, Beat Hargrove." During the last period of the day, when everybody was supposed to be getting help with that impossible load of work, we would be ordered to report again to the chapel, where the whole period would be given to synchronized cheers, team introductions, frenzied outbursts like the ones in the morning, halting flustered speeches delivered sincerely by the team captains. Even between classes, traveling around campus, you'd be stopped by a senior in your path; he'd stare into your eyes until you blinked and had to look away, then would speak, in a flat menacing tone. "You going

45

to the Hargrove game?" I'm sure if you hadn't answered immediately, a crowd of upperclassmen would have gathered around, paring their fingernails with switchblades, but of course you said yes right away. "All right," he'd say. "I'll see you there."

Naturally the Rose and I were planning to go. But the day before the game, he came down with something, aches, chills, and a high fever, no doubt psychosomatic, so it looked as if I would have to go alone.

"Of course you don't want your old man along," my father said, and I'm afraid he was right. As much as I would have liked the company, you can't take your father to a thing like that. It would cut you off from everything. He let me out that Friday night at a corner of the parking lot, and said he would be back in a couple of hours. "Bring home a winner," he said.

Something about that game impressed itself on my mind, perhaps the fact that it was nearly the first thing I did at the Academy; maybe the fact that I went alone, that it was all new and strange, has made it loom larger in my mind than other games. When I have dreams about football, they are on almost that field—the enormous bleachers, high gleaming light standards—on that kind of dark starry night, and my team is the enemy, surrounded by hordes of hostile fans. A game at night always looks different, the field a pale green and freshly lined; the players seem farther away and in sharper focus; under the lights their uniforms wear a kind of glow. Just the fact that it is night makes the game more of an event. In my memory that Hargrove game has a kind of mythical quality. Our ragged little crowd of fans was cheering against incredible odds. The Hargrove players were mammoth, skilled, fleet of foot. I recall it as an epic battle. I know it was just a crummy high school football game.

Looking back on it now, since we got to be friends later, it seems natural that Nick Kaiser came down to talk to me, but at that point, we hardly knew each other, had just sat together in chapel, and it was an unusual thing to do. At first the game wasn't going too well, Hargrove starting a steady drive, and the freshmen were all taking it very seriously, scowling, screaming the cheers, shaking their fists; they weren't exactly fraternizing. Nick slipped down a couple of rows to sit beside me. He was a funny-looking kid, lean, flat-headed, with a narrow face, wide jaw, a tight circular mouth. He never seemed quite happy; sometimes he got a little hilarious, but always as if there were something on his mind that he wanted to get away from. I have often speculated since as to what that thing might have been.

"So you made it to the big game," he said, sitting beside me.

"Wouldn't miss it. Afraid somebody might kill me if I did."

"And look at them now. They don't even know we're here."

It was true. All those seniors who had been threatening and bullying all week now sat up in the stands trying to look humble and sincere to impress the girls. They couldn't have cared less that the freshmen were there.

"You think we can win?" I said.

"I don't know. They look big. God. Awful big. Look at that tackle." Hargrove had just broken from the huddle, and the tackle who had led them out was huge, torn dirty tape on his hands, the tail of his jersey hanging out. "I hope we do. You know this is my stomping grounds."

"No."

"Hargrove Township. Yeah. I couldn't exactly brag about it at those pep rallies. But this is where I'd be going, if not to Arnold. And I've heard about it from my friends."

"I'm sure."

I could imagine how I would feel if Arnold were playing the public school in my neighborhood.

"You like Arnold?" I said.

"I don't know. I guess. But it's so hard over there. So fucking hard. There's more work in a day than we had in three weeks. And living there." He looked at me with his sad sleepy eyes, his mouth tight. "I have to live over at the school. You take so much shit." He looked back at the game. "I know it's a great opportunity. A great place."

"Yeah."

"I just don't know if I'm going to make it."

He was sitting with a knee drawn to his chest, an arm wrapped around it, and staring toward the field. Hargrove had penetrated into our territory, then stalled, had to punt; our offensive unit was into the game. As if coming out of something. Nick nodded toward the field.

"You see that kid? Number twenty-nine? He's a freshman."

"Come off it."

"So help me God. Pollett. He's a freshman. Played for Southwest Catholic last year. Grupp got them to give him a scholarship. Look at him sometime when we walk out of chapel. Sitting with those little kids. He looks like a gorilla back there."

"I had no idea."

"There's another one too. Cortese. Just a freshman. Plays linebacker. He starts. You don't know these things, Dan. You ought to be a boarder. Like hell." He smacked the stands with his fist. "You're lucky you're not. God, I can't wait for freshman football to start."

"I know."

"Show those bastards. I can't wait for it to start."

He was intense when he spoke, apart from everything around him, then when he'd turn his attention to the game he'd be the same way about that, screaming himself hoarse, pounding the stands, chewing on his lip and grimacing. He didn't even seem to be with me.

For a while he didn't have much to cheer about. The whole first quarter, and some of the second, seemed a desperate impossible effort. Hargrove did look huge, big hunks of meat on the line, while our team examined closely was a motley crew: one tackle with a big slow lunk while the other was lean and wiry, more like an end; one of the guards was quick but looked way too small. The whole first quarter was just a defensive effort, with Hargrove constantly in our territory; it took rugged gang tackling, incessant pursuit, a couple of last-second desperation tackles, to keep them from

48

breaking through for a score. Every time we got the ball we'd run a few ineffectual plays and get off a desperation punt. With every exchange we were losing ground.

Until that one play. Fifteen years later, I can still see it as if it were happening in front of me, and that night it was, a couple of yards from our goal line, right in front of where all of us were sitting. At first it just looked like an end run, one of the Sherrill twins sweeping around to the short side of the field, toward us. Even that seemed a daring enough play, backed up against our own goal; usually you'd just try a quick opener. But then we saw—I'm sure those of us in that little block of stands saw it before anyone else in the stadium—that he'd handed it off on a reverse to Pollett. And that seemed insane. Because naturally on a reverse Pollett was going to sweep wider, going the other way. He was a tall kid, heavy from the waist down but lean up above, and as he started that run, about the time he took the ball and turned to look upfield, he stepped with one foot into the end zone.

Just as he did, a Hargrove linebacker, the one man who had diagnosed the play, was knifing in behind the line, diving for Pollett's front leg, and got it. But the one thing about Pollett—aside from the fact that, for all his leaness, he was strong as an ox, with legs that seemed to have been taken from a 200-pound tackle and grafted onto the torso of a skinny kid—was that he was very bowlegged: with Pollett you might get one leg, and a good grip on it too, but you just couldn't reach the other, and if help didn't arrive in a second you'd feel your arms grow helpless as the one leg you had was ripped from your grasp. That is what Pollett did to the Hargrove tackler, leaving him buried face down in the dust of the goal line, sweeping way wide to that far side of the field and turning the corner, then just letting it out, eating up the ground with that long loose stride of his, the ball a forgotten trinket in his hand, and he took it all the way, 100 yards plus that six inches or so he'd stepped into the end zone, for a score.

After that the whole game was different. Hargrove

came back to score, the way it so often happens, as if one team gets the idea from the other, but from then on it was a battle, fought the whole length of the field and with full arsenals. It could have gone either way, and as a matter of fact Hargrove wasn't much of a team that year, finishing two and eight and down in the bottom of their league. But that night it was the big game, and as if it were fated, just because it was my first big game at the Academy and just so I could remember it all the rest of my life, Arnold did score last, holding off Hargrove in the final few minutes. When the gun went off, the rest of the stadium was silent and turned for the exits, while our little cluster of fans jumped and spilled onto the field, going wild in a victory celebration.

I have one other memory from that evening in the stands. It may really stem from some other game; it seems unlikely that everything could have started on the same night. It is a most vivid recollection. Up in the stands I see a man in a herringbone jacket, blue tie, dark slacks. His mouth smiles slightly, just to one side, and his brow is wrinkled ironically, as if at a faintly amusing joke. His hands are in his pockets. Beside him Mr. Bates is talking incessantly, though the man does not look at him; occasionally, in fact, he nods, gestures, toward the field, as if to direct Mr. Bates's attention there. To his other side is a girl. Her hair is blond, so light it is almost silvery, and in large ringlets; her complexion a pale white but rich, a mole on one cheek; her cheekbones are high, her mouth tender, sensitive; in her eyes is the trace of a sad smile. She seems to be watching not the field, but the fans below her, as if what she enjoys is not the game but our enjoyment of it. Occasionally she takes the man's arm. I figured he must be her father.

I lost Nick in the victory celebration. By the end of the game he was so worked up I think he really did forget I was there—I can still see him, when the gun went off, his fists thrust into the air, head thrown back, eyes closed—and he ran onto the field and dove head first into that mass of players, fans. I ran onto the field with everyone else, but when I got there I didn't have anything to do. Everybody was hugging, laughing, jumping around, pounding each other on the back. It was a good feeling, being part of the victory party, but I felt a little ridiculous too, not particularly knowing anyone. I followed the crowd back toward the bus, gradually let them get further and further away. Soon I was walking alone.

When I first saw those four guys, they were standing under one of the high streetlights of the parking lot. They were vaguely familiar—the kind of guys you see hanging around all the time at a school, who never seem to go anywhere—especially the one in front: short, his curly hair tinged by a trace of red, the big grin he always wore chipped by half a tooth in front (no doubt somebody punched it out for him). So I wasn't all that surprised when he spoke to me. I wasn't too happy about it either. Those are the kind of guys that never play it straight with you.

"How you doing?" he said, stepping out from the rest of them. "Hey. What was your name again?"

"Dan," I said. "Dan Keith."

"That's right. Dan. God damn. I knew it was something. Dan, or Sam. These are a few of my friends, Dan. Ted. Piggy. O'Toole. Dan here's at my lunch table."

"Yeah," one of them said.

"And my Latin class, I think."

"I take French."

"Oh fuck, that's right. You told me." No I didn't. "Great game, huh Dan."

"Yeah great." I was sure as hell wishing I hadn't run into those guys, the little one with his hand on my arm, the others with their solemn nods, cigarettes all around.

"Listen, Dan. We were wondering. How were you getting home?"

Oh, hell. "My old man. He's picking me up."

"Great. Great. Listen. You don't think the old man would be in a mood to give a few of your friends a lift? Just into town. Drop us anywhere."

Friends! I didn't know about the old man, but what

51

about me? "Sure, I guess." There wasn't much I could say.

The whole situation made me sick. On the one hand, I didn't care for my father to be seeing them, with their cigarettes, scent of beer, dark turtlenecks under their oxford cloths—though this little Piggy wore an ascot—since they were hardly the kids he wanted me mixing with. On the other hand, I didn't really want them to be seeing him. Not that there was anything wrong with my father. But it's hard enough trying to make an impression at a new place yourself without having to worry about what kind of impression someone else is going to make. I guess everybody at that age is a little embarrassed about his father. We had just been seeing those trustees in the stands, wearing their hundred-dollar sports jackets, and here he was sitting in that beat-up old Nova, in his shirtsleeves, with the top down.

I was just wondering what to say, realizing that I was giving those guys a ride because nobody else would do it, when the little one stepped up and spoke for himself.

"Mr. Keith. J.T. Frankenheimer. I was just asking Dan if my friends and I could bum a ride into a town."

"Sure. Since you're bringing home a winner."

"You heard," I said.

"I asked one of the girls from Hargrove. She was delighted to tell me. But it's Dr. Keith, J.T. I think your father's a patient.

The kid reddened. His smile faltered. "Dr. Keith. I didn't realize this was your son."

"We even have the same last name. But sure. I'll be glad to give you a lift." O'Toole was lighting a cigarette with a huge flame from his lighter. "Just make sure your friend doesn't burn up my car with that blowtorch of his."

"Sure. Maybe you'd rather we didn't smoke at all." He turned to O'Toole in a stage whisper. "Ditch it, asshole."

"It's okay. They're your lungs. Though as your father's doctor I don't recommend it."

I used to love riding in that junky little car, just as

my father did, with the top down. The top wasn't automatic, all kinds of trouble to lower, but he used to do it anyway, every day it was anywhere near warm, riding home from work in Oakland over those shady back streets. I was even enjoying it that night, with a warm breeze blowing, though I would have enjoyed it more if those four guys hadn't been there. But I wasn't uneasy anymore. I knew Frankenheimer was wishing he didn't smell like a beer hall, sitting beside my father.

"Hargrove doesn't schedule you guys to get beat," my father said. "You're just supposed to be a tune-up."

"I noticed they didn't look too happy," Frankenheimer said.

"Everybody thinks you've got to be a coal miner's son to play football. Give me a team with some brains."

"That's right."

"A good coach or two. How long have you been at Arnold?"

"Since third grade. I'm a sophomore this year."

"You must be kind of used to the place."

"Kind of. But the upper school is a whole new thing. Much harder. And there's so much else you have to do. So many extra things."

I wish I could have been in on that conversation a couple of months later. I would have appreciated it more. Frankenheimer's only extracurricular activity turned out to be sneaking out to the woods behind the library for a smoke.

"It won't kill you," my father said.

"No."

"It's a good school. I don't really like private schools. Don't like the idea. But I consider the alternative. One thing bothers me, though. Always has. With all those wealthy families around, kids who have been there since first grade, I can't help wondering what kind of reception everyone gets."

I could have answered that one already. Frankenheimer was beside me considering the question as if he were an expert on the matter. It has always amazed me that my father carried on a serious conversation with that kid. "It varies. I don't know. I guess everybody finds a niche." If those four guys did, everybody did. "But it can be an exclusive place. Pretty cruel at first. What helps is if you've got some special talent. Something you can give to the place." He looked at me. "What's it going to be, Dan? You've got good size. Maybe you saw your spot out there tonight. That wouldn't be a bad reception. People swarming all over you."

"I'm going out," I said.

"He's got good size," my father said. "But he's got to get rid of that baby fat."

I wish he hadn't said that. I know he didn't mean much by it, just some kidding among men, and I know there was some truth to it. But I wish he hadn't said it. Frankenheimer was staring at me with that sarcastic grin—I'd like to shake the kid's hand who chipped that tooth—and those guys in the back seat were probably laughing so hard they bit through their cigarettes.

"I'm going out," I said again.

But I don't know. I'm not sure what the problem was in those days. I wanted to find a place in that little world I had stumbled into. I suppose I also wanted to prove something to my father. But he didn't care about that—he had never said he did—and my way of finding a place was roundabout, to say the least. I was a mild kid, soft, quiet. I had no trouble making friends. Somehow I decided I had to be different. Three years later I was hard, stoic, slabbed with muscle—and I did start at tackle, in front of all those people, played a hell of a game: there was nothing fake about it. But somewhere inside me was still that kid who thought he had to be something else, had to gird himself up for a massive effort and prove himself. That kid who watched the game breathlessly from the Hargrove stands. He stayed with me forever.

Chapter 4

IT MUST HAVE been early in that freshman year that I happened to read a book about a high school football team. It was no kid's book, but an adult bestseller; at least that's what it said on the back of the paperback I bought. The school was somewhere out in California, and the team was in the running for the state title, though I don't remember whether they won it or not. All the players were fabulous athletes. Even the tackles, instead of being ugly ill-tempered kids who had always been the fattest ones in the class and were now developing acne, were graceful and agile, just larger versions of a fullback, with wide shoulders, deep chests, trim waists. Since most of the social life took place at the beach, everyone was tanned a deep bronze; they would do acrobatic stunts on the sand, throw the ball around, ride the surf, have bonfires and wiener roasts. They drove home in their new sports cars. All the first-rate players on the team dated cheerleaders, and all the cheerleaders screwed.

In one of the early scenes in the book, the right tackle (heroes always play on the right side; there's something sinister about being on the left) told the quarterback he had just scored (that's what they called screwing in the fifties) with his cheerleader. The quarterback rather solemnly congratulated him, as if he'd just been named All-State. It turned out she had been the last holdout among the cheerleaders, and this was only about ten pages into the book. There was so much

55

screwing going on that players started to have affairs with each other's girls, like suburban business executives. The plot of the book hinged on one such affair, which came to light before the championship game; the danger was that the two players would start feuding on the field. It was a very long book, and I didn't read the whole thing, just the dirty parts, and the passages describing football. But the general plot was easy to follow.

Of course, it was not that book which established for me the link between sports and success with women. That was a connection I had sensed for a long time: I *knew* it existed. But the book spoke deeply to what I already knew. It gave form to the myth that until then had lived only vaguely in my heart.

In the sudden bashfulness of my adolescence, when just the prospect of speaking to a girl left me in a cold sweat, I pictured a more hopeful future when I would play for the varsity. At home games, down on the varsity field, a play would drift toward the sidelines, the opposing runner feinting, taking a step to change direction, about to shake loose, when I would come hurtling in about chest-high from the side, belting him out of bounds, flying over him and tumbling into one of the roped posts that kept the spectators back; they would rise to their feet as one, gasping, but I would already be up, jogging back to the field, as if I hadn't even noticed the post that lay now in splinters on the field.

After the game, when the fans had swarmed onto the field, I would find myself walking beside a girl (various young ladies in my imagination held this honor) who would shake back the hair cascading over her shoulders, bite her lip, smile, say, "God, Dan. I was so fascinated. Watching all of you charge like so many animals. Then when I looked in the program and saw it was you, who I've known all these years. I just don't see how you do it." I would pull off my helmet, smile, wiping away the grime and sweat, begin to explain. . . .

It wasn't just to win the love of many women that I wanted to play football. That would, however, be a nice auxiliary benefit.

Edwin Kirtley had lived in my neighborhood for years. He was a thin, sallow kid, with sleepy eyes and wide nostrils. He had never gone to public school, started at Arnold in kindergarten, and didn't have much to do with the rest of us. When we had ball games he would come around and stand there, or sit on the bank of grass off to one side, but if we asked him to play he would just shake his head, sit there and watch. He was always popping Necco Wafers into his mouth. He seemed to live on the things.

He hadn't exactly rolled out the red carpet the first time he saw me at Arnold—he did manage a nod—but after a couple of days he stopped me in the hall.

"I'm having a party this weekend," he said. "Kind of a back-to-school bash. A bunch of guys from the class are going to be there. I'd like you to come."

"This your birthday?" I said.

"God no." He frowned. "My birthday's in April. This is a party. With music. Dancing."

"Dancing?"

"For Christ's sake. With girls." There was a disgusted, angry expression on his face, as if to say, Why did I ever try this? "I thought you might like to come."

Edwin went to the enormous Episcopal church attended by the city's bankers and corporate businessmen; he attended the most exclusive dancing school; his family belonged to the leading country club. His crowd had been having parties since they were twelve. He was trying to do a nice thing—though obviously he had some reservations—by inviting an old friend to join them.

"I don't know how to dance," I said.

"God," he said. "You don't have to know how to dance. If you can walk you can do the dancing we do. If you can just stand there."

"I won't know anybody."

"You'll know the boys. I'll introduce you around. Just show up."

"Oh Lord," my father said when I told him of the party. "Now it begins." Actually, he was pleased. He loved to hear of any kind of contact between boys and girls.

There had been something of a hiatus in my romantic life, of about five years. I had had a girlfriend in fourth grade. In fourth grade, in fact, I could have had as many as I wanted. The other boys all pretended, or actually felt, that they wanted nothing to do with girls, but I never felt that way at all. I loved girls. Always had. Since I was almost the only one paying any attention to them, they all liked me too, even if I was a little chubby. "I like your little curl," Karen Cordrey said, reaching up to touch my cowlick. She was my favorite. She was a little stupid in class, had flunked one grade—no mean feat at Point Breeze—but was very friendly, always smiling, with her eyes all squinched up. She was bone thin, with a narrow face, long nose, and her drab clothes just hung on her, but when she smiled like that her face seemed pretty.

During free time at school she hovered around me constantly. Finally she invited me down to her house, near a large woodsy park a couple of blocks from school. We walked into the park, and she took me into a leafy little ravine and asked if I wanted to kiss her. She had a very thin mouth—I had always imagined kissing large voluptuous lips—but I did kiss her, repeatedly. She kept smiling every time, and hugged me hard. She would hold my face in her skinny little hands and look at me. Eventually she said, "I'll show you, but you promise not to touch. Today." I said all right. I wasn't entirely sure what she was talking about. Stepping back and looking down, she slowly raised her skirt—she had on no underpants—and looked up at me solemnly. But after a moment she couldn't resist, and grinned.

"There's just one thing," she said later. "Don't ever tell my brother. He'll kill you. I mean kill."

Her brother was a big lunk of a seventh-grader, with dark greasy hair hanging down into his eyes. Far outstripping (pardon the expression) his sister, he had flunked three times.

"Why?" I said.

She shrugged. "He wants to be the only one."

I decided it would be better not to go to her house anymore.

For some reason, through the years, I had lost the confidence I had once had with girls. Maybe it was that they had grown more reserved. They no longer made a point of coming up to me and touching my cowlick.

"It may seem a little strange," Edwin said to me the day before the party. "But you've got to wear a jacket and tie to these things. The girls dress up too. The parents expect it."

It seemed I was dressing that way for everything those days. Pretty soon I would be like Rosy's grandfather, who put on a blue vested suit and dark tie just to come downstairs and listen to the ball game on the radio.

"Dan," my mother said to me when I came downstairs on the evening of the party. "Don't *you* look nice!"

Would I hear those same words every day for the rest of my life?

"Don't make her any promises," my father said to me quietly at the door. "You're too young to support a family."

Quite a sense of humor the old man had.

Edwin's place was three stories, rough red brick, solid and imposing. His mother was waiting to greet us at the door. She was a handsome woman, but had dark thick eyebrows that slanted in and met above her eyes, one of the severest glances I had ever encountered. In my whole life until then, I had seen her all of about three times, and every time she seemed weary, pale, just plain angry. But the night of the party she was bright and animated, elegantly attired, her striking brows just accenting her beauty. "Dan," she said, taking my hand. "We're so happy to have you. You especially. Our old friend." She seemed to be staring at the middle of my forehead. I started to say something, but already her animated gaze had bounced away to another guest.

The house was warm and dim. The large living room

was mostly cleared of furniture; what was left was along the walls. A single soft lamp was on in the near corner. In the dining room the table was covered by a sumptuous buffet, small crustless sandwiches, potato chips, pretzels, cupcakes, cookies. A bright fruit punch was in a large glass bowl at the center. Not a crumb had been touched when I first saw the table. It was like a picture.

It would be hard to exaggerate the impression that first party made on me. I was used to the girls from Point Breeze school, pallid, a little silly and giggly, in drab colorless clothes that I never much noticed. The girls at Edwin's party had gone upstairs to leave their coats—a task which took roughly ten minutes—and gradually, in little clusters, began to wander down. They weren't all pretty, of course. But they wore dresses like their mothers might have worn, lavender, or scarlet, or a deep yellow, in soft material that clung to their bodies. Their faces were lightly made up, with a little rouge or lipstick; it seemed they were just flushed from the warmth of the house. They wore a little jewelry and their hair had a kind of glow. They smiled politely at me, even though we hadn't met. It didn't seem they could actually be more mature than the girls I had known before, but they were curvaceous, bosomy, and they looked older. In their little clusters they spread through the hallway and living room. They were lightly and deliciously scented.

As he had promised me he would, Edwin introduced me around. In a bright plaid sports jacket, he looked like quite the man about town, though his eyes still had that sleepy leer. "This is Dan Keith," he would say. "An old friend of mine from the neighborhood. Arnold. First year." That apparently classified me in some obscure way.

"You can dance with any of them," he said to me, as if he were outlining the ground rules in an expensive brothel. "All you have to do is ask. They never refuse. The ghost of Mrs. Bond would haunt them all their lives." Mrs. Bond, apparently, was the old bat who ran the dancing school. "And they want to dance. Believe me. If one of them misses a dance at Mrs. Bond's she has a fit."

The dancing was another thing that took me by surprise. Throughout the evening the living room remained dim, almost dark at the far side, and on the hi-fi one slow ballad after another played. The girls stayed together in little groups near the hallway, as if giving us a better light to see them in, and if I asked one to dance—Edwin was right—she would always smile appreciatively and nod. Together we would walk into the far shadows of the living room, she would put her hand in mine, rest her arm on my shoulder, and—to my astonishment—move her body warmly against mine, head to toe. Apparently this was a way of dancing that the girls had not been taught by Mrs. Bond, but had picked up on their own. I could feel the press of their breasts against me. Their hair was soft and fragrant. Now and then my mouth would brush the smooth skin of their necks. When the music ended, my partner would step back, smile, and thank me. *She* would thank *me*.

Probably that first evening I traveled along a couple of inches above the floor. I danced with nearly all the girls, not remembering their names, not particularly caring. I didn't eat much from that huge spread of food. I wanted everyone to think I was dieting. "I don't know how he got so fat, he never eats a thing," or, "He may be fat, but he understands his problem and is trying to improve himself. Once you get past all the blubber he's really a good kid."

I did drift out to the dining room table, though—it didn't hurt to look—and was stunned at one point when I ran into a familiar face.

"Rachel," I said.

"What's the matter?" She bit lightly on a potato chip. "You weren't expecting me?"

Rachel lived in the neighborhood too, of course, had been around forever. I had known her as long as the Rose. At Point Breeze she had always been the smartest kid in the class, so far and away the smartest that it was a little as if she weren't there at all; she was just off in her little world thinking whatever she thought.

She had been a short pudgy little girl with red hair and freckles and glasses with white frames. I always pictured her out in the driveway watching her father work on his car; despite the fact that he had one of the largest dealerships in the city, he still did the work on his own car, and liked to do it at home. When we were kids she joined in the little games we always played. She would do anything you asked her to, take any role, join either side. She did whatever it was very seriously. Somehow, though, she just wasn't any good at it. She couldn't run fast, couldn't pretend very well. She didn't really seem to care whether she was doing it or not. It was as if she had made a mature decision that she should be out there with us children, that it would be good for her.

As we got older and didn't have much to do with the girls, we ignored her, but sometimes she would come over and watch our ball games, just as studiously and seriously as she did everything else, as if she wanted to know, objectively, what boys were like. She had thinned out a little as she got older, but she still wore those glasses. It wasn't that I thought there was anything wrong with her; I just didn't much notice her.

For some reason, though, my father always did. She had been a patient of his. "You watch that Rachel Hardy," he said. "Those redheads take a while. But she's going to be a beauty someday."

For the life of me I couldn't see what he was talking about.

Once when we were younger and playing in her garage, on a whim, I had given her a kiss, and—damn those fifties movies—she had slapped my face and run away.

It was as if, at Edwin's party, my past had risen up to greet me, just when I was doing so well. Get out of here, I wanted to say. Go away. Forever.

"I guess I wasn't expecting to run into anybody I knew here," I said. "Any girls, I mean."

"I'm going to Ellsworth now," she said. "Maybe that explains it."

"And I'm going to Arnold."

62

"So I hear." She took another little bite of the potato chip. "I'm not sure that means we belong here."

She would say that. I don't know why it had crossed my mind—it was just like me to ruin things when I was having such a good time—but suddenly it had occurred to me that maybe Edwin hadn't wanted to invite us, that his mother had forced him to because we lived in the neighborhood. I could just hear a mother saying that. "You can't have a party without Rachel Hardy and Dan Keith. They go to the right schools now. And they've lived in this neighborhood all their lives."

"Do you want to dance?" I said. I had no idea why I'd said that.

"You don't have to dance with me."

"I know." She made everything so difficult. "I was just asking."

"All right, I'd love to."

Rachel, however, did not dance the way the other girls did. Somehow—and I'm not sure exactly how, since she didn't seem to be exerting any force—she held her body away from me, so I could never quite get to her. It was frustrating and uncomfortable. It's much easier to hug a woman than to look at her. No wonder I hadn't seen Rachel on the dance floor with anyone else.

"Do you know what it means for a girl to be catty?" she said.

"Yes." Actually, I wasn't sure. That was one of those expressions I heard all the time but whose meaning seemed vague, more just a feeling that people got. Often such expressions had to do with women. Women's intuition, for example.

"These girls are catty," Rachel said.

"They haven't been catty to me."

"You don't know what it means," she said, "if you say that."

"Maybe not." She was such a pedant.

"Girls are catty with other girls."

"All right, all right. Jesus Christ, Rachel. What's the matter?"

"You don't have to get mad. I thought I could talk to you. My feelings are hurt."

"*I* hurt your feelings?" That was the limit.

"No. Not you. You're nice. You asked me to dance."

I could explain all that. I didn't really want to dance with her.

"It's other people," she said.

"Who? Show me. I'll tear out their cruel hearts with my bare hands."

She laughed.

For a funny moment, though, I meant it. I felt a twinge of sympathy for Rachel. I had known her for years. I wanted her to be happy.

"It's not anything anybody's done," she said. "It's just a feeling. Like these people don't want me here."

I wished she hadn't said that. Some people went ahead and said such things. It was like a fear that was hovering in the back of my mind. I hated hearing someone put it into words.

"You don't know that," I said.

"I feel it."

"It's all in your mind. You can't expect everything to happen at once. You've only known them a little while."

"I understand that. But there are things I can see even now."

She hadn't up to that point looked like she was going to cry. She just looked very intent.

"You've got to give it time," I said.

Suddenly it did look as if she were going to cry. Her eyes seemed to cringe, and her face was trembling.

"Rachel," I said. "You're pretty." I didn't mind lying. "You've got a great personality. You're fun to be with." I seemed to be going a little bit overboard. "You're the smartest person I've ever met. Point Breeze. Anywhere. I know you're going to make it over at Ellsworth. You'd make it anywhere."

It had worked. Her face composed itself, grew serious and intent.

"You don't have any idea what I'm talking about," she said.

The pendant was back.

"I'm not talking about my looks," she said. "My

personality. Whatever that is. I know what I've got for brains. I'm not worried about how I'll do. I'm talking about feeling welcome at a party."

She was right. I didn't know what she was talking about. I didn't see the distinction.

"You can belong," I said. "If you'll try a little harder." She could quit being so critical. She could quit telling people what they didn't know. She could dance a little closer, for God's sake. "I know I will."

She shook her head. "I just don't think you see it yet."

"See what? Lord. Speak for yourself. Don't try to bring me into this."

"There's a lot about us that's alike."

I hoped not. "How can you say that?"

"I've known you a long time."

"You haven't known me that well."

She shrugged. "Call it woman's intuition," she said.

I was glad the song was coming to an end.

Later in the evening we played a game that, as far as I knew, those kids had invented themselves, where you danced around awhile until the music stopped and the one lamp was turned off, then groped in the pitch black until you came up with a new partner. The groping was pretty much fun. You never knew what you might run into. Girls that age certainly come in all shapes and sizes. I had just been dancing with one who was much bigger than I, taller and more muscular— though when the light snapped on, she had a lovely face—when the music stopped, and we all bumped around again, and the girl I found in my arms felt no bigger than a child. Her back was lean and hard, like a dancer's. The light came on. Her skin was soft and white and smooth, a small mole near her mouth, her eyes a pale blue. Her hair was blond in large ringlets, and her mouth seemed taut, and delicate, and tender, so that you wanted to touch it with the lightest of kisses. Her eyes, too, had a vulnerability to them, as if the slightest thing would make her blink.

"I don't believe I know you," she said.

It was the girl I had seen in the back of the stands with her father at the Hargrove football game.

"No," I said. I was tongue-tied.

"You must be a friend of Edwin's."

"Yes." Slight exaggeration there.

A small light of amusement shone in her eyes. "Do you have a name?"

"Dan." I had been reduced to monosyllables. If my name had had more than one syllable we'd have been out of luck. "Dan Keith."

"Well." She gave my shoulder a little pat. "Dan Keith. I'm very glad to meet you. I'm Sara Warren."

I just smiled. More than even the beauty of some of those girls, it was their poise that astounded me. I couldn't get over their poise.

If a girl could have been catty to a boy—if Rachel would have allowed that exception—Sara was being catty to me. Perhaps condescending was the word. She wasn't always to be that way, of course. I think it was just a reflex, nothing personal. But I loved just being with them, with Sara, with all those elegant girls, dancing with them, hearing the interesting things they had to say. I didn't see—I suppose I didn't want to see—the looks in their eyes.

Chapter 5

THERE HADN'T BEEN any freshman sports the first week at Arnold. Apparently they thought we needed some time to adjust. They were right. I couldn't have played a stiff game of horseshoes at the end of those first days. They did, however, let us know that nothing was to be supplied for freshmen. We had to buy everything ourselves.

"New football equipment?" my mother said.

"The stuff I have is for kids," I said. "This is the big time. We're going to be playing other schools."

"It seems like such an expense." She was frowning deeply, as if we barely had clothes to get through the winter.

"And I'll need good shoes. Football shoes. With spikes."

"You wear *spikes* on your shoes?" You'd have thought I said we wore spikes on our helmets, long ones with sharp points, so we could impale the ball carrier as we tackled him.

That evening at dinner she was silent when she was serving us. She had a way of clenching her jaw when she was angry, as if to bite the words back, and she did everything more hurriedly than usual, walking out with quick little steps and throwing the plates down. My father seemed not to notice. We were having a beef and noodle dish, and he started to dig into the noodles, mixing the gravy in.

"I don't like this thing of buying new football equipment," my mother said.

"It's just this once," I said. "Next year they supply it."

"He needs new equipment," my father said. "The old stuff is cardboard."

"I want to get good stuff," I said. "For once."

"I mean I don't like the idea of going out for football at all," she said.

I looked up from my plate, stunned. "You knew I was going out for football."

"I've heard you say things. I thought it was just the kind of thing all boys say. Like they want to be a fireman someday."

What did she think the stacks of magazines were all about? The hours I played day after day? I hated not being taken seriously.

"What's wrong with football?" my father said, sucking a noodle up into his mouth. He was always sloppy with noodles.

"Your arm is what's wrong with football for one thing. Your hand. It's never been the same since."

"I seem to get by with it." He had been a doctor all those years.

"It could just as easily have been something else. Your leg, so you'd have limped the rest of your life. Your neck. Your skull." All kinds of interesting possibilities.

"That was backyard football. A bunch of kids fooling around who didn't know what they were doing. This is going to be supervised. With coaches who know the game. Good solid equipment."

"Boys get hurt playing football every day, high school and college, no matter who's supervising them."

"There's some danger in everything. Just riding out to school on the bus." More danger in that than he knew. "You can't wrap yourself in a cocoon."

"It isn't just that it's dangerous. It's the game itself. Beating and kicking and tackling people." She was a little fuzzy on the particulars.

"You don't know the first thing about the game."

"I know enough to see that the object of it is to hurt people. Hopefully maim them for life."

"Good Lord, Martha."

"I can see plenty just passing by the television. Men with scar tissue above their eyes. Teeth missing. They can hardly put together a coherent sentence." Those were my heroes she was slandering. "Talking about how much fun it is to *get hit*. That isn't what I want my son turning into."

"He's not going to turn into anything."

"Do you think those men started out that way? As boys? Do you think they just grew up without teeth?"

"This whole argument is besides the point. Dan's old enough to make this decision for himself. We're not going to tell him what to do. If it's football he wants, that's what it's going to be."

"Then don't expect me to have anything to do with it. You can take him to buy his equipment."

"I can do it myself," I said. "I'll take a streetcar down." I didn't exactly want my mother along anyway.

"Now let's *eat*," my father said. "In peace." He gestured with his hands up, pleading over his food.

My parents didn't argue all that often, but their major arguments were always the same. They would both be up in their room, as if they knew what was coming and wanted it to be there. From downstairs, where I was reading or doing homework, I would begin to hear their conversation clearly; normally they spoke softly enough that their words were just a murmur, but when a fight was coming on I would hear them distinctly, louder and louder. There was a pause at some point, and their door was closed with a sharp click. That was a little ridiculous, because from downstairs I could hear them about as well with the door closed. Then they would really start to shout, my mother—normally a quiet woman—making as much noise as my father. I pictured them at either end of the room, stomping and gesturing.

"Your mother and I had a little argument last might," my father might say to me the next day. He didn't want to keep it from me.

"I noticed," I'd say.

That night it was mostly the same as at the dinner table, my mother shouting about what imbeciles football players were, how dangerous the game was, my father saying she didn't understand.

"You're just like my parents," he shouted. "Protecting me from a danger that didn't even exist."

"We're not talking about your parents. We're talking about a game. Played by idiots."

"A boy's got to have something. The work's hard, and the school's hard, and he's at the hardest age he'll ever be. I can wish it weren't football too. But I'm not going to take it away from him."

Actually, I liked having my parents argue over me. I liked it that my mother was afraid of what we were doing. That made it seem more important.

The salesman at the sporting goods store in Oakland wore a big smile the whole time, even though he was chewing gum. He had huge teeth, including a big gold one up front, and was short and thin. He looked like he had forgotten to take the coat hanger out of his jacket. He had all the color of a cadaver.

"So you're going to be a football player," he said, lacing up my shoes.

"Yeah." I hated the sarcastic tone some people took.

"A guard or tackle or something."

"I guess." I had finally given up my hopes of the backfield.

He grinned up at me, chewing away. "You'll have to lose that spare tire."

II

Arnold seemed a different place after 3:14. The shrill bell in the academic building rang for the last time, and outside the loud gong from the clocktower sounded. There was a perceptible relaxation all over the campus. Even if a teacher was in the middle of a sentence, there was a difference to the words he spoke after the bell, as if suddenly he were just a man talking to some boys, taking up their time, and he could smile, and be half-human about it, and try not to be so boring. After 3:14 students lingered awhile in the hallways, and down around the lockers. There was an unspoken rule that at that point books could be dropped anywhere, and they lay in piles all over the building. The doors leading out front were flung open. A few of the older teachers stayed in the classrooms, or went home, but the rest of the school—especially in fall and spring—walked down the hill to the gym, with at last a little looseness to their strides.

Somehow it was not that way for me. Not the first year, anyway. Maybe because it meant so much, or it was all so new and strange, the athletic period stood at the end of my day like a firing squad. The last period was free, for extra help, and usually I spent it in study hall. I could do no work. From the front of the room I watched the silent second hand of the clock, felt the nauseous fluttering in my stomach, the large drops of sweat that plopped from my armpits and raced down my belly; I took deep breaths, trying to calm down. The passing minutes tightened around my chest like a steel band. The final bell cinched it. While everyone else loosened their ties and threw their jackets over their shoulders as they walked down the hill, I got stiffer and stiffer, my feet slapping the pavement, as if someone were pushing me along.

That first Monday, I remember, I had been kept late doing extra work for French, and as I ran down the hill, with the combination lock and the slip of paper bearing my locker number, all my equipment stuffed—as I had seen other guys do —into my football pants, I realized I had no idea where my locker was. I had not been to the gym before.

It lay just at the base of the hill, high and wide, the driveway running around it. The bright green doors that faced the hill led onto the gym floor, but were closed most of the time. I found my way into one of the smaller doors around to the side. The hallway was long and dim, doors down either side. A few guys walked around half-dressed, paying no attention to me. Around me sounds echoed, shouts, laughter, singing (certain men, it seems, must sing as they take their clothes off). The place was stuffy, smelled of stale sweat and the hot balm athletes use for sore muscles. I tried a door to the left, but somebody was banging his way out from the inside, and just about took my hand off.

"Sorry," he said, stepping out. He was half a foot taller than I, wearing just a supporter. His midsection was lean, carved as if whacked out by a chisel. The rest of him up top was also lean and hard, his hands—I had noticed them as he banged through the door—twice the size of mine. He slouched a little, as if swaybacked. His thighs were massive, slabbed with muscle.

"You don't come in here," he said. He had gotten a quick look at me, sweating, disheveled, toting my store-bought football pants. He was just stating a fact.

It was Pollett, fresh from the Hargrove game. I had made a point of looking for him that morning in chapel. He was a freshman, one of the scholarship kids, with special dispensation to play varsity.

"You know where I do go?" I said.

"No idea."

"Must be the freshman locker room."

"I guess." He had had no experience of the place. Fortunately another guy was passing by and overheard. "You're in the shithole," he said helpfully. "Other end of the hall."

"Oh thanks." It was good to know where I belonged.

I had glimpsed enough of the varsity locker room to see that it was a large empty space, lockers around the walls. The room I wound up in was big enough, but must have housed three times as many people. The lockers were in rows, little benches in between, so you passed by row after row where naked kids were huddled in together, bumping butts with the guys behind them, trying hurriedly to pull their stuff on. I got a locker in the farthest row back, so there was a little space to move around, but a lot of other guys had abandoned the narrow rows and brought their stuff there too. Nick Kaiser was there—the kid who had talked to me at the Hargrove game—naked from the waist up, fooling with his football pants. He looked sturdy enough, but a little soft, or just smooth, none of the muscles showing that Pollett had. He grinned sheepishly as I arrived.

"I swear to God," he said. "I don't know how to put half of this stuff on."

"I'm not sure I can be much help." The cadaver in the sporting goods store had showed me a little, jerking at straps and knocking things around, but very quickly, as if any man would know how to do it.

"You're late."

"I had to stay for French."

"Jesus. I'm shaking so hard I can't even do these straps."

So I wasn't the only one. I started tearing off my clothes, throwing them in the locker.

Wearing a lazy embarrassed grin, a kid named Sennett stood back against the wall, stark naked. Even in the second week I knew his name. Everybody knew his name. He had a big reputation as a fighter, based mostly on a shrewd sense of who would back down from a fight and who wouldn't. His stiff brown hair hung down over his forehead in a little point. His face was splattered with pimples. His soft white body gradually widened, pear-shaped, into a fleshy gut and jiggly fat ass. He was a scrub on the JV football team, spent that whole year getting in for three plays at the end of a game and immediately starting a fight. While the rest of us hurried to dress, he stood around naked, reaching for his balls every couple seconds to make sure they were still there. He liked to get to practice late so he would miss calisthenics.

"No, kid." He had stepped up to a skinny freshman at the end of our bench. "It's a nose guard." He grabbed the kid's jock from his hands and jammed it down over his head, pulling it tight.

The other sophomores at that end of the room laughed heartily, in deep mock baritones. The freshmen were pretending not to see what was happening.

"At least that way he's got something to put in it," somebody said.

"Someday he might grow some balls," Sennett said. "Anything's possible."

Another freshman was leaning to get something, and Sennett pulled back his jockstrap like a slingshot, letting it snap. The sound was like the crack of a whip.

Sennett knew all the jockstrap jokes.

"You're a fairy, Sennett," somebody said. "That's your problem."

Sennett just grinned, red-faced (the kid was bigger). "I ain't no fuckin' fairy," he said.

"Jesus, Dan," Nick said to me. "Now what?"

He had just gotten his shoulder pads on, his arms through his jersey, but he was stuck there; it was all too tight.

"Little help, Sennett," somebody shouted.

"That's okay, kid," Sennett had materialized behind us. "I'll help you out. Put it through." Nick got his head through, and Sennett gave the jersey a yank, pulling it down over his back, then kept yanking, and pulled Nick backwards over the bench, and hard, with a loud crack, onto the floor.

General falsetto hilarity from the sophomores. That tone was reserved for occasions when somebody might be hurt.

"Christ, kid." I helped Nick up. It was a good thing he had the shoulder pads on.

"Yeah?" Sennett said.

"You could have hurt him," I said.

"You want to do something about it?" Sennett said.

He was smiling with one side of his mouth. That was the first time I had been challenged by a kid who was naked. At least there would have been plenty to grab on to.

"Leave him alone, Sennett," somebody said. "That poor kid's got something wrong with his finger."

I knew that would come back to haunt me. I had badly cut my middle finger opening a can, and my father had wrapped it with gauze and tape so I could practice. No disability was funnier to a bunch of teenage kids.

"What happened to your finger, kid?" Sennett said. "Somebody kick you in the ass?"

That joke, probably dredged up from his youth and told to Sennett by his great-grandfather on his deathbed, brought a huge burst of laughter from the sophomores. Sennett's mouth was moving convulsively, flesh jiggling all over his body.

"No," I said, reaching back for an old one myself. "Your mother crossed her legs."

A sudden hush fell over the room.

Really, I didn't mean a thing by it. It came to me as naturally as blinking, just one in a long series of mother jokes. So's your mother. Guess who I saw your mother with the other day. That was so funny your mother and I both fell out of bed. Why is your mother like a cup of coffee? Why do they call your mother the spider? Let's get off mothers, I got off yours. Among my friends we used them all the time.

Sennett was in agony. A wave of red was slowly spreading up his face. His mouth was twisting and writhing into all kinds of fierce expressions. His head tilted gradually to one side, and he walked slowly toward me, grabbing my T-shirt and pushing me up against the lockers. He shoved his face up to mine.

"Listen, kid," he said. "Nobody talks about my mother."

"Okay." I was staring at the spit bubbling at the corner of his mouth.

"You can say what you want about me." That a promise? "But leave my family out of this."

"All right. I'm sorry." I was just as glad he was holding my shirt that way, because my knees were shaking so hard I probably would have fallen down otherwise.

"You'll be sorrier if you do it again."

He let me go and walked away slowly, so that he only jiggled slightly. The sophomores were gagging to stifle their laughter.

Apparently we were to understand that, like many another vicious brawler, Sennett cared deeply for his mother.

"I guess you shouldn't have said that," Nick said to me, as, finally, we were trudging back up the hill. The freshmen practiced up on the main quad. They didn't even let us down on the athletic fields.

"I guess not. Lord. I really feel ready to play football."

Nick nodded. "You should have to go to school or play football. Not both."

We were beginning to see—as we hobbled along in the high-cut shoes that were still stiff, the jerseys that were tight and practically choking us—that freshman football wasn't going to be all we had hoped.

The quadrangle was not too wide, but very long, probably a quarter-mile around. Every day before practice we ran four laps, our shoulder pads flapping, cleats crunching awkwardly through the turf. I had never run that far before in my life. Our calves would be searing, lungs bursting, when Rosy and I finally dragged ourselves in. Immediately—everyone else had had a nice breather waiting for us—calisthenics would begin, jumping jacks, toe touchers, windmills, neck bridges, sit-ups, and leg raises (cramps in our stomachs as if strong hands were clawing there), an attempt at push-ups with the shoulder pads digging in at our clavicles. The ground was cold and hard, the scent of grass heavy in our nostrils. We all hoped the campus dogs hadn't done anything in our spot. We finished up with a brisk grass drill, running hard in place, throwing ourselves recklessly now this way, now that. By the time it was over every muscle in my body ached, and I was limp as a rag doll.

At that point it was time for practice to begin.

"Jeez," Sickert would say, pacing back and forth in front of the group. "Doesn't look like too many you men are in shape to me."

His face in a deep frown, one hand bearing our thick play book, he walked slowly up the long hill to the field every day. He wore an old ragged sweatshirt and some faded football pants without the pads. His hairy belly poked through beneath the sweatshirt. For the first few minutes of practice he instructed us in fundamentals. With rapid violent lunges he demonstrated falling into a stance, throwing a block, sticking a shoulder into a tackle. He would select a volunteer from the audience to work with; now and then he got carried away and knocked some poor kid down. His favorite maneuver to demonstrate, and our favorite one to watch, biting our lips, was a pass pattern, as he came blasting out of a stance with short digging steps, throwing his arms this way and that making fakes, gazing into the air for an imaginary ball. He looked like a frightened man running from a flock of predatory birds. Later in the season he mentioned he had been an end in college.

Probably he knew his football, but somehow, try as we might, we could not learn from him. It was the same problem as in math class. Every practice began with one-on-ones, and every day he paired me with a kid named Kretchmer. "Keith, Kretchmer, get in there." Sickert always emphasized staying low, so we would shove out of our stances and collide—with roughly the sound of a quiet handclap—about a foot off the ground, both of us digging away with our feet, getting nowhere. "You gotta get low, men," Sickert would say, straining his eyes to see what the backs were doing across the field. It always seemed he would rather be with them. "Keith, you gotta get under that man."

Tackling drills were brutal. The linemen in two rows formed a tunnel; the backs lined up to run through it. No fools, they kept inching further and further back to get a better start. Soon they had about ten yards to work with. A lineman heard his name barked out, jumped into the tunnel, feet dancing; the back took dead aim and came roaring down; there was a terrific crash, a loud whoosh, as the lineman's lungs collapsed, and he was clutching desperately, grabbing and clawing, trying to take the runner with him as he went over on his back. The other linemen looked away, or covered their eyes with their hands.

The rest of the afternoon we scrimmaged, full-speed, full-contact, every day. We had an incredibly complicated offense that would have done the Green Bay Packers proud. We stumbled through a play three or four times, never quite sure what we were doing, never really getting it right, while behind us Sickert was flipping madly through the play book. Must be something in there we could run. The last twenty minutes he kept saying, "One more play, men. Just one more play." We played the equivalent of a full game every afternoon.

Only twenty-seven kids had gone out for the team in the first place and, what with our expert instruction and conditioning, injuries picked off a slew of them. It wasn't long before the defense had only eight guys on it in practice scrimmages (The offense looked good under those circumstances.) Everybody was going to play. Rosy and I were starting at the tackles, going both ways. Nick was in at end on offense—he had tried out for halfback but didn't have the speed—and linebacker on defense. He looked funny in a football uniform, skinny up top, and with a bad slouch when he walked; he wasn't strong, but played with an intensity nobody else could match, lowering his head and pounding into anybody who got in his way. He shouted at the rest of us, ran around slapping the butts of the linemen as they got down in their stances. Sickert had named him defensive captain.

Our first game was only two and a half weeks after practices began. My father said he would cancel his appointments that day and come on out to the field.

"I don't know," I said. Before the season I would have wanted him to see every minute I ever played, but now I wasn't sure. "We're not really too good yet."

"No reason you should be," he said. "You just started. But I'd like to be there for your first game."

That afternoon turned out to be gray and wet. It had rained hard the night before, and all day long a heavy mist hung in the air. We met in the varsity locker room, where there was a blackboard, all of us pulling on our equipment nervously, white-faced, taking big gulps of air. We didn't even have matching uniforms, just some old jerseys that looked as if they had been used by the varsity in the roaring twenties. Coach Sickert came in, looking as if he wished there were something he could do to help. He kept saying, "Listen, men, I know you're nervous, but you gotta remember, this is our first game as coaches too. We're just as nervous as you are." That really made us feel better. When we broke out of the locker room, skidding and sliding down the hallway on our cleats, shouting, I brushed by Grupp, the varsity coach, as he stood there wearing a fat grin; it was a big thrill for me, thinking I might play for him someday.

Outside it had started raining again. The field was a mudhole. In bright new green uniforms, the other team was sharp as they ran through their drills. Lined up for the kickoff, they seemed huge, and looked fierce as they charged down under the ball, heads down, legs pumping; I made only a halfhearted attempt at a block. The kid over me at the line of scrimmage was much taller, rock hard. His face was shadowy under the helmet; I never really saw what he looked like. I expected to get clobbered, but he didn't really hit me. Instead he stood up pretty straight and just muscled me out of the way, as if to let me know he could hit harder but wouldn't if he didn't have to. One good low crack would have put him on his butt, but at that point I was scared, and bewildered, and forgot what little I did know. I let him take me out that way. Probably he was just as scared as I was.

Not much football got played that day. The field was so wet nobody could move on it. Early in the fourth quarter there was still no score, and I was out for a couple of minutes, when an end run drifted toward us over on the sidelines. Everyone was running gingerly, their feet making loud slogging noises as they moved along. Nick managed to get in front of the play, the only defender there, facing the interference. One kid went in on him low, a halfhearted block that anybody could have gotten away from, but then a big fullback came along and hit him high, a real shot, that would have knocked him head over heels. Probably he would have been all right if he could really have gone over. You could see him start to rise in the air, but his foot got caught—maybe the kid on the bottom was holding—so he didn't quite leave the ground, just crumpled over backwards where he was. The fullback came down on top of him. Somebody said later you could hear the scream all the way down on the soccer field.

Everyone rushed out onto the field, and a big crowd gathered around, but my father worked his way to the center of it and got everyone else away. It must have been nearly ten minutes that he was out there, just a little crowd of coaches around him. Finally they carried Nick off on a stretcher, very slowly, and almost immediately an ambulance came down on the field to pick him up. We heard the siren and saw the red light spin slowly through the mist and rain as the ambulance drove up the hill and away.

"It's just his leg, men," Sickert said. "We gotta try to forget it and go on." For once, though, the man seemed genuinely shaken, pale and swallowing hard. He had heard that scream as well as the rest of us.

There wasn't much game left anyway. It ended in a scoreless tie, and we all hurried off the field, cold and wet and tired. That was the only game we didn't lose all season.

I would rather have taken the bus home afterwards, but of course my father waited for me. I knew he had seen me out on the field, shying away from that kid who never really threw a block. I didn't want to face him.

But he didn't say much about the game. "At least you didn't lose."

"Yeah."

"That field was terrible. Probably the game shouldn't have been played."

"Is Nick all right?"

"It seemed to be a broken leg, but in a bad spot, up on his thigh. He was in a lot of pain. I know that must have been scary for you guys, sitting there watching that."

"Not really." Nothing like that could have happened to me. I wasn't getting in the way of any plays. Nick, I knew, was the only kid on our team who had really played.

"I don't think we'd better tell your mother about that. Not today, anyway." He looked like a man who was facing an ordeal. "That'd be all she needs."

It was early October, but there was an Indian summer that year for the week or so that I went every day to see Nick; the days were hot and dry, the blazing sun beating down through a haze onto the dusty practice field. The first time I didn't even know where the school infirmary was, and spent a while looking before a teacher directed me down to a side road of the campus, in front of a small bumpy field that was used sometimes for football drills. The varsity was there that day, in the off-white practice jerseys, torn and dirty, that made them look so tough; drymouthed, sweating, they hit the sled with loud grunts and hissed as they pushed the metal skidding over the hard dry earth. I watched awhile. Even just watching football at that point made my stomach clutch in a knot.

Coach Grupp was there, off to the side, watching his assistants put the team through their paces. He was a short round man, and stood with his arms behind his back, so his belly rested before him like a great boulder. He had a bushy mustache, and a large underlip that he characteristically pushed up and out in contemplation. His hair was unkempt and graying. Mostly he was a quiet man, with a low, hoarse voice, but regularly—already I had heard—he exploded into violent fits of temper.

"Is this the infirmary?" I nodded toward the building beside us.

"That's it," he said. "You came to see your friend."

"Yes."

"He's a tough, brave kid. All his friends should come to see him." Coach Grupp nodded with approval. "But he should never have let that guard get in on him with that low block."

"No." That was an angle I hadn't heard. It was Nick's fault he had broken his leg.

"You never get hurt if you play this game right." He took a few steps my way. "You're Keith, aren't you?"

"Yes." A shiver ran through me at the thought that Grupp knew my name.

"Sickert told me about you. One of his big boys. You're not at practice."

"I hurt my knee."

"You seem to be walking."

"My father said I should stay off it for a few days."

"Your father?" He spoke the word incredulously, as if surprised I had a father.

"He's a doctor."

"Oh." He pushed out his under lip, considering. "I suppose he should know." He turned his attention back to the field and watched for a while. "I bet you figure that'll be you out there next year."

His face had creased in an odd smile. Laughing at me? I didn't know what to make of it. But he was right: I did hope that some miraculous transformation would take place, that suddenly I would learn how to play, I wouldn't be afraid, and the next year I would be one of those hard-muscled varsity linemen pushing the sled around.

"I don't know," I said. "I'd like it to be."

"You'd like it to be." He deadened the words, saying them. "You've got to make it be."

"I know." I'd said it wrong. Had I ruined my chances?

"It's a big jump from freshman to varsity." He was going to cut me right now. "You don't get any breaks." He stared at the ground, digging at it with his cleats. "When I was a freshman I played freshman ball. The next two years I was junior varsity. Fighting to make that. And my senior year they dragged up this new sophomore, six-two, two-forty. . . ." His face wore a bitter sneer. If that sophomore had been around he'd have gone after him on the spot. "Nobody's going to give you any breaks."

He looked up at me, and I nodded.

"You need to gain some weight, don't you Keith?"

"I guess." I was a little surprised. Anyone in his right mind would have said I needed to lose twenty pounds.

"You need to gain some weight." He walked over and lightly punched my chest with his little fist. The man was a couple of inches shorter than I was. "I want my linemen big. That's what I don't have this year. I got a back field like a dream. Those Sherrill twins. This kid Pollett. He's college material. I mean big-time college. And Scovill. But I got no blockers for them. In a few years . . ." He nodded, his face just inches from mine, fixed in an odd smile. "When Pollett's in his prime, I want some big tough linemen to block for him."

"All right." I felt myself swell a little. What he wanted I wanted.

"You think about that, Keith. Now go see your friend. I'm going to work."

I walked toward the infirmary, a little relieved to get away. It was exciting to hear him, but also a little strange, too intimate. It was as if we were a couple of kids, dreaming together.

"Oh Keith." I turned. Grupp had been walking away too, but turned back with an afterthought. "You don't want to be a pussy, Keith."

I just stared at him. He couldn't have said what I thought he had.

"I know your father's a doctor. He knows all about bones and tendons and things. But you're hardly even limping. A man's got to play with the little hurts."

I swallowed, humiliated. "All right."

In his quiet, hoarse, intimate voice, he spoke the words again. "You don't want to be a pussy." He gave one small sharp nod.

We both started walking again.

It was great having a coach who urged you on with memorable moral precepts.

The infirmary was a dim, stuffy building, like a small hospital corridor. As far as I could tell when I entered, no one was around. I wandered down one wing looking for a room that was occupied. The air was heavy, stale, smelled of rubbing alcohol. As after every other day at the Academy, I felt wrung out like a rag. The conversation with Grupp hadn't helped any. The close narrow corridor made me feel faint. I saw a door that was halfway closed, pushed it open.

It might be an exaggeration to say that what I saw shocked me; probably my feeling was more like embarrassment, but it was strong and sudden. Everyone had told me how bad it looked, the cast that covered his right leg and extended partway up his torso. But when I entered, Nick was lying across the bed, on his stomach, asleep. His face was red from the heat, mouth hanging open, hair disheveled. The pillow and sheets were in tangled disarray. The cast looked dirty, huge; his one good leg and small flat butt were dwarfed by it. The room gave off a stale odor. My entrance must have awakened him; he took a moment to focus after he'd opened his eyes. "Keith. God. You should have warned me." As awkward as his position was, he couldn't change it. He couldn't move an inch. He fumbled for the buzzer. "Wait a minute. I'll call the nurse."

She came hustling down the corridor as soon as he buzzed, a heavy gray-haired woman who walked with a limp. I had seen her around campus before. Her eyes seemed always tired and preoccupied, her mouth set in a constant frown; there was a large growth to one side of her chin. Her name was Pearson, Nursie Pearson, as everyone called her. There were a lot of stories about her that even in those early weeks I had already heard, how she kept coming in suddenly to check on you if you stayed there overnight, how, no matter what you came in for, the first thing she made you do was drop your pants. Probably there were stories like that about every school nurse. "You boys aren't supposed to come in here without checking with me first," she said, but not in a mean way. "You step out in the hallway, while I get Nicholas ready for a visit." That was the first time I'd heard anybody call him Nicholas.

He looked a lot better when I came back in, over on his back, the pillows pounded and sheets straightened out. His face was pale, but that was better than when he had been lying there as if someone had clubbed him over the head. He was gazing out the window at the varsity. "Look, Keith." As we had gotten to know each other better, he started calling me by my last name. "Our favorite game. She put me in this room especially because she knew I'd want to watch." He turned to me with a sickly smile. Then he remembered. "Hey. You aren't supposed to be here."

"I hurt my knee."

"Huh. Bad?"

"I couldn't bend it at first. But it's just a little sore now. My father says I should lay off the rest of the week."

"That's a shame." I don't suppose anything short of a broken neck would have impressed him. He was still staring out the window; we both were. In small groups the linemen were running blocking drills. "How do you feel when you look out there?"

"I don't know." But I did know. I wish I could have said how scared I was even at the thought of freshman football, much less varsity. I had learned early at that school to hold things back, cover up. If you revealed a weakness at that place you got torn to shreds, as if by sharks smelling blood. "It looks rough. Harder than anything we ever do. But I guess that'll be us next year."

"It'll never be me."

"Come on, Nick. You'll be out there." I thought he meant his leg wouldn't heal.

"You just don't know, Keith. You don't know what I went through. It was like I was splitting apart. It wasn't like pain. That came later. But for a minute or so it wasn't like pain. It was way too awful for that. It was just fear. Like something had reached down out of nowhere to break me in two. There wasn't a thing I could do. It was the most helpless feeling. I never knew what it was to be afraid until then."

Nick's jaw was set, tight, as he spoke those words, spitting them out, his face pale, drained of blood. I didn't know what to say. He must have known he had embarrassed me.

"God, Keith. I hate this place. Everything about it. Three months I've got to spend here. The cast smells. I smell. It's so damn hot in here. My leg gets to itching like crazy, and there are places I can't even reach. I sleep in the day and it gives me a headache. Then I can't get to sleep at night. I got to piss in a pan, shit in a pan. You don't know how embarrassing that is. And that lady. My God. She means well. But she's always around. She gives me the creeps. You can't even hear her coming. I wake up in the morning and there she is."

That was the one thing that was to puzzle me, what came to seem his obsession with that nurse. He complained about her every time I was there, frowned fiercely when she even came into the room. I suppose it was understandable, his being that age, exposed to her all the time. A couple of days later I noticed in the back of his notebook some grossly obscene drawings, mocking her; I shut it quickly without mentioning them.

"You know my mother's got to work."

"I know." People had mentioned it since the accident, that Nick lived alone with his mother.

"She'd like to take care of me but she can't. She still comes and stays with me most evenings. I hate putting her through that. But if she didn't come, Jesus, I'd go nuts in here."

"Anybody'd go nuts in here."

"She didn't want me to go out for football. That's all she could talk about all summer." He was staring fixedly down at the cast. "But now she doesn't say a thing."

Finally he turned to me. He had hardly looked at me since I'd been there.

"You know Sickert hasn't come to see me once."

"Really?"

"He didn't even call the hospital. So many people have. You. Shit, I knew you'd come. A bunch of guys from the team. Some teachers. Helping me with my work. And Bates came down here with his whole family, a big cake, books for me to read. I swear I could have cried. But Sickert hasn't come once. Not so much as called me on the phone. The stupid prick."

Outside the varsity was hustling to gather around

Grupp, shouting and clapping as they huddled up. Nick wasn't looking out there. He was staring at the foot of the bed.

"I wish to God I'd never heard of football," he said.

Part Three

Part Three

Chapter 6

THE PROBLEM WITH the Nova was that it didn't hold anything. My mother had a perfectly good sedan, but nothing would do for my father but that we took that Nova to the beach. "We'll want to have the top down once we get there," he said. I had gotten the plates stacked on the floor in the back, sixty pounds on each side, but the bar wouldn't fit; it wouldn't begin to go in the trunk, and it wouldn't lie anywhere in the back seat without scraping the upholstery. It was beginning to look as if I would have to leave it partway out the window, holding it the whole way so it wouldn't decapitate somebody on a sudden stop. I kept trying to figure out an angle, resting it this way and that.

"Maybe if you just bent it in half," a voice behind me said.

I turned. It was Rachel. It would be. Usually Mrs. Hardy took the dog for a walk, but summer mornings, once school was out, Rachel took over. The Hardys had a squat heavy bulldog. His sloppy mouth, showing pink gums and prehistoric teeth, looked as if it could mangle your leg like a giant garbage disposal. He always growled down in his throat when anybody got near. He had stubby legs and a huge torso, so he padded along on his fat paws almost scraping bottom. Probably it would have beeen easier to roll him along, or dribble him like a basketball.

"That would be easier," I said. "Maybe we could get your father to do it."

"Are you taking that to throw it away somewhere?"

"No."

"Where are you taking it?"

Rachel was wearing her usual expression, blank of anything but a vague curiosity. Behind that mask, I knew, was a critical intellect that sliced like a razor.

None of her business. It was hard enough to admit to anybody what I was doing, but it would have been fatal to reveal it to Rachel, who had known me since kindergarten and still treated me the same way.

"To the beach," I said, reddening.

"The beach isn't for lifting barbells," she said. "It's for relaxing, and getting a tan, and going swimming, and taking a rest. It's called a vacation."

"I just want to.'"

"Even my father doesn't take his weights to the beach."

"Your father has weights?" I had a new respect for the man.

"He lifts them every morning. He's strong, *really* strong."

And you're not, her words seemed to be saying.

"The only way to get strong is to work at it."

"I think he was strong from the day he was born."

He probably came out smoking a cigar, too.

"Then he didn't have to lift weights," I said.

It was the same with everything. If you were weak and lifted weights everyone thought that was very funny, that you'd never stick with it and never get strong. Who should be lifting weights except somebody who was weak?

Just then my father came out the door, carrying a couple of suitcases.

"Dr. Keith!" Rachel beamed, blushed a little.

"Hello, beautiful," my father said.

No two high school kids flirted more than those two. It was that way with my father and most of his female patients. Women seemed to worship their doctors. He was always suggesting I take her out. "What's wrong with Rachel Hardy?" he'd say, trying to jazz up my social life. He should have taken her out himself. That was what she really wanted.

"It looks like a nice day to get out of the city," she said.

"Any day," he said, straining with the luggage, "is a nice day to get out of the city."

"What do you think of your son here with his barbells?"

"Dan." He stopped, frowned in consternation. "Not at the beach."

"I don't want to lose everything I've got," I said. "I've been working all spring." It was true. I had really improved.

"They'll rattle around back there."

"I'll hold them down with my feet."

"There's no place for the bar. You'll be fighting it the whole way down."

"It's going to be *me* back there with it." I'd have ridden on the hood to take my weights along.

"All right." He shrugged. "I don't want to hear them rattling."

"You won't hear a sound."

Rachel took a step toward my father. "I was sorry to hear you're going into the hospital," she said.

Actually, we were taking our vacation a little early, so that when we got back my father could go in for an eye operation. It had surprised me, a few months before, when he had told me that. "Cataracts? I thought only old people got those," I said. "Maybe I am old," he said, grinning. "No. People different ages get them. They're complicated for me because my eyes aren't much good in the first place. Probably I could wait awhile. But sooner or later you have to operate. We thought I might as well get one out of the way this summer."

What really surprised me was that anything at all was wrong with my father. He didn't, to my mind, belong in a hospital. I still thought of him as the burly man who had come out a few years before to throw the football around.

But he was not. Though roughly the same proportions, he was thinner than he had been, diminished at the shoulders and chest. He had always had streaks of gray in his brown hair, but now he was mostly gray, and beginning to wear his hair short, so you could see it thinning. He was starting to look old, older, really, than a man in his early forties. He didn't come out with us anymore; every evening, in fact, he went upstairs to sleep after dinner. A nap! When bedtime was only hours away. Sometimes afterwards he would come down to the basement when I was working out. "You're the one who ought to be lifting weights," I'd say. "Never," he said. "I don't want to get all knotted up." But now and then he would do a few exercises, getting me to hold his feet for the sit-ups. "I really ought to get back in shape," he'd say.

I didn't want a father who was getting old. I wanted a father who was young, and as strong as I was going to be, who would be strong with me.

"We thought August was the best time," he said to Rachel. "So many people away. Alice can take care of the routine checks. And it won't be too long before I can come in. But I'll have a patch over my eye. I won't be able to do any close work."

"We'll all miss you," Rachel said.

"Thank you, dear."

They were shameless, the two of them.

Rachel continued on her walk, and my father watched her as she went, trailed by that monstrosity on a leash. "I'm telling you, Dan," he said. "Now is the time."

"She loves another," I said.

II

Out on the road he still drove with just one hand on the wheel, the other arm resting out the window, tapping a rhythm sometimes with his fingers on the top. The Nova didn't have much pickup, but showed some speed once we were moving, and we whipped along the turnpike, the speedometer nudging toward seventy-five. "Are your eyes good enough to be driving like this?" I said. "I could make this trip blindfolded," he said. That didn't say anything about the other cars on the road. But my father had an instinct for driving, never seemed to ride too close or come up on a car too fast. It was always a relief to get off the rush of the turnpike and onto the straight flat two-lane roads, through grassy meadows, of New Jersey. "Smell the sea!" my father would say, inhaling deeply, as we got closer. "Fish!" he shouted, as we passed the overwhelming odor of a grubby commercial fishery on the outskirts of a little town.

We never really felt we were there until we crossed the drawbridge over the harbor; in the red summer sunset, yachts, sailboats, small inboards and outboards would be bobbing in the quiet ripples of the water by the docks.

"It never changes," my mother said. "It's like a picture."

We always rented the same cottage, a two-bedroom place a couple of blocks back from the water. Much of that resort was like a small town anywhere, with little houses and scraps of lawn, clothes flapping on clotheslines out back, a couple of blocks of stores and a movie theater downtown, but on back streets you came across huge white magnificent Victorian structures, hotels or rooming houses, that had been restored years before and maintained ever since. Inside, the hallways smelled of mildew, lights were dim, floors sagged and creaked, windows were filmy from the salt air. There had been a splintery, rickety boardwalk when I was a kid, but it had been wiped out by a bad storm one winter and replaced by a sea wall, into which boards had been built on the top, the same battered, weathered ones as before, it seemed. On sunny days the beaches, sectioned off by long black rock-walled jetties, were jammed with people, and at night, in families, couples, small groups of young people, they walked the boards, eating popcorn and ice cream cones, while down past them the black sea crashed in wave by wave.

There was a fun house with pinball machines and Skee-Ball, a hot dog stand where by the window the meat was sliced lengthwise and cooked over a slow grill, a cavernous high-ceilinged hall that smelled overwhelmingly of popcorn and where there was a dance every night, a little building for auctions, where old people sat stiffly, obediently, and up front a greasy man spoke in an impatient nasal tone, as if they were keeping him from something important. "Take this in your hands. Pass it around. Examine it." He jerked at his collar, glanced vaguely off toward the back. "You'll be able to see without a doubt that it is sterling silver."

I was at a stage when I didn't want to be with my parents. I wasn't sure what I wanted. In the daytime, dressed in a bathing suit and knit shirt, I walked the beaches, sitting by myself here and there. I hoped my shirt seemed to conceal a barrel chest, bulging with muscle. In the evenings, as if I had a vital appointment, I would hurry out of the cottage ahead of my parents, walk the boardwalk endlessly. I never stayed anywhere long. If I saw my parents coming, I ducked in someplace, trying to avoid them. It seemed I didn't even want to acknowledge them with a courteous nod.

"You doing any good on these walks?" my father said. "I never see you with anybody."

"I'm just walking," I said. "I like to get off alone by myself, and walk."

"Sure," he said.

He thought he knew what I was after.

But in a way—though of course he did know what I was after—I was closer to the truth than he. In those days the seashore held great promise for me. I thought that if I could be where people didn't know me I would suddenly be transformed, or at least people would see me for what I really was. One of the knowing, self-assured girls on the beach would understand my shyness and speak to me, or, among the Skee-Ball games and mock bowling alleys where you aimed at plastic pins with a metal puck, I would suddenly become glib and know what to say.

Anybody could get a girl at the beach. On a back road of the town a beautiful woman—preferably a hundred-dollar call girl on her way to Vegas—would have a flat tire and need my help (oh how can I ever thank you?); a girl would be overcome by the towering surf while the lifeguards were away and I would be the only one left to save her; on the far stretches of the sea wall late one night I would come across a solitary, lonely girl, blinking back tears. . . .

Somehow I never seemed to stumble across such situations. Girls traveled in packs (like wolves) or at least in pairs, and when I hovered around they eyed me with amusement. We know what you're after, fat stuff. At the dance hall they stared at me when I got near, then pointedly looked away. Even when they stayed put, at the beach, the game rooms, I couldn't think of a word to say. I would remember the weights back at the cottage, the sprints I would run in the morning, the football season coming up, and think: there will be a time.

So maybe I was right. Maybe I did just want to go off and walk. What I wanted was not to be with a girl, but to be alone, among girls, and dream of being with a girl.

I was out of the cottage every morning long before breakfast. Later in the day the sun would be high and hot in a cloudless sky, softening the tarry streets, but at that hour there was the hint of a chill in the air. At a restaurant on the corner, waitresses spread tablecloths and set out flowers on the outdoor tables; the scent of coffee floated on the breeze. I walked down onto the sand. The water was a slate blue, nearly gray, with the sun so low. Gulls sailed quietly above the surf. I trotted for a while down near the water, where the sand was hard, then began my sprints, falling into a stance, charging out low and hard, running for what I took to be forty yards. Slowly I walked back to where I had started. The scene around me—gulls soaring, waves crashing—was peaceful and majestic, but I was picturing another scene, the cold crisp afternoon when I would pick up a fumble and run for a touchdown, forty yards, or the play in the final seconds of the game when, running forty yards, I would make the last-ditch tackle that saved the game. Sometimes at the end of a sprint I hurled myself through the air, skidding with a thud into a bank of sand. I would lie there a moment and stare at the sea. Really, I didn't run too fast, or work too hard—not nearly hard enough. I would be pleasantly tired, glowing, as I made my way back to the cottage.

Later in the morning, out in the backyard, I worked with the weights. That was more in earnest. From the moment I touched a barbell I had loved it, the strain as I worked against a heavy weight, my muscles flushing and pumped with blood, the progress in my workouts week by week. I had read up on training—I was a great one for reading about sports—and I knew all about it; I worked the big muscle groups—thighs, lower back, shoulders—with heavy weights. Between sets I pictured the snap of the ball, my quick first step, the right uppercut I delivered with a forearm to the blocker's chest.

"Do me a clean," my father would say, walking around from the side of the cottage. "Let's see a couple presses."

He had no idea what the terms meant, had heard me use them and was just repeating.

My parents spent most of their time sunbathing that summer. My father had never been one for sitting around before, but that summer he seemed content with it. "Just to watch the ocean," he said. "I could do that by the hour." They would wander back from the beach about the time I was finishing up.

"Let's see you lift that," he'd say, touching the bar with his foot. "Lord. More than I can do."

He had been a physical culture buff in his own day, employing a primitive method of isometrics, which, along with more conventional exercises, included such things as pressing your palms together until you nearly blew a blood vessel, entwining your fingers and straining to pull them apart, and sleeping at night with a cold washcloth on your balls (a routine which he dispensed with). Back then, weightlifting was taboo for athletes, said to make you musclebound and slow; he used to kid me about weightlifters who got all cramped up trying to comb their hair. He claimed to have had quite an athletic career at his military school, running cross-country, wrestling; to hear him tell it, he practically inaugurated the track program, ran the mile, the half, the hurdles, high-jumped, put the shot, threw (what he called) the disk. He made it sound as if the other team would show up and there would be just him, one guy on the track, surrounded by all the equipment.

"Were you really on the track team?" I said, when we were out there with the weights and he was telling me those stories.

"I *was* the track team. Cross-country too. The only thing I didn't do was schedule the meets."

"Were you good?"

"Good? My name's still on the wall down there. At least I think it is. We'll have to go down there and see." He made it sound as if we were leaving any minute.

He had some great stories. I never knew whether to believe him or not.

III

When I was a kid, all I had ever wanted to do at the beach was go fishing—I used to beg my father to go out every day—but that summer it hardly came up, I was so busy with other things. We did go once, as if it were unthinkable to give it up completely. We always drove back into town, away from the water, it seemed, parked in the driveway of an old battered cottage on the outskirts. "Willy King," the small handpainted sign said. "Boats." We walked around the side of the house through some tall weeds. Out back were the canals, and he had a marina there, just a low dock—at high tide the water nearly came up to touch it—with some little outboards at either side. Willy was a big blond guy, just a kid when we first went, but every year he blew himself up eating until by that summer he looked like a middle-aged man, his eyes staring out from within a heavy weathered face. He always wore just blue jeans, more often than not was standing thigh-deep in water, working on a boat. The skin of his body was a bright red, looked painful to the touch; it never seemed to tan. As soon as he saw us, he started to gaze around at his boats. "Hiya, Doc," he said, as if he had just seen us the day before. "I got just the craft you need."

"Just a little outboard, Will," my father said. "We're just going to putter around."

The canals were narrow and shallow, surrounded by islands clumped with high green grass, as if we were sailing into the African bush country. Our little motor sputtered along, giving off a heavy scent of gasoline. Around the muck at the side of the islands little sand crabs had dug their holes, and would skitter around nervously as we passed by. I never understood how my father knew his way around in there, but eventually we emerged into the wider canals, pebbly beaches at their sides, where people fished, and sunbathed, and some even swam. I couldn't imagine why they preferred that to the sandy beaches and high breakers of the ocean, but there they were. Other years we might go from there into the bay, or even, on a calm day, out into the ocean, but that afternoon we fished the canals for flounder, drifting along almost imperceptibly without anchoring. We caught a few. You would hardly feel a bite, just a dull dead weight on your line, and they barely put up a struggle as you pulled them in.

"Not much of a sport fish," my father said. "But good eating."

"Yeah." I didn't like to eat fish, but I enjoyed catching anything.

We drifted slowly down the canal, the sun blazing away. A Jersey day, we used to call it, when the sun was just a silvery blaze in a pale cloudless sky.

That afternoon, it turns out, was the last time I ever went fishing with my father.

"You know," he said after a while. "I kid around a lot. But you are getting stronger."

"You think?"

"It's hard to tell day by day. But coming back here, after a whole year, I can see it in your shoulders and back. Up around your neck."

"All those cleans," I said, grinning. Shrugged it off. But I felt myself swell, a little catch in my throat. I hadn't realized how much I had longed for those words until I heard them.

He shook his head. "My son turning into a strong-man."

He was leaning back against the gunwale, his eyes closed to the sun, the rod resting across his knee.

"You looking forward to September?" he said.

"Football."

"I know, football. I meant school."

"I guess." I hadn't given it much thought. As far as I knew, you had to go to the school to play on the team.

"I've been wondering how you like it after a year." His old obsession.

"It's way better than public school," I said. "Ten times better."

"But do you *like* it?"

"Sure. Sure, I like it." At least I wanted to like it. I wanted to like it for him.

"I worry sometimes that it's too much for you."

We were beginning to skirt a dangerous subject. I could feel myself tighten.

"I know I could have studied harder last year."

He shrugged. "Sometimes I thought you could have studied harder."

"I'm going to study harder this year." I meant that. I felt that way every year.

"Fine."

It wasn't that I didn't spend the time. After the first semester, my father suggested, and I agreed, that I spend two hours every evening with the books. I did spend that time. But after a few drowsy minutes, over algebra, or physical science, or ancient history—you name it—I would have read the same sentence eleven or twelve times, and back in my mind I would hear the whistle for the opening kickoff. . . .

"Sometimes," my father said, "I wish you weren't so wrapped up in one thing."

"Football's only in the afternoons," I said. "One season a year. It doesn't take up study time." That wasn't entirely true. My fantasy life, for instance, took a huge bite out of the day.

"I'm just saying, Dan. I wish you weren't so wrapped up."

He knew.

"Schoolwork means nothing to me," I said. "I've heard all the arguments. You're training your mind. You've got to get into college. You're doing this now so you can do something interesting twenty years from now. But my Lord. The tombs of the Egyptian pharaohs. Barsconi's principle, or whoever he is. The irregular -ir verb. And word problems, my God. A boat is sailing down the river, and how soon will it get to the town if a wind comes up and everybody paddles with just one oar. Wait and see. Or everybody paddle with both oars. Or go drown yourselves and let the boat sink."

My father smiled. He knew my arguments were irrefutable. Did *he* care passionately about the Greek city-state?

"Football means something," I said.

"All I'm trying to say," my father said, "is that you don't have to be a football player."

I pounced on his words like a fumble.

"You don't think I will be," I said.

"I didn't say that."

"You've never thought I would be."

"I think you've got a good chance. You're really shaping up. But I hate to see you drive yourself. Beating yourself with the same thing over and over. I think if you relaxed about the one thing the others might get easier."

"I know I wasn't good last year. I didn't know what I was doing. I was out of shape. Probably still a little fat." A hell of an admission for me. "I was nervous, and scared, and I let those guys . . ." With a fist I whacked my thigh. "Sometimes I wish I'd never played those games." I knew I wished my father had never seen them. "But I think I had to go through them. This year I've got that behind me. I know it's going to be different."

"I'm sure it will."

"Nobody believes me."

"I'm just trying to say there's more to life. If you don't make the team, or don't make it like you want to,

102

or if something happened to you like happened to your friend Nick . . ."

I figured I'd kill myself.

"I'm afraid you'd be crushed," he said.

"I'll crush *them*." I whacked my leg again. Once more and that would be the injury to end my career.

"Who's this 'them'?"

"There's no use talking about it." I was beyond the point of being rational. "I'm going out. I'm going to play. What happens is going to happen. Let's wait and see."

"I'm behind you in this, Dan. I want you to be happy."

"I know."

But I didn't believe that. The forces that loomed to keep me from what I wanted were overwhelming, and I saw them everywhere. My father was just trying to prepare me for a disappointment, but I thought he was telling me not to try.

The glare was dazzling in the water, but I stared at it, hurting my eyes, because I didn't want to look at him.

Chapter 7

THE WEEK BEFORE preseason we could go any day to get our equipment; Rosy's mother drove the two of us out. "I feel as if I'm driving my son off to his execution," she said, frowning deeply with her dark heavy eyebrows.

"We're just getting fitted," Rosy said.

"For the noose." The woman had an incredible frown. "Do I come in?" she said when we reached the gym.

"Good God," Rosy said, an expression of violent distaste on his face. "No." He winced an apology at me.

The equipment was scattered all over the wrestling room, and Mr. O'Malley, a tall old bald man who was deaf in one ear, and lisped around his dentures, was there for assistance. You walked around trying to find stuff that might fit you that wasn't too beat up. It was said that first-rate players, like Pollett, had stuff ordered especially for them and were fitted in another room. I didn't see any of them around. The only guy who was there the day we went out—just my luck— was Sennett, my old pal from the locker room, standing in a T-shirt while Mr. O'Malley checked the fit of his shoulder pads.

"I probably never got in real good shape last year," Sennett was saying. He sneered, reddened. He was the kind of kid who, racked with guilt, might rattle off a confession to anyone. "I wasn't dedicated enough. I never gave what you might call a hundred and five percent. I probably didn't have the confidence in myself."

"That'th fine, thonny," Mr. O'Malley said. Sennett, unfortunately, was talking to his deaf ear.

"This year it's going to be different," Sennett said.

Where had I heard such sentiments before?

"Uh huh," Mr. O'Malley said. He himself had undoubtedly heard—or rather, not heard—such things many times before.

I didn't bother to ask after Sennett's mother.

The shoulder pads I found were massive, half again as large as any I had ever worn. The pants, unlike the ready-made ones I had bought the year before, were skimpy and empty; you slipped the thigh pads in yourself and strapped your own hip pads on, where you wanted them. The helmet was thickly padded inside and had an elaborate face mask. My shoes were new, of a soft dark leather. The jerseys, also new, were soft and white.

"The real thing," I said to the Rose, as we decked ourselves out.

"It's a new year," he said.

At least we were all in agreement.

It seemed crazy the next Monday to be getting up at the crack of dawn to go off somewhere and play football. I stumbled around pulling on some old clothes, fixed a classic athlete's breakfast of boiled eggs, toast with honey, tea. To this day I am not able to eat those foods together. One or the other of the weary martyred mothers drove us out. The old nervous jitters fluttered away in the pit of my stomach as I walked gingerly on my cleats down to the varsity field. A heavy dew was on the grass, a whitish mist on the outskirts of the field, but already behind it, melting it away, you could feel the latent deadly heat of the August sun. Most of the other guys were passing a ball around or standing in little groups, but I paced nervously among them. "Don't move around so much, kid," somebody said to me. "You'll get enough of that." An eerie silence hung over the whole scene, the white mist, quiet players in their white uniforms. Finally somebody said, "Here they come," and from up at the gym we all saw the coaches walking down in a pack, Grupp in the lead. When he hit the top step he gave a sharp blast on his whistle, and everybody gave off hollow nervous shouts, gathering around in a group on the track.

We were cheering because he was about to put us through hell.

On the first day Grupp always had a kindly glint in his eye, a beaming face, as if he anticipated a glorious experience. The first mistake anybody made, though, usually about ten minutes into the first practice, threw him into a deep gloom from which he didn't recover until well after the season was over.

He spoke in a husky intimate voice, like a lover. "This summer, fellas, I had one of the marvelous experiences of my life. The opportunity, the privilege, of visiting a professional football camp." For Grupp, the equivalent of two weeks on the Riviera. "I was able to observe a number of their training routines. Some of them I've decided to institute for us. Their method, for instance, of calisthenics." His face seemed to say he envied us all this experience. "It's marvelously economical. It has a kind of mathematical purity. The first thing we're going to do this morning is run for sixty seconds." He gestured toward the track. "Wide open.

With a sudden savage frown he gave a blast on his whistle. "Move your tails!" an assistant screamed.

The training program *was* economical. Wore us to a frazzle in no time. It involved all the old exercises, but for periods of time—thirty or sixty seconds—instead of repetitions, and always, as Grupp never tired of repeating, wide open. Jumping jacks, toe touchers, windmills, push-ups, sit-ups, bridges, grass drill. Twice we ran for sixty seconds, and once thirty. Also two times, mercifully, we rested for sixty seconds, collapsed on the grass like battlefield casualties, while Grupp, at the front of the group, proclaimed what fantastic shape we would soon be in, what miserable shape we were presently in.

"Jesus Christ, Grupp," a big lineman near me muttered. "Kiss my ass. Sixty seconds. Wide open."

I soon realized that, however much better I was than

the year before, I wasn't in good shape—those piddling little sprints on the beach had barely tuned me up—and I had never really known what it was to work on a football field. After calisthenics we hurried to the seven-man sled, and for twenty minutes or so worked on that; a burst from Grupp's whistle, a lunge and a grunt from the blockers, and we were pushing it—feet digging, sweat dripping onto the ground—over the thick dewy grass of the field. We had blocking practice, one-on-ones, two-on-ones, three-on-twos. At the end of the morning, with the late summer sun at its height, we did sprints, or, if the coaches were feeling particularly brutal, ran The Hill.

The Hill was down on the cross-country course, though not actually a slope that the cross-country team ever ran; they used a path that was much more gradual. It was not a hill that, properly speaking, you could run at all. It was nearly straight up, so that once the coaches—those little guys up on top of the cliff there—gave the word, we started clambering up on all fours, and since the grass and clover were never cut—who could negotiate a lawnmower there?—we always disturbed a number of bees who had been peacefully grazing. "God!" players would shout, as they were scrambling along and got stung. "Christ!" Anyone who would actually die from a bee sting was excused from that drill, Grupp said. Sennett immediately confessed to the life-threatening allergy that had plagued him for years. Going back down we slid on our butts, or just took a dive and let ourselves roll. Often, at the bottom, a couple of linemen took a quick break, just long enough to throw up.

In scrimmages the sophomores were used as cannon fodder, lined up in rudimentary defense while the first and second strings ran play after play to learn them. They put me over the strong side guard. Never before had I run into anybody who could block like that. He was shorter than I, and lighter, a very handsome blond kid named Hoffer, the wrestling captain that year. The ball was snapped and his shoulder was into my thighs; the two events were simultaneous. It didn't hurt to be hit by him. I just suddenly found myself backpedaling furiously until I hit the ground, wham, on my back, and saw the bright peaceful sky above me. Light and quick as a welterweight, he was up and gone, back to the huddle, while I dragged myself slowly to my feet, hobbled back into position, so I could go through the same thing all over again. I should have stayed about five yards from the ball, on my back. Would have saved us both a lot of trouble.

At lunchtime—before the light workout, without pads, in the afternoon—the scrubs all sat together in the shade of one of the trees in front of the gym. We would have showered, taken our time getting dressed, but we were still flushed and sweating, incredibly dry: from a milk truck that drove by each of us bought a half-gallon of lemonade or orangeade, and drank the whole thing. For a while you didn't even feel it going down, you needed it so much. We chewed slowly on sandwiches, strained to swallow, our hands trembling weakly as we held the bread. We didn't talk much. There wasn't much to say. Off under another tree the older kids sat, talking and horsing around. They looked ready to start again. It was tiring to knock the day-lights out of somebody for two hours, but not as tiring as it was to be on the other end.

One afternoon I had just sat down with my lunch, slumping back against a tree, not even bothering to open the bag, when I saw Nick Kaiser trudging up from the track. He was wearing an old ragged sweat-shirt, baggy and loose on him; his face was flushed a bright red and his hair damp and hanging down in his eyes. He always walked with that slouch, and he was limping that day, though he didn't most of the time, only when he was tired. He looked as if a tap on the shoulder would collapse him into a bag of bones on the ground. Slowly he walked over to where I was sit-ting—his mouth was dry as dust—and sat down beside me. I gave him a drink from my lemonade.

"You could at least take off the sweatsuit," I said.

"I'm not supposed to. It keeps my muscles warm."

"Warm? Jesus Christ. It's the end of August."

"All I know is what the man said."

"Who?"

"The coach." He smiled sheepishly, looked away. "This is the first day of cross-country."

"You? Cross-country?" Of all the kids on the freshman football team, only Rosy and I had run laps slower than Nick. He had been the first one to get there when the hitting started, but he hated to run.

"Since I was always so fast."

"You figure to make it?"

"Everybody makes JV. They just throw the whole crowd in there and let them run together. The perfect sport for a scrub. And there's not a chance in the world of making varsity. My fate is sealed." He reached over and took another drink from the lemonade. "You know what I finished out there today? Last. Dead last."

"What the hell. The first day."

"I'm hoping it'll make my leg stronger."

"How is the leg?"

"Right now? About to fall off. I had to stop out there twice."

It was the Nick I remembered talking, his face set, eyes staring. I couldn't believe he'd finish last too many times.

"I'm also going out for wrestling," he said.

"Really? You ever wrestled?"

"There's a first time for everything. It seems to be what's left for me. There are weight classes, and skills you can learn. Everybody's starting off about even. I've been working out some. Light weights. But this leg has got to be stronger."

"You've got a few months."

"God." He shook his head. "I hate the thought of finishing last in those meets."

We just sat there awhile. I opened my lunch. Peanut butter and jelly. Great. With that and my pink lemonade I was all set for kindergarten.

"I've decided it's all right, Keith," Nick said finally.

"What?"

"Everything." He nodded toward the varsity, off under another tree. "I watch you guys practice, and I remember when I wanted that. A part of me still does. I mean I'm watching you, and remembering, and it's

109

like I still want it. That's ridiculous. The doctor said never again. He's not any too wild about the wrestling. Besides, I think if I put those pads on again I'd shake so hard I couldn't even leave the locker room. But all those hours lying in bed, and hating football, and hating the school, and the guys on the team, and Sickert, and the nurse, and the varsity outside my window, all of it, everybody." He nodded, his jaw clenched. "I hated you. All of you had done that to me. And then one afternoon, like it came out of nowhere, I suddenly thought, 'No. It was an accident. It didn't have to be football. It could have been anything. Anybody.' And all of a sudden, as much as I was hurting, it was all kind of funny. Like what were the odds that it would happen to me. But I wasn't hating anymore. It was all right."

I wished I could have believed him. I believed in that moment he was describing, of course: he wasn't lying. But there was something in the way he slouched, and limped, the weariness in his eyes, the way he talked about cross-country, most of all the way he was staring over at the varsity. Part of the old bitterness was still there.

"What about you?" he said. "Am I going to be seeing you out there against Hargrove this year?"

"They haven't made any cuts yet."

"Great."

It was hard for me to admit. With myself I could face the truth. But it was hard to say it to someone else.

"I don't think you better count on it," I said.

He smiled weakly. He understood. Did my eyes have the same look as his, as I stared over at the varsity?

"You hang in there, Keith," he said.

II

At the beginning of the second week a new coach arrived. After the first day I had gotten in the habit, like the others, of just standing around on the field before practice began, watching the gym for the pack of coaches to emerge with Grupp at the front, but that morning just a single man came out, already running—we could hear his cleats hit the cement—with an easy stride, a whistle in his mouth giving off little bursts with every other step. "Oh God," somebody near me said, "he's back," and around me all the older kids started quietly to swear, though a few of them, as if at a private joke, were smiling a little. Stopping dramatically on the top step, the man gave a long shrill blast on the whistle, pointed down the track. "I give you fifty yards," he shouted. "Take off."

We were not much beyond the first turn when I heard his voice behind us, "Move. Move. Move." Unbelievable. A coach was actually running. In fact, he seeemed to be gaining on us. Until that day, if he showed up for the running at all, Sennett had always brought up the rear, a mask of agony etched on his face, but that morning the voice continued—"Harold Sennett. If I catch you on this lap, you run again"—and it was amazing the reserve of speed that Sennett found, flying past me and the rest of the linemen, gaining on the big pack up front. "If you report late to practice once this year, you run twice. You run with me. If you seem to be having trouble with calisthenics, I'll give you help with them after practice." I couldn't understand how the man had so much voice; I'd have been hard-pressed to choke up a death rattle at that point. But it wasn't Sennett, it was all of us; we were all running faster, as if that were the voice of doom that was gaining on us.

He did not, like the other coaches, stand around during calisthenics adjusting his jockstrap and burping off his big breakfast, but jumped in with us, the first one up in front of the group. "Sixty seconds. Fast as you can. Jumping jacks. Go." He was of medium height, had a hard trim muscular build; his brown hair was cut short as if to be out of the way, and his face registered no exertion. "Faster, faster," he shouted, and the older kids grinned, shouted back at him, but they were moving faster. He went after particular players, challenged them to exercises, and played no favorites; that morning he challenged Rosy to sit-ups and Pollett to push-ups. I had never seen the Rose move so fast, but the man beat him two to one, and he edged Pollett by three push-ups, his body straight as an iron rod and his arms powering him up and down as if he weighed nothing at all. We were all working harder, though it didn't feel that way; maybe we were going too fast to notice. By the time the other coaches got down to the field we had already finished.

"They're all yours, Mr. Grupp," the new man said.

"Thank you, Mr. Wiggins." Grupp was smiling contentedly. He had just unleashed his secret weapon.

After the sled drill—Wiggins had stood at the center, directing us with bursts from his whistle, cajoling us to hit harder—Grupp said, "Mr. Wiggins. Would you like a group for the drills?"

"I would love one." Loud groans from all the linemen.

Grupp seemed to pause, considering. "All the kids from the defensive unit," he said, "the scrimmage defensive unit, follow Mr. Wiggins."

That, in fact, was the first cut of the year, though it was so unobtrusive—or we were so tired—that we didn't notice.

Wiggins was running to the far end of the field, as if the mere presence of the older kids would contaminate us. We stumbled after him. "Two lines," he shouted as he got there. "Facing each other. Hurry hurry hurry." One by one we straggled in. "Manager," he shouted. "I want water up here. My boys first. Then the varsity." A chorus of hoots from the other end. He gazed at the ragged motley group that was standing in front of him. To anyone who looked around—and I was looking around—the light was starting to dawn. Wiggins himself had said it: the varsity was at the other end. "All right, boys," he said. We were not men. "One knee."

While the manager passed around the water—"Take all you need," Wiggins said, "but don't bloat yourselves"—he finally came down a little, talked more quietly, and we heard our first of the Wiggins speeches.

"Blocking in football is fairly simple. It's surprising, really, how many wrong ways it's done, when the right way is really so simple. You drive your body into the other guy's body and make it move. There are a few things you need to get pretty close to right. There's a place for your head. There's an angle for your back. Your feet have to keep moving, or he'll never go anywhere. But the basic operation is very simple."

It was downright insulting. Here we were, after a week of scrimmaging the best players the school had to offer, and he was telling us what a block was. He made us get in our stances, hold them while he checked every little thing. According to him, something was wrong with all of them. We had to walk through a block, step by step, like a stop-action camera. If somebody's head, foot, elbow, was in the wrong place, he came over and moved it. We did it again. Again. Then we went through the whole thing at half-speed.

Meanwhile the varsity was whacking away like a herd of rams, sharpening themselves to grind us up. I kept thinking, "When's he going to give us something we can use?" But the first time we ran a block full-speed he started screaming as if he'd stumbled over a corpse. "No no no. Terrible. Terrible. You ducked your head. Your feet didn't move. You took two steps and both fell down. Again. Again. We don't leave here till you do it right." The varsity had stopped, was looking up at us and jeering, but he seemed not to hear. After a while Grupp yelled up, "Mr. Wiggins. When will your boys be ready to scrimmage?" Wiggins's voice was shrill and definite. "Three weeks at the earliest."

But we were scrimmaging that day. During a scrimmage Wiggins concentrated his efforts, let the rest of us get beat all to hell while he worked with one man. After a while it was my turn. Hoffer had just hit me a particularly vicious shot, practically depositing me at Wiggins's feet, and my lungs were empty, ears ringing, when Wiggins helped me up.

"Dan Keith." He had learned my name in the one-on-ones. "Who's your insurance with?"

"What?"

"You're getting killed out there, son. How long has this been going on?"

"However long we've been practicing."

"You must really be enjoying it."

I shrugged. Enjoyment had nothing to do with it.

"I take it you're open to suggestions," he said. I nodded. "All right. Forget about beating him head-on-head. Forget about making tackles in a varsity scrimmage. Forget there's even a man running the ball. I want you to watch for the snap. When you see the ball move, the second you see it budge, I want you to dive for his ankles. Take them out from under him. Imagine you're going to drive them a couple yards back. But the important thing is to be down that low. If you've got his ankles he's not going to move you anywhere. You understand what I'm saying."

"Yes."

"You've got to quit thinking about making the varsity for a while." Already he knew me. "It's getting you killed. I want you to concentrate on one thing. Grabbing ankles. Eating dirt."

I tried it. It was an odd sensation, hardly felt like winning. Hoffer grunted in surprise and came down on me hard. A couple of backs were coming through that hole, and one of them kicked my helmet; it sounded and felt as if the whole team were coming down on me. But it didn't hurt. I wasn't on my back. Was that what they called making the stop?

Hoffer stood up sneering, red-faced. "Come on, kid. Play football."

Wiggins was already there. "That's football. Can't you take him?"

"I can take him if he'll come at me, instead of digging a hole like a worm."

"You mean if he stands up and gives you the block. He just decided to quit that. You've got to make an adjustment."

Hoffer spat, turned away, shaking his head.

Wiggins laid his arms on my shoulder pads, looked me in the eyes, nodded. "We're going to do it again," he said.

By the end of the morning our whole line was submarining, clogging things up something awful. When a play didn't go, Wiggins would whoop, holler, in a shrill falsetto; Grupp turned away and slammed his clipboard to the ground. I sensed a certain antagonism between the two men. Grupp liked it when Wiggins trained and conditioned the players; he didn't like it when Wiggins did it *too* well, so the younger kids showed up the varsity.

Wiggins taught us simple stunts, the linemen crisscrossing on their charge, to confuse the blocking. We weren't beating them every play, or anything like it, but much more than you'd have ever thought a few days before. Most important, the game was beginning to make sense to us. We were beginning to know ourselves. The varsity was better, but they weren't a fearsome implacable force. There were certain things we could do. Some days we held them almost to a standstill.

Finally I had something to talk about on visits to my father at the hospital. Sleepy after dinner, bruised and weary, I took the streetcar into Oakland most evenings to see him; my mother would have spent much of the day there. The August evenings were sticky, the air stale and heavy. Some nights the streetcar moved haltingly through ball game traffic; I got out a few blocks early and made my way through the tide of people on their way to the game. The hospital was partway up the steep hill on the other side of Fifth, toward the football stadium.

When I was a kid my father had taken me along when he made calls at the hospital. We walked quickly—with that air of authority a doctor bears—over the marble floors, past the people waiting in the lobby and the nurses moving quietly through the hallways. He had to leave me in a lounge for the doctors, where they usually came only to pick up their coats or leave them; there were some old crumpled magazines there, and I would leaf through one looking at the pictures, but then begin to think, as gradually the minutes passed and he didn't return, what if he doesn't come back? What if something happens, and I just sit here and sit here, and my father never comes back to get me? The longer I waited the more worried I got, as one man after another passed the doorway and wasn't him. Why, I wonder, did I want to go to the hospital if I always got so scared? Finally I would hear his peculiar stride and immediately recognize it, that little extra click to the right heel. He always did come back.

So it seemed strange to be entering the hospital without him. I walked uneasily through the halls, expecting that any minute someone would stop me. His wing of the hospital wasn't air-conditioned, and it was deadly in there that summer, with the heavy scent of hospital alcohol and that other hospital smell, that seems to be old bandages, and the scent of people lying too long in bed, and the perfumes and powders of women visitors. The windows were open, letting in stale outside air and the sounds of traffic. In the dying light of the day my father still would not have turned a lamp on in his room, and he had his glasses off because of the big bandage of a patch on his eye; as he turned to me when I entered, his head rolling slowly on the pillow he lay back against, I must barely have been a shadow. "Hello, Danny," he said.

People shouldn't be held responsible for the way they look in the hospital, but I hated the way my father looked. His hair was disheveled, and his face was pale, and he lay back against the incline of the bed as if he couldn't lift his head, though I knew he was just trying not to put a strain on the stitches. He seemed thinner around the face and neck, and sometimes he wouldn't have shaved, because all he could use was an electric razor and that was rough in the heat. He smiled at me, but his mouth was dry, and the smile seemed weak, as if he barely had the strength for that. His one good eye didn't really seem to focus. I felt as if I were visiting an eighty-year-old invalid.

"Lord, it's hot," he'd say, the first thing he said every evening. "The nights in this place. I never knew."

"Don't you want me to turn on a light?" I'd say.

"If you want. Doesn't matter to me."

I would turn a lamp on or not, and sit down in a chair in the corner, by the open window.

Once I was there it was pretty uncomfortable, looking for something to talk about. It made no sense to ask about his day. He would ask about football, and the first week it was hard to talk about practice without getting too specific about what was happening. After

Wiggins arrived, things were better. I was more animated, would catch myself being cheerful, would actually have something to tell my father as soon as I got in the room. I talked about the workout, the scrimmages; I didn't describe it as the JVs against the regulars, but just a big varsity scrimmage, where I happened to be playing defense. "They never knew where we were coming from next," I said to him one evening. "We knew they were practicing passes, and we kept stunting, the guards going wide, and just about the time they'd sit back on their heels, we'd play one straight and go right over."

My father was smiling contentedly, peacefully, as if he were about to doze off; he didn't seem to care what I said, as long as I was talking with energy and had something to say.

"So this Wiggins is quite a man," he said.

"Sure." I didn't think I'd been talking about Wiggins. I thought I'd been talking about football.

"You really like him."

"I guess." I frowned, thinking about it a moment. "I like what he's taught me. But he's a hard man. Hard to like."

"Come on, Dan. You love him."

I reddened. "Let's not get carried away." The old man was obviously delirious.

"No. It's good. One man can mean so much. More than all the rest of your education put together. It doesn't matter if it's on the football field, or where it is. It doesn't even matter if it's at school. He sounds like an authentic man."

"He is." I had spoken quickly, but stopped to think about it a moment. If he was authentic, that didn't say much for everyone else. Already I had noticed that, even in casual moments, he and the other coaches didn't seem to have much time for each other.

"Anyway," I said, "I can't wait for you to see me play. It's not going to be like last year."

"I can't wait either. Lord. I can't wait to get out of here."

It turned out there was a problem about that. Obviously there was a long and delicate convalescence after a cataract operation—my father told me he even had to be careful about the way he sneezed, because of the stitches—but we thought a lot of that time could be spent at home. One night, though, after I had gotten home on the streetcar and gone to see my mother in the bedroom, she said, "They've decided to keep your father at the hospital a few extra days."

"What for?"

"Just to make sure everything's okay." She wasn't looking at me, was staring at her fingernails as she put polish on them, trying to sound casual. "That everything heals all right."

My mother was busy those days, what with seeing that I got to and from practice and that she got in a long visit with my father every day. She didn't go just for a few hours, but spent most of the day there, even eating her lunch at the hospital coffee shop, and if the visits were hard for me they must have been worse for her. When she was tired she seemed to get hurried and impatient; I would hear her moving in the kitchen with loud quick little steps, pans clattering all over the place, and in the evening she rushed around doing all kinds of trivial things, dusting, fluffing pillows, straightening rugs. She smoked constantly, expelling what seemed to me an incredible amount of smoke with her words as she spoke, and in little gusts between phrases, and long exhalations at the end of a sentence.

I did not like the new tenseness about my mother, the hard sad look around her eyes when she was tired, the way she rushed off to the hospital every morning like a soldier going into battle. Her jaw clenched a little as we talked about my father, as if she were angry, or impatient with what I was saying.

"The operation's been a strain on him," she said.

"I know."

"He's tired, and weak, and doesn't feel like doing much. There's no reason for him to be home."

"You make him sound like an old man."

"He is *not* old."

"You're the one who's saying he's weak and tired."

"Your father is not well." She glanced up toward

me, then looked back at her fingernails. "He's been through a major operation."

"He was well enough before."

"No."

"But he didn't look like that. I think we should get him out of there. It's what he wants." It was what I wanted.

"The doctors just want to keep him an extra week."

"Another week!"

"They know what's best for him. As much as he wants to leave, he understands that."

But I didn't understand. I only knew what I saw. They had taken him into the hospital for an operation he hardly seemed to need, and now, as if to prove them right, he seemed to have fallen ill.

Chapter 8

THE THING TO DO in those days, when school was out
and you had some time on your hands, was go to
Poplar Street. Three blocks of elegant fashionable
shops were there, and a couple of bars, and some
eating places. On Saturday nights the streets were
jammed, especially the corners around some pizza
places, and it was hard to negotiate a car, because
people kept spilling off the sidewalk. Only a single cop
patrolled on those nights, a small stocky Italian, and
beside him, on a short leash, walked a German shepherd that came to his waist; the air of eagerness, and
restraint, in that dog, and the apparent bad temper of
the cop, who walked around scowling and spoke to no
one, served to keep the crowds from getting too unruly.

There hadn't seemed much to do, though, on the afternoons early in the summer when the Rose and I had
gone down. We could have gone in the shops and
looked at the clothes, though that held little fascination
for either of us. We did go into a small record store
and looked over the albums. There was a bar on the
street where it was said anybody could get served, but
at the age of fifteen, in the middle of a summer afternoon, we weren't about to try.

What you had to be able to do, that we had not yet
learned to do, was to stand around on a streetcorner
and look as if you were doing something.

One Saturday afternoon the Rose and I had walked

the street three times when he said, "Why don't we go see somebody?"

"Like who?"

"I don't know. Sedgefield is walking distance." He was wincing, as if the whole thing were a pain. "How about Sara Warren?"

"Okay." My heart took a dive and bounced off the pit of my stomach.

He couldn't just have thought that up, I decided, as we were making the long trip up among the hills on the other side of Fifth. He must have been thinking about it for days, and let us tour Poplar Street all that time while he was getting up the nerve to suggest it. Casually.

Sedgefield was a long winding road of very expensive houses, off from the crush of the city. It was like a pleasant woodsy park where a few wealthy people had been given the chance to build; houses sat back among high stands of oak and maple, or surrounded by soft sweeping lawns. It seemed we traveled forever to get to Sara's, an enormous white brick place in a little valley, with a gravel driveway that curved down past the front door. One look at that house by myself and I'd have turned around and headed back, no matter how far I had walked, but the Rose just bore down the driveway as if we were picking up a friend to play ball and gave a loud whack on the door with the heavy knocker.

My problem at such moments was a vivid imagination. I figured probably Sara would recognize us ("Hello, Bobby, and ah, um . . ."), but maybe our visit would make no sense to her. What do you mean you came to see me? A tall severe butler would open the door and frown in distaste at the spectacle that presented itself. Sara's mother would answer and slowly admit us, her face frozen in horror at the incredible faux pas we had made in coming over.

The door clicked open and Sara was standing there. "Bobby and Dan. How nice. Come in."

Magically, to my mind, the door swung open to let us enter.

If anything, on that afternoon and the others that summer when we went to see her, Sara looked better to me than she had at the parties. She would be wearing a light sweater, maybe a pale blue or yellow, and tight jeans that hugged her small shapely butt; she kept stuffing her hands into the front pockets, as if doing an imitation of a teenage hood. Usually she was barefoot. She wore just a touch of makeup, the color so faint on her mouth that you weren't sure it was there. Her hair was that bright blond in its natural curls.

Just inside the door was an Oriental rug over the thick white carpet that covered most of the house. A little down the hall was a living room, where I could glimpse a huge marble fireplace, a grand piano to its left in a corner. There was a wonderful silence to that house; even the door closed behind us quietly.

"We could sit in the living room," Sara said. "Or we might be more comfortable downstairs."

"Maybe downstairs," Rosy said. Anything would be cozier than what we had seen.

I couldn't imagine being comfortable anywhere in that house.

But it was different downstairs, a long low-ceilinged room with dark wooden paneling and wide low couches against two walls. There was a Ping-Pong table and a plush regulation pool table. Sara's brother was there that first day, shooting pool and listening to a piano sonata. He was a tall man with floppy sandy hair and a friendly smile; his face, disconcertingly, was a dead ringer for his sister's. She kept insisting we'd be glad to have him stay, but he said no, no, he'd just been about to leave, and with rapid accurate shots rammed home the last four balls on the table.

"How old is your brother?" Rosy said, after we'd seen him around a few times.

"Twenty-three."

"Does he work with your father?"

"He doesn't work at all at the moment. Father's all upset."

"He's not married?"

"He doesn't seem interested. Happy the way he is." She looked up at us with a little smile. "He's a dear person, and I love him more than anybody."

122

The Rose and I nodded, as if we ran into such situations all the time.

The wonderful thing about our visits to Sara, which soon became regular, was that they were effortless. She would put on a record, usually one of the dreamy romantic ballads of the late fifties, and sit—with a leg drawn to her chest—between us on the couch. Always she talked for a while about what she had been doing. She owned her own horse and went riding in Schenley Park nearly every day. Often she went to the club—wherever that was—and played tennis; we were invited to come sometime. Gradually, about the time my palms stopped sweating, she worked the conversation around to us. Rosy immediately piped up about football, something I would never have done, and she didn't know beans about it, but didn't shy away from it. She asked specific questions—"I want to know about this," she said—and seemed to make sense of our answers. Later in the afternoon we played a game of pool or Ping-Pong. She was a crack player in both and didn't try to hide it. She could play Ping-Pong with spins and lobs, but put us away with speed. She had us lunging all over the place, the Rose giving off his usual grunts and shouts, landing on the table like a beached porpoise when he missed. In pool, with her delicate hands and small body, she leaned across the table and snapped the balls into the pockets with deft hard shots; obviously she had learned from her brother. The Rose and I stood there watching, holding our cues.

Unfortunately there were often other people there when we went to visit, older guys from Arnold, but also occasionally some total strangers. She organized little groupings, people playing doubles at Ping-Pong or gathered together around the pool table, but that never helped, because we were all there to see her, by herself.

It was no wonder that Sara hadn't been surprised that first day by our visit. Half the city seemed to visit her.

One visitor in particular annoyed me, a thin smirking chap with almost no chin. He always wore a blazer, even in the hottest weather, and smoked cigarettes in a holder; he had just graduated from boarding school and was off to Yale the next year. When he was there, Sara's brother stayed downstairs sometimes to talk to him. In a way Sara paid less attention to him than to anyone—he just sat there on the couch, never joined in the games—yet I had a feeling, almost because she didn't seem to notice him, that he had the inside track. Maybe it was just his way of being in the house. He seemed to belong. I could imagine him staying after the rest of us were gone.

II

Making phone calls had always been a trauma for me. I waited until the downstairs was deserted, stepped softly back to the den, and quietly closed the door. I got the phone down from the table, set it beside the couch, not even attempting at first to approach it: I was brave, not reckless. I opened the phone book and stared at the number for a while. Every time I reached toward the phone, my heart began to thump, a pulse fluttering in my throat, palms beginning to sweat. All that would have been all right—I didn't *think* Sara would be able to hear my heartbeat over the phone— except that something drastic had happened to my breathing: I found myself suddenly gasping, then gulping for air, blowing it out with gale force. When finally I had screwed up my courage, stretching and pacing and hyperventilating as if awaiting the kick-off—be aggressive out there! *hit* that phone call—I heard the slow tread of the footsteps coming down the stairs: my father leaning against the wall, feeling his way.

As soon as he had come home I felt I had been right all along. His color improved. He no longer seemed weak and weary. With just a small beige patch on his eye, he could wear his glasses, and see a little better, though it still made me nervous when he hesitated at the stairs, feeling out with his foot before he came down. He still couldn't read for too long, and didn't have much to do, but would sit downstairs with me in the evening in the old plaid bathrobe he liked to wear around the house, and we would listen to a ball game on the radio, and talk some.

By the time he got back to the den I had the phone put back and the book put away.

"You want to watch the game?" he said. "They're in Philadelphia. It's on TV."

"Maybe later," I said. "I don't feel like it right now."

"You got to feel like it when the game's on."

"It's going to be on a couple hours."

"The middle innings are always the dull ones. Half the time I just want to turn it off."

I had already stood. "I'll be down in a couple minutes. I probably won't miss a pitch."

He was staring around the room with his one good eye, trying to figure out why I'd been sitting there.

"You were doing something important? I could have stayed upstairs."

"Stay here. Please. Just sit down." Sit anywhere, as long as you stay put.

So I had to take the whole operation upstairs and start over again, very quietly closing the door to the guest room, putting the phone in position, opening the phone book, staring at the number. From the downstairs den I could hear the blare of the pregame interview.

Finally (he spins the chamber, puts the gun to his head) I made the call. The first moments were the worst, when I heard a soft distant voice at the other end and was choking out a request to speak to Sara, but it was she who had answered, and by some miracle—no doubt from the agonized gasps—she knew who it was, and interrupted me.

"Dan. How are you tonight?"

"Fine." Having a coronary, but otherwise okay.

"I guess you've started practice."

"Yes."

"It must be exhausting."

Nothing compared to this phone call. "It is."

"I can imagine."

I hoped she kept to the short easy questions.

But as she started talking—long soothing sentences, as if she knew I was near collapse—gradually my pulse slowed, my breathing grew calm. As it turned out, the Rose started seeing another girl that fall and we stopped our visits to Sara's house—I wouldn't go alone—but I replaced them with phone calls. I grew to love those conversations. As if she had nothing in the world to do but talk to me, Sara spun them out, told stories with endless digressions, ran through the banal details of her day, whispered mildly risqué jokes. It was as much a fantasy for me as anything else, picturing her lovely blond head, limpid eyes, taut tender mouth, being lulled by her voice. Always she was patient—"Mmm. Sure"—when I finally got around to mumbling my invitation, that first night, to a Labor Day party at the country club the Rose belonged to.

"It's supposed to be the last big thing of the summer," I said. "The first of the fall."

"I know." Couldn't get one up on her with the social schedule. "It sounds wonderful."

Ah, success.

"I was wondering if you'd like to go with me."

"I'd love to. Really. I really would love to. But somebody already asked me."

"Oh."

"I do hope to see you though. I will see you there, won't I? We can talk, or dance or something."

"Sure."

"I'll really be looking forward to that."

I don't know how she did it. A refusal from her was better than someone else accepting. Relaxed, drained, my ego swelling fit to burst, I knew I would call her again.

I had barely hung up when I heard my father coming up the stairs, with that same slow tread. I opened the door and walked out into the hall. He was staring down at the steps as he walked, as if his neck were tired, or as if he could barely see them.

"That team's got no pitching," he said. He had heard the door open. "There's not one starting pitcher on that team."

"I was just coming down," I said.

126

"Forget it. The game's over. They might as well throw it up there underhanded."

"It can't have been more than a couple of innings."

"That's all it took."

I was disappointed. I had wanted to watch the game with him.

He had gotten to the top step, and turned around, fooling with the sash of his robe. He focused in the dim light with his one good eye. His face relaxed into a smile.

"What did she say?" he said.

III

We had the Labor Day weekend off from practice, and I spent Saturday afternoon over at Rosy's house listening to records. We lay on the twin beds of his attic room, moving only to turn an album over or put on a new one.

"What do you mean you're not going?" he said when I told him. "Everybody's going."

"I called Sara and she's already been asked."

"So call somebody else."

"I wanted to go with Sara."

"Ah." He touched his heart, fluttered his eyelids. "Young love."

"Up yours."

"You hang on everything she says when you're there. You practically pass out if she looks at you. It's perfectly obvious."

"I bet she's going with that guy in the blazer." Change the subject.

"So come anyway. He'll probably die of lung cancer in the middle of the party. And if he doesn't, there'll be plenty of girls there. Not everybody'll have a date. All of Arnold's going to be there, I swear. The whole football team."

That settled it. If the whole football team was going to be there, so was I. Maybe they'd introduce us at a break in the action.

But without a date I couldn't double with the

Rose—that had been the plan—and my father wasn't able to drive yet, so that left only one way for me to get out. A hard-nosed lineman on the football team, risking my neck every time I stepped on the field, I swore on the way out that I would never again be driven to a party by my mother.

Her mood had improved since my father had gotten home, and she was full of herself that night; she thought it was wonderful that I was going to a dance at the country club and she kept talking about parties in her day, where it sounded as if everybody spent most of the night eating, and all the girls got together and squealed every few minutes, and seven or eight of them went to the bathroom every now and then to smoke a cigarette (one drag apiece), and at moments of high excitement they all raced out on the dance floor and did the Big Apple.

"I know you're going to have a good time," she said when she dropped me off.

Just get out of here fast, I wanted to say. Somebody might see you.

As I headed down the walk, she leaned out the car window. "Be sure to dance with the Blair girl."

Christ! I made it a practice to avoid at all costs the girls my mother wanted me to dance with.

At the top of the driveway was the clubhouse, an elaborate white rickety structure like a hotel at the seashore. Inside—I had been a few times with the Rose—it was silent and cool and furnished with quiet taste, huge picture windows looking out on the putting greens and ninth fairway; the wooden floor of the grill were pockmarked with golf spikes, and upstairs there were living quarters for a few old gaffers who still tottered around dreaming of the days they had been able to handle a mashie and niblick. Outside, down to the right, through a small grove of trees, was the swimming pool where the party was, its water blue and peaceful on that soft evening. After a blazing afternoon the air was still warm, but as night came on we felt a chill, like an omen, and out over the golf course the sunset had an autumnal copper tint.

Everyone arrived in summer clothes, the girls in cotton dresses that were a bright white against their deep tans, the boys in lightweight jackets—madras and seersucker—and dark slacks. People went swimming first, and I wasn't wild about that—I hated to ruin the neat impression made by the cut of my sports jacket—but it wasn't any good to be standing around in street clothes while everyone else was swimming, as if I were disfigured by a hideous birthmark, so I got into my suit and tried to keep my torso under water most of the time.

After a while the buffet was announced, and everyone got dressed—their hair still damp and skin still ruddy from the swimming—for the food, grilled hamburgers and hot dogs, corn on the cob, potato salad, fresh tomatoes, plates of summer fruit, homemade cookies and cupcakes. While we ate, a little band was setting up in one corner, a couple of saxophones, a drummer, an electric guitar and a little electric piano, and just about the time everyone was leaning back from their plates it started to play.

Up until then it had been all right. A lot of people, though mostly boys, had showed up without dates; at the pool everybody was thrown together and at dinner just scattered at random around the long picnic tables. But once the music started it was obvious who was unattached. The remaining girls were snapped up immediately. A lot of the boys, myself among them, stood around the fringes of the patio and tried to look as if we were jazz aficionados and had just come to appreciate the subtleties of the band.

What was bothering me at that point was that I hadn't seen Sara at all. After a while she did show up, when dinner was over and the dancing had started, and she was with the guy who I thought had the inside track, the man with the miniature chin. He was wearing—surprise, surprise—a blazer, and smoking his cigarettes in that holder. Probably they had come late because he never ate, just lived on cigarettes, and I didn't think, from the looks of him, that the guards would have let him in the pool without an inner tube. He didn't dance any of the fast numbers, but did try the slow ones, holding Sara's arm out straight and spinning around dramatically as if they were doing the tango. Between the slow numbers they just stood around, he with his arm still around her waist, she with hers around his shoulders. She didn't need a very long arm.

I had been watching them steadily for some time, noticing, actually, how thin his neck was, and how easy it would have been to snap it in hàlf, when, from behind, somebody grabbed me around the waist and hoisted me high in the air. The arms were clasped tight just under my diaphragm, shaking me like a rag doll.

"Say you give, you son of a bitch," a hoarse voice growled. "Or you're gonna get wet."

"I give." This was all I needed.

"Chickenshit." The arms dropped me and I turned around, trembling. It was Nick.

"Jesus Christ." I could have killed him. "You're pretty strong for a skinny kid."

"You're not such a big load," he said. "For as fat as you are."

His date, beside him, and eating from a big paper plate of fresh fruit, burst into laughter.

"I'm kidding, Keith," Nick said. He turned to her, blushing, more embarrassed than I was. "He used to be fat. But now he's all muscle. He plays varsity football. He's going to be in there against Hargrove."

She was grinning irrepressibly, and slipped a melon ball into her mouth. "He looks tough," she said.

"I'm serious," Nick said.

"I know, Nick." She was still grinning.

"Say hello to him," Nick said, taking the plate of fruit. "He's my best pal. I tell him things I don't tell anybody."

"Hello," she said, nibbling at the end of a strawberry.

"Say *hello* to him," Nick said.

She stepped forward and, softly, kissed me on the mouth.

"That's the way we say hello out in Hargrove," Nick said. Now he was grinning, had grabbed my arm. "You like that, Keith?"

"It's definitely the way to say hello," I said.

"Her name is Kathy," Nick said. "I think she likes you, Keith."

Nick was all jazzed up. If I had dropped him into the pool he would have sizzled. His hair and Kathy's was plenty disheveled, and their faces were red—along with the grin, Kathy seemed to wear a perpetual blush—and Nick's mouth looked as if he'd been off practicing the bugle.

"We were out looking at the golf course," he said. "It's pretty nice. Especially when you get close up. Like about an inch away. Lying down on it."

"It's so . . . ," Kathy groped for a word. "Grassy."

I wouldn't have called her a raving beauty. She was a little on the heavy side, and had big round cheeks. Her brown hair curved around them and made a little frame for her face. She actually seemed slightly bigger than Nick. He'd better be careful what he said. But every inch of her was friendly, and she had those large soft lips, and she was attentive to Nick, leaning against him, giving him little squeezes, tugging at handfuls of his hair.

"Where's your date?" Nick said.

"I don't have one."

"Keith." He frowned belligerently. "Is every girl you know here? Every single one? With a date?"

"No."

"Then where's your date, Keith?"

"All right, all right."

"We could have fixed him up," he said to Kathy.

"We could have fixed him good," she said.

"He could be out there on the golf course right now."

Now they told me.

"You got to know how to get girls, Keith. Isn't there somebody here you wanted to bring? Somebody you like?"

"Yeah."

"Who?"

"Sara Warren."

"Which one is she?"

I pointed her out, across the way, with her date. Now he not only had one arm around the small of her

131

back, but had the other around the front of her, with his hands clasped.

"The pretty little blonde with the fairy?" Nick said.

"Yeah."

"Jesus Christ, Keith. You got to know how to get girls. Should I show him?" he said to Kathy.

"Show him," she said.

"You stay here." He took the arm that had been draped around himself, and draped it around me. It was quite heavy. "She's all over me, Keith," he said. "I can't get rid of her."

"It's terrible," she said.

"Wish me luck, babe."

She gave him a long, active kiss. "Go, tiger," she said.

He was a sight, with that funny little slouch to his walk, the jutting defiant chin, flat head, hair all messed up. He walked through the dancers, who, lunging and gesturing to a fast number, kept bumping into him. He bore down resolutely. Sara and her date were standing a little to one side and didn't see him coming; he just appeared before them, and they looked at him. He said something to her ("What was it?" I said later. "I asked if she was Sara Warren," he said) and she nodded, smiled. He took her face in his hands and kissed her lips.

I would have expected the music to stop with a jolt, everyone to turn and gasp in astonishment, but of course no one even noticed; I was watching through the bodies that were gyrating weirdly between us. Sara just looked at him a moment, a little stunned, and then (would she scream in horror? deliver a ringing slap to his face? would her date produce a gauntlet from his waistcoat and challenge Nick to a duel?) she beamed, started laughing. Incredibly, the chinless wonder patted Nick lightly on the shoulder, as if to congratulate him on his enormous wit. Nick lurched away, headed toward us.

"So that's how it's done," I said.

"That's how *he* does it," Kathy said. "Isn't he great?" I could feel her swell with pride. "I love him."

"He's great," I said.

132

"Say hello to me, Keith," Kathy said.

Sometime I would have to tell her that wasn't my first name.

"Hello," I said.

She wrapped me in her arms and kissed me. Her lips were soft, soft; her arms were strong; her slender little tongue darted into my mouth as if to tease me. She tasted, on that balmy evening at the end of the summer, like strawberries.

Chapter 9

THE WEEK BEFORE the Hargrove game, a list was to be posted of everybody who was to be issued a uniform. All kinds of rumors existed about how many uniforms there were, how many would be issued that year. The Rose and I, and the other kids on the third string, still had hopes of playing—some days, after all, we still rocked the offensive unit—but in the shadow of those hopes was the dark fear that they'd run out of uniforms before they reached our names. In practice we busted our tails, dogged by that fear. It was unthinkable that we might have to watch the Hargrove game from the stands.

On Wednesday that week I was bored stiff in the half-speed scrimmage; on the line we kept doing the same thing over and over. On a play partway through practice, Sennett was standing up straight and could see, apparently, that no one was looking. I had gone out on him with a fake block, sticking my shoulder softly into the jelly of his gut. He held down my helmet and jammed his knee into my face.

Three weeks before I wouldn't have done a thing. People could punch me, bite me, kick me, spit in my eye. Just let me lie down here while you wipe your feet. But Wiggins had changed all that. I wasn't just there for the varsity to batter around anymore.

Jumping out of my crouch, I caught a glimpse of Sennett's grinning face and swung a wild right. He must have been leaning back, never expecting that. The thick pad on my hand crashed into the side of his face mask. To my astonishment he crumpled to the ground.

"Keith!" The voice boomed across the field. It was Grupp's. His stubby little legs pumping, he was charging at us from the defensive backfield. "I said this scrimmage was half-speed."

"Tell it to him," I said.

"I didn't do nothing." Sennett was scrambling, red-faced, from the ground. He was the kind of kid who thought a lapse in grammer conveyed sincerity.

"He kneed me," I said.

"It was an accident," Sennett said.

"Sennett kneed him," somebody said. "I saw it."

"Je-sus *Christ!*" Grupp raised his clipboard high in the air—as high, that is, as the arms of a five-foot-six-inch man can raise a clipboard—and slammed it to the earth. "I got an important game to prepare for, two days away, and here I've got worry about JV kids starting a fight in a half-speed scrimmage."

"I'm ready to end it anytime," Sennett said. "Just let us go down over that hill."

"I've got things to do here," Grupp shouted. "To some of us this is important." He was throwing his little arms around, clenching his fists. His face was blood red. A fleck of spit clung to his lower lip.

"You're not varsity material." He swung his wild eyes on me. "Not you." He poked a finger in Sennett's chest. "Not you. Not a bunch of you guys. Even if I do get big-hearted and let a couple of you sit on the bench. You're not varsity material, and won't be, until you cut out this kind of crap. Quit playing games."

All the JVs were standing there white-faced, hoping he didn't mean them. I noticed Wiggins standing with his arms folded, staring at the ground.

"God almighty." Grupp's voice had suddenly dropped to a hoarse whisper. "I don't know why. . . ." He ran a hand through his hair, stooped to pick up his clipboard. "You two start running. Maybe after a while I'll let you stop."

In a dead silence we headed out. That was Grupp's favorite punishment, especially for his big linemen, the endless laps of the field. I should have been crestfallen after all he'd said, but at that point I was still pretty charged up from standing up to Sennett.

"So help me, Keith," Sennett said when we were about fifty yards away. "You keep me from that uniform and I'll get your ass."

For some reason I suddenly knew it was all hot air.

"They don't have one shaped like a pear, Sennett," I said. "They'd have to send away for it special."

"In the locker room, Keith." He was already gasping from fifty yards of running. "In the locker room."

I lengthened my stride and pulled away from him.

When we got back to the scrimmage—Grupp had let us run seven laps—there were two older kids in our places, and Grupp just let us stand around. If he passed near where we were he made sure his back was to us. By that time I was feeling pretty bad. Probably I had known all along that I wouldn't be playing varsity, but I hadn't expected to have it spelled out so bluntly. I thought I'd been playing hard. I couldn't believe he saw things so differently.

Sennett and I were allowed to run sprints after practice. A rare honor. As I was walking afterwards up the steps to the gym, Wiggins appeared beside me. He didn't go so far as to open the conversation.

"Did I do the wrong thing?" I said.

"What do you think?"

"Probably." I smiled weakly. "But it felt good."

"You can't always do the thing that feels good."

Sometimes I wished he would come right out and say what he thought.

"You could have said something to him," he said. "You could at least have tried that. I saw the whole thing."

Why, I wondered, hadn't he said something in my defense?

"I just hope I didn't hurt my chances to play."

"You didn't."

By that time we were standing up near the front door to the gym. Other people had passed us by and gone in. It was good to hear him say that. He knew Grupp better than I.

"You wouldn't have played anyway," he said.

I stared at him. "Oh?"

"Grupp doesn't use a lot of players. It's just the way he coaches. Some of those kids on the second string won't get in. Much less the third."

"You know that for a fact?"

"I've been here four years."

"Why don't you tell those guys? They all think they got a chance."

"They'd never believe me. They'd think I meant somebody else."

"Do you think we're good enough to play?" I meant myself, but I couldn't say it.

"What's the difference? I'm not the coach."

"If you were."

"If I were the coach everybody would play. I'd have a squad for everything. Kickoffs, punts, third-down situations, the works. Everybody would have a small particular responsibility. I'd use a kid like Bobby Malcolm on the goal line. When I needed a fireplug. I'd put in a hothead like Sennett when things were dragging and we needed somebody to shake us up."

When would you use me? I wanted to say. What would I be good for?

"My players would always be fresh," he said. "They'd know just what they were in the game for. If I didn't have use for a kid I wouldn't keep him around."

I was stunned at the thought of it, a team where every player had a use.

"I repeat," he said. "I'm not the coach."

"You should be," I said.

He didn't flinch. Flattery got you nowhere with Wiggins.

"You've got to stop wishing things were another way," he said. "And face them the way they are."

He stood there a few moments, letting that sink in, then walked toward the gym.

The next morning, on a bulletin board in the main hallway of the academic building, the list of kids who had won uniforms was posted. All the rumors—about how there was a league rule that only twenty-five kids could be carried, only that many uniforms were ever bought—proved to be untrue. Thirty-four names were

137

on the list, all the kids who had been out for preseason since the first day. Beside my name and Sennett's there were red asterisks, and at the bottom of the page, beside another asterisk, was the word probation. I finally got up the nerve to ask one of the team captains what that meant. "Beats the shit out of me," he said.

The uniforms were new, bright gold and a deep blue, and were a good fit when we tried them on that afternoon for our light workout. They also looked good the next night, the gold giving off a kind of glow under the lights, as we sat on the bench at the Hargrove stadium, all of us sophomores lined up together. We had tried to get a little dirt on them before the game, falling down hard in the grass drill, but the field had been too grassy and they still looked spanking new. We yelled ourselves hoarse on the bench, jumping up frequently to wave our fists, but we never got any closer to the field than that. Seventeen kids got in. I counted. The game was never particularly close. Hargrove had recovered from their off season the previous year, and went on to finish second in their league. They won, 28–6.

II

Our JV games were on Monday, so as to interfere as little as possible with the varsity schedule. We got out of class a period or two early.

Wiggins on the day of a game was all business, far less excited, for instance, than on that first day he had showed up for practice. While we finished getting ready, he came in and read the lineups, announced the captains—they were on their own there, made all the decisions—and reminded us always of a few simple things, playing together, keeping alert, guarding against mistakes.

During the game he yelled a lot and shouted encouragement. At half-time he made us loosen our pads, lie back, and relax; he diagrammed their alignments on the chalkboard and noted changes in our assignments. After a game he told us immediately what we had done well and what we hadn't. He might blow his stack in practice, ride you all afternoon in fact, but never at a game; he didn't embarrass you in front of outsiders. And he knew you were putting out. You always would, for him. "That was a better team out there, boys," he said one week. "Nothing we could have done would have beaten them." Grupp wouldn't have admitted the Four Horsemen of Notre Dame were better.

But we won under Wiggins, four out of seven games that season, the same kids, basically, that hadn't come close to winning a game the year before. It wasn't exactly his dream squad, that mythical team where everyone had a use, but he did play everybody. Our kickoff team, for instance, was a crazy mix of kids who hadn't gone out for preseason; they sat open-mouthed in the locker room as they heard their names announced. Half the time they were the first team we put on the field; we all held our breath as the ball went sailing through the air, but they always managed to stumble down and bounce around and make the stop. Pretty soon they got cocky, calling themselves the suicide squad, crack specialists, like the pros. Whoever he had to work with, Wiggins stuck to his guns.

Still home from the office, my father managed to get to the first game. He hadn't been sure he'd make it, and all through the drills I kept looking for him; it wasn't until just before the kickoff that he arrived. My mother drove, of course, brought the car down beside the field. Through the odd crowd of people standing around—soccer players on their way to practice, sisters and girlfriends and parents of players—they picked their way slowly, she with her arm in his hand guiding him. At that point his patch was off, and the lens for his bad eye looked like a magnifying glass, giving him an eerie ghostly look. His clothes fit loosely because of the weight he had lost. I tried to smile at them, give them a wave, but they were both concentrating too hard on their navigating to notice me. JV games were informal, everybody juust standing around among the players, and they were the only people, on that bright autumn afternoon, who sat in the bleachers.

I'd never been in a game where both teams played

well—in fact, I'd never been in a game where my team played well—but that afternoon we both did, both scoring twice. At half-time our manager said something to me about how their kicker had a lot of leg, but got almost no loft on the ball. So, for the second extra point, I moved over the center, just stood up with the snap, and sure enough, much faster than I would have thought, the ball whistled through the air and hit me square in the face. We had been taught to cross our arms in front of us, but I'd never really thought I'd block a kick. The point of the ball jammed in above my face mask, banged the bridge of my nose; when I went over to the sidelines and held a towel to it there was a huge splotch of blood. But I had blocked the kick, and we ended up winning by a point, so I was a hero, except that it happened early in the third quarter and nobody much remembered later.

My parents waited for me outside the gym after the game. My father didn't move from beside the car, my mother on his bad side. There was a dignity to him, but it seemed the dignity of an old man, or a statue.

Wiggins came over when he saw me with my parents. "He's a little the worse for wear," he said. "A lot of blood, but nothing broken."

"Blood?" My mother paled.

My father leaned back a little more, staring at me. "You take an elbow?"

"He blocked that extra point," Wiggins said. "Saved us the game."

"Somebody said that point was blocked. I couldn't tell what happened." I gestured toward his eyes. "I've got these new glasses."

"Unfortunately, he blocked it with his nose," Wiggins said.

"That's the limit," my mother said. "Was he supposed to do that?"

"Only if he couldn't find anything else," Wiggins said.

"This is Mr. Wiggins, Dad," I said.

My father turned slowly to face him, shook his hand. "Dan talks about you a great deal," he said. "He enjoys football now."

"They're coming around," Wiggins said. "I think we'll have a good season."

"He keeps telling me he's learning the game."

"He'll get there," Wiggins said. "He works."

For weeks I had wanted those two men to meet. I wanted them to see each other, know each other, be impressed; I wanted them to talk about me. I was glad it had finally happened.

"I don't like all this blood," my mother said.

I was full of myself that evening, after the first win ever for me. I'd been worried up to then that I might only be able to perform in practice, with Wiggins backing me up, but having him on the sidelines was just the same. In the living room I talked about play after play with my father.

"I hope you can get to some more games," I said.

"I'l try." He had reddened a little, nodding. "It's still pretty hard for me to get around."

It wasn't until the next morning, before he came down for breakfast, that my mother told me he really hadn't seen the game at all. "He kept asking about you," she said. "Trying to tell me where you'd be. But it was all so confusing to me. It was a frustrating afternoon for him."

That afternoon at practice Wiggins made a point of speaking to me. "I was glad to meet your father. I've heard about his problems with his health. I'm sorry for his trouble."

"He's better than he was," I said. "Pretty soon they'll fit him with a contact lens."

Wiggins was staring at me, the way he did; his glance never wavered. "He's a brave man," he said.

I thought Wiggins's solemn manner a little ridiculous. It made more out of something than there really was.

Chapter 10

AFTER THAT OPENING-GAME loss, the varsity turned its season around and won three straight, including a close third game that they just pulled out in the closing minutes. With the Sherrill twins in their last season, Pollett a year bigger and stronger, the backfield was superb, and the line got the job done. But in the fifth game they ran head-on into Asbury, league champions two years running, and a team that also had a star sophomore fullback, Ted Kotar. He was a different kind of runner than any we had, bulled four yards with people hanging all over his back; he finally wore down our line and led Asbury to the win, 28–20. We won the next three, and technically had a shot the last week at a tie for the title if Asbury lost and we beat Northrup. There was a big push for spirit around the school, a huge bonfire down by the gym on Thursday night, a massive pep rally on the quad Friday morning, but against Northrup our line was really outmanned and we got clobbered, 24–6. Asbury won their game anyway and took the title for the third straight year.

Something about that last week of the season was slightly askew. People were weary from the long fall term. Sure we're going to beat Northrup, people were saying, we'll get a piece of that title, but nobody really believed it. We were just going through the motions. It was like the little kid who is late getting to bed, strung out, keeps saying no, no, he's not tired, he is not *grumpy*, he just wants to stay up a little longer.

It was in the week after the Northrup game that the seniors had their tea party for Nick Kaiser.

The tradition went way back. In front of the academic building was a large rectangle of grass with a few trees and a high flagpole. Only seniors were allowed to walk on it. It would have been convenient, if you were late to class, or in a hurry to get down to the gym, to cut across it, but you never had to. The faculty, who of course had full permission, rarely used it. But every year a few underclassmen—in defiance, or by accident, or in a moment of bravado—stepped on a corner, or ran across. If they were caught, a ceremony followed, with the whole school in attendance, the senior class as hosts. It had evolved through the years, and changed from year to year, but always the offender appeared with next to nothing on, carrying his pants, and participated in an elaborate ritual, at the end of which his pants were strung up the flagpole.

"I don't get it," I said to my father after the first one I'd seen. "I don't see why they let it go on."

"Lots of places have a custom something like that. Boys' schools. Fraternities."

"It seems so childish."

"Even young men have some little boy in them."

"They don't have to take it that far."

"A group seems to find a way to do that. Strip you of everything, so to speak, so you'll be just like them. Or maybe it's just that the older group has to do that to the younger, put them in their place, because they're a threat, or going to be. They'd do it anyway, so the school lets it be out in the open, in a ritual. At least the teachers are out there supervising."

"To me that makes it worse. Like they're saying it's okay."

"At least they're there. To keep it from getting violent. Or being really cruel."

At first I heard only by rumor about Nick Kaiser's tea party. He and I hadn't seen each other as much that fall as in the past. We didn't have any classes together, and rarely had time to talk at athletics. He never did get much better in cross-country, running back in the JV pack, but he still looked forward to wrestling, and went up to the gym to lift weights after practice. Trying not to seem too eager, I asked him now and then when he and Kathy were going to set me up, and he kept saying to be patient, he'd be driving by springtime, we could all double together. Then he'd tell me about the parties he'd been to the weekend before, show me the little marks of affection Kathy had left on his neck or chest, say how surprisingly heavy her breasts were, and soft, and how large the nipples seemed in his mouth. Really, I'd been glad to take a cab out there. But he started also to hang around with guys I didn't know too well, kids on the fringes of things, who slouched around together, signed out of study hall for a smoke, left school before athletics. I began to see him pretty often with Jack Wedman.

Jack was a genuine eccentric at the school. He was a fabulous natural athlete, had muscles tough as rope, and though he spent the athletic period intensively lifting weights and went off on long runs, he never went out for a sport. He wore old clothes, barely within regulations, sneaked off to the woods to smoke short black cigars, spent most of his free time in the dormitory commons rooms shooting slick expert pool. It was said he spent his weekends in low dives downtown, hustling.

The Monday of that week in November, late in the afternoon, he and Nick had strolled out on the senior campus on a dare. Supposedly a senior had told them it was all right, that they had his permission, then later claimed, red-faced and smirking, that he'd said nothing of the kind. Nick and Jack made various appeals, but everyone said it was a student matter. The seniors said there was no such thing as permission to walk on the senior campus.

Probably it wouldn't have been so bad if it just hadn't happened that particular week, when everybody was already grouchy and giddy and slightly out of their minds.

The rumor was that Nick and Jack weren't going to let the tea party happen. There were other rumors, too, that the seniors were going to make this the tea party to end all tea parties. Always there were incredible stories about what they decorated the kids with, but this time it was said that the seniors in one dorm had been preparing a jar all fall, that there was spit in there, sperm, shit, piss: you name it, some perverted senior would claim it was in that jar.

It turned into a real battle. Jack took off out the basement door of his dorm, high-tailing it for the cross-country course and the woods beyond it. Nick signed out toward the end of his last period study hall and made it unseen to the basement of the chapel. But a party of seniors went out to beat the bushes, while some idiot secretary who was rumored to hump for the business manager told another search party where she had seen Nick go. They finally spotted him up in the rafters behind the curtains of the chapel stage. Nick and Jack had made the tea party pretty late in starting, but things had gotten so bad that everybody was just standing there waiting for it, bunched around the squad, letting athletics go by, shivering, hands in their pockets, in the cold gray afternoon. Even the coaches were up there, laughing and joking, waiting for all the excitement to be over so they could start practice.

I was there with everyone else. It wouldn't have occurred to me not to go. That was a big school tradition, and I suppose I thought you had to be there, that it would be like missing a class if you skipped out.

There was often a little chase at the beginning of a tea party, but usually by the time things started the guests of honor were sheepish, good-natured, went along with the whole thing. Nick and Jack, on the other hand, had to be pushed, dragged, practically carried, out to the quad. At first everyone laughed, as if it were some kind of pantomime, prisoners of war, but soon you could see they were serious, adamant, bitter. Already they were stripped, decorated with shoe polish, and as they stood shivering in the center of the quad a small group of seniors moved around, pouring on maple syrup, molasses, squirting on whipped cream. The quad had grown almost silent, just some quiet conversation, as if watching a solemn ceremony. Nick kept staring at the ground. You could see the scars from his stitches running down his leg. A few of the big jocks had to go with them, constantly shoving, to get them to run their laps. Most of the seniors had stepped back, just a few went on grimly, as if finishing something they had to do. There was not a sound, just a kind of shudder that went through the whole crowd, as somebody poured out the contents of the fabled jar, now on one head, now on the other.

I saw Nick afterwards down at the gym, slumped in front of his locker, when he had done what he could to get that stuff off him, out of his hair. He was red-faced, sobbing. Even at school, Nick wasn't afraid to show his emotions; that was one of the things I most admired about him. Everyone got dressed quickly and silently around him, hurried away. I stayed awhile, trying to think of something to say. "They shouldn't have done it" was all I could come up with. "They shouldn't have done it, Nick."

"I'll get even for this, Keith," he said. "So help me God. I'll get even for this if it's the last thing I do."

II

That Saturday I went to school first thing for the tutorial sessions. I went most Saturday mornings that year. I was taking biology and geometry, and needed all the help I could get. A lot of people had given up on extra help, that late in the fall, not long before vacation. The school sent around a van for the few of us who didn't drive, and that morning I was the only one on it.

I got to campus a little early, and the place seemed deserted. Nearly all the boarders at Arnold went home for the weekend. In the dim hallway of lockers beneath the chapel—I went there to pick up some books—a few guys were lined up washing something off the walls, with brushes, sponges, buckets of water. I knew scholarship kids helped out with work on the weekends—the janitors were off on Saturday—but I hadn't realized they ever did any work like that. Pollett was there, Cortese, Kasunich, classmates of mine, though I hardly knew them at that point. They hung around with the varsity athletes, or among themselves.

As I stepped through the door they turned on me

with looks of sullen anger. I suppose that in their minds I was the landowner and they the peasants, though to me, what with the aristocracy of talent around that place, it was just the other way. I felt inferior in their presence, and like an intruder. My impulse was to slink past them down the hall. So maybe we were even.

Todd Grunfeld was there too, and I knew him a little better. "What's going on?" I said.

His eyes were frightened. "Somebody broke in here last night. Must have been a bunch of guys. Tore the place up. Wrote on the walls. This isn't too bad. It comes off. But go up and see the chapel. It'll make you sick."

I walked up the stairs into the back entrance. The chapel had been horribly desecrated. With black spray paint, obscenities had been scrawled on the walls, wantonly and at random, coupled with the names of teachers and administrators. There were drawings, too, crazy obscene caricatures, even up on the podium that was used for a pulpit. Xs were marked in certain seats in the pews. The windows had been sprayed, the window curtains, the stage curtain, even the keys of the organ.

However you felt about the school, the chapel was the heart of it. It was the first place we went every day. It was where Bates gave all his talks, tedious and boring as they were. All the school ceremonies were held there, wild student skits and crazy displays of spirit. If you had to pick one room that was the school, held all its contradictions, the chapel was it. Now someone, some one of us, had done all that to it.

I was scared, astounded, alone in that silent room, but it wasn't until I got to the front of the chapel, noticed the back wall, that I felt a clutch like a fist in my guts. That was a wide wall, and there was a huge drawing there, of a nude woman, wide-eyed, grinning, with wild curly hair, long pendulous breasts, a mass of pubic hair dripping moisture; she was facing a huge erect phallus on a nondescript male figure. Above the drawing, and below it, were words: "Nursie Sucks."

I had seen that drawing before, or almost that drawing, in the infirmary, in the back of Nick Kaiser's notebook. I made a connection I should have made immediately. It was the Saturday morning after that Wednesday afternoon tea party.

The tutorial sessions had been called off. People just stood around the chapel in groups, teachers talking to students or among themselves. A few of the teachers were openly fearful, and I was in awe of that. I didn't talk with anyone. I felt guilty. Guilty for what I knew, guilty for the way those guys had turned on me in the hallway, guilty because Nick had warned me he would get even, guilty because he was my friend, guilty because I had stood with everyone else at that tea party the week before, guilty perhaps most of all because it seemed such a terrible thing, yet I understood what had led Nick to do it. We had come up in the school together.

I talked it over that night with my father. He had returned to the office by then, had a contact lens that helped him see better. He looked better, too, though he had never regained the weight he had lost. I was pretty agitated, probably said some crazy thing, but he just heard me out.

"You're sure it was him," he said.

"There's something about those drawings. I'm not sure I could even say what it is. But I'm sure he did them. When I saw that wall I just about passed out."

"It puts you in a bad spot."

"For all I know the whole class has seen his drawings. They all used to visit him in the infirmary. Maybe he showed them off. Maybe everybody knows. But I don't see how I can mention it to somebody when I'm not sure."

"No. You can't."

"And I've got to see Nick. I've got to face him. Sit beside him in that chapel."

"That'll be rough."

"If you could have seen that tea party. The stuff they poured on him. Things they made him do. It wasn't in fun. They weren't doing it that way, and he couldn't have taken it that way. It was like it was personal, they really wanted to humiliate him. It shouldn't

148

have been allowed. And now everybody will be so self-righteous about what he's done."

"I know you think it's the school, Dan. That it shouldn't let that happen. But you've got to allow certain things. Then they're taken too far. Boys are worse than you'd want them to be."

"They can get away with that, and now, for this, he's going to be treated like a criminal."

"I know. I can't tell you what to do. But I do think one thing, if what you said about those pictures is true. Nick Kaiser may have been justified in what he did. But the way he did it . . . He needs somebody's help. And he's going to need friends. All he can get."

The next few weeks were even worse than I had imagined. Bates gave lecture after moralistic lecture. The student council president, Brian O'Casey, gave a long chapel speech in which he said that information could be passed on anonymously through him to the administration. The senior class president, newspaper editor, all the campus bigwigs spoke, squeezing every drop of meaning from the incident they could. Through it all Nick sat beside me—we were seated alphabetically in chapel—hunched forward in the pew, silent, grim, trying now and then to look unconcernedly at the speaker, as anyone else would.

One morning I came in late, and Bates was already launched into a talk. "They've disgraced themselves. They've disgraced their parents. They've disgraced their school. . . ." For a moment, suddenly hopeful, I thought they had found the culprits—Bates seemed to be talking about specific people—and that Nick wasn't one of them. Stupidly, I turned to him. "Who's he talking about?" He paled, stared at me as if aware of what I knew, as if, cruelly, I were making him say it. "The kids who painted the chapel," he said.

A couple of years later I might have felt differently, but at that point I was terribly torn by what I knew. I thought of all that seemed wanton, irrational, blasphemous in those pictures. I thought of the genuine sorrow I had seen in the faces of some teachers. I suppose I thought of what my revelation might win me, the favor I might gain. A struggle was raging in me between loyalty to my school and loyalty to a friend. I have often wished since that my friend had won.

A couple of weeks after that Saturday I had approached the student council president, O'Casey. He was a likable kid, with scruffy hair, sloppy clothes, a nervous hurried manner.

"I want to talk to you about the chapel," I had said. "I have an idea who might have done it."

"Where'd you get the idea?"

"Well. I was here that Saturday morning. I saw what it looked like."

"And you recognized the pictures."

"Yes."

"A lot of your friends have told me the same thing. It's what you'd have guessed anyway, after the tea party. Everybody knows. All this talk is just psychological warfare. I don't see how he can hold out much longer."

So all my agonizing hadn't mattered; as the student body sat morning after morning in the chapel, hearing those words, everyone knew where they were directed. I was never sure what finally happened. The rumor was that Jack Wedman finally spilled the beans, because he just didn't care, began to tell it around that it was him and Nick and a couple of malcontents from the class ahead of us; they had gotten drunk on beer that Friday night plotting how to get even, got the paint and spray cans from Jack's garage, drove out in a wild spree and painted until the paint was gone. They hadn't sneaked around or even tried to be quiet; it was incredible they hadn't been caught that night. In any case, the end was quick. On Monday morning I heard on the bus that Mr. Bates had discovered and confronted the vandals. That morning Nick wasn't in chapel, and though the incident wasn't officially mentioned again, we heard that the headmaster had expelled them. The place beside me in chapel remained empty. I didn't see Nick the rest of that year.

Part Four

Chapter 11

IN HIS FATHER'S Olds 98—that was the summer we
started to drive—the Rose leaned back and wedged a
fistful of fries into his mouth. "There's Baumgardner at
one tackle," he said. "Krause at the other."

We were at a drive-in down on the boulevard. The
August air clung to your skin, sticky and hot. The
night was filled with the rush of traffic. Rosy had a
couple of hamburgers and a strawberry shake with the
fries. He liked a substantial snack.

"Krause can't stay down," I said. "He can't move."

"He can't be moved either. At six-five."

"So how's he going to block?"

"Maybe he'll fart and blow the guy away. How the
hell do I know? I just heard Grupp's starting him."

"Christ. Go on."

"There's a new scholarship kid named Ryczek. A
sophomore, tackle. Unknown quantity."

"Wonderful."

"Mattheson's at one guard. Falcone at the other.
Baker's being moved to center. You couldn't get him
out of there with a load of dynamite. Bert Foley and
Giles as utility men."

"Giles is chicken. Half the time he's in there he
looks like he's going to cry."

"I know. But his mommy wants him to be a football
player. If not a priest. She follows Notre Dame all over
the country. Anyway. You try to move the lard in his
ass out of there on defense."

Look who's talking.

"All right," I said.

"Then there's Sennett."

"My God, Rose. We don't have to get ridiculous about this."

"He's a senior. Grupp likes seniors. He's got him pegged as some kind of hatchet man."

"So where does all this leave us?"

"Fighting for playing time is what it looks like to me."

"I can't buy this crap."

"The man makes his lineup in January. He could hand in his half of the program to Hargrove right now. That's the way it is."

The Rose never said how he knew these things. He gave up on his food, leaned back to sip from his milkshake, light a cigarette. His new girlfriend had started him smoking. He sucked in the smoke as if he'd been at it for years.

"Good for the wind, Rose."

"I'll stop. I'll stop next week."

"It's going to feel real good on those sprints."

"When did they ever feel good?"

"You don't have to make it worse."

"Listen. If I'm going to make it this year, it's not going to be my superb condition. Or my blinding speed. It's going to be size. Size or nothing."

By that logic, his nightly snack—a new feature of his life since he got his license—was a major part of his training program.

"I guess," I said.

"At least I'm not like you. Mr. Barbell. Any day I expect to see you on the back of a comic book."

It was true enough. That whole summer I had hardly missed a session with the weights, in our dank basement, the prickly summer heat crawling along my skin: I spent most of the evening, with heavy weights, bouncing the weight off the tile floor when I finished a set. Every morning I was up early to run. I still wasn't a gazelle—in fact, I still hated to run—but I plodded along the sidewalks of the neighborhood, toughening up my legs and lungs. I was in a lot better shape than the summer before. Barely five-nine, I nudged the scales after a heavy meal past the 200-pound mark. My shoulders had widened, chest bulged, arms hung heavy. If you saw me on the street you didn't mess with me.

We hadn't made it to the beach that summer. In June my father had gone in for his second eye operation, and if anything—despite the fact that we knew more or less what to expect—the whole ordeal was worse. His stay in the hospital was just as long, and his problems seeing afterwards bothered him even more than before. He seemed thinner than ever, especially in the arms and shoulders and neck; often, in fact, when he was having a conversation, he would reach up to support his chin with his hand. "My neck's a little weak these days," he said when I asked him. "I have to do it." His voice, also, was hoarse and weak. He seemed to labor to swallow his food. His hands had started to tremble—nerves, I thought, from all the trouble he had getting around—and when he held a cup and saucer, or a glass with ice, it rattled away like castanets.

Something in me—a part I wasn't much listening to—knew that something more was wrong than just a problem with his eyes.

I wanted to shout at him sometimes: "Stand up straight! Don't shuffle along. Don't act like an old man. You're not old." I don't know what was wrong with me, that I couldn't be more sympathetic to a man who was plainly ill. At the dinner table, when his head was sagging, and he was laboriously chewing his food, straining to swallow, I didn't look at him. It was as if I had blinders on. I ignored his end of the table altogether.

I know I didn't want to see him looking older like that. But at the same time, I think, I didn't feel ready to face him. I was embarrassed by all the talking about football I had done, which had come to nothing. I had to finish what I had set out to do. I have sometimes thought that all the training I did that summer, the long hours with the weights in the basement, the mornings out running, were an odd combination of those two things, avoiding my father and working to prove myself to him.

Around the middle of August he had to go back in the hospital again.

"Your eyes?" I said.

"No," he said. "The eyes are okay. It's some trouble with my stomach. Ulcers, that have started to bleed." He was smiling benignly, as if that were an everyday matter.

"Ulcers?" I was almost angry, hearing it. It was like that hint of something more that I knew must be wrong. I didn't want to know. "Are you worried?"

"You don't always get them from being worried."

"From what then?"

"Nobody knows. But it's not a serious thing. The doctors just think I need a rest."

He went into the hospital a week before preseason began.

II

The big man around the locker room that year, or anywhere else down at the gym, was Pollett. Just a junior, he was already one of the co-captains of the team, and closing in on the school rushing record. Smelling of talcum powder and a light after-shave, he liked to hang around the gym by the hour, wearing just a jock, sitting in the whirlpool or slowly getting taped or just talking. All eyes were on him in that place. His upper body bulged with muscle, but it was the rest of him that was really impressive: he had a rear end, all muscle, that belonged on a beast of burden, and the thighs of a circus strongman. Already he walked with the rolling gait and wobbly knees that showed the kind of pounding he had to take. His bright blond hair shone in waves above his narrow hard face.

It was on the third day of practice, Wednesday, that week, that he spoke to me in the locker room, early in the morning.

"Coach Holden wants to see you," he said. "Right away."

156

"Who?"

"Coach Holden." He had an odd look around his eyes, almost frightened. He seemed a litttle green around the gills.

"I don't even know him," I said.

"He said Dan Keith."

"I wonder where he heard my name."

Pollett shrugged, stepped back. He seemed to want to get away.

"Where?" I said.

"Out front. Somewhere out there."

That helped a lot. I was wearing just gym shorts, those little flimsy gray ones that tie in the front with strings, but the man said right away, so I walked out, barefoot, just like that.

Holden was the new backfield coach that year; the first time I even heard of him was when he was out on the field the first day of practice. At first I had thought he was somebody's father, from the way he was so familiar with all the players, from his New England accent, from a certain ruddy look he had about him that reminded me of the corporation executives who showed up at Arnold on ceremonial days. He walked with a slight limp and munched constantly on apples, which he pulled out of the pockets of an old letter jacket he wore and kept offering to his favorite players. The story was that he had been the head coach at a well-known prep school, had been most successful and even a little famous, known for sending first-rate players off to the Ivy League. Nobody explained what he was doing coaching under Grupp at Arnold. He had a characteristic odor about him that I associated vaguely with men's places, the bar and grill where my father ate lunch downtown, the den of our next-door neighbor. It seems funny to me now that I didn't know at the time what it was.

As the year wore on he grew stranger and stranger. Always a bit of a buffoon, with wild bug eyes, a childish grin, he had an endless supply of football anecdotes, about players way before our time. He was a math teacher, and it was said he often told the same stories in class. He seemed hardly to follow the modern game. In the middle of the year he was suddenly relieved of his teaching duties. The rumor arose that he had been in the war, suffered from shell shock, and that his memory had been affected: in the middle of class he would suddenly lose his mathematical train of thought and rescue himself with a football anecdote. It's funny the crazy stories that arise to keep students from knowing a simple truth. He was given odd harmless jobs around the school, mostly proctoring study halls. He applied himself to them with a fierce zeal. In the spring of the year his wife suddenly left him. He had come to be an embarrassment to the whole school. The following year he was not asked back.

But that early in the season, the third day of practice, I didn't know him; nobody did. I padded along on my bare feet toward the main part of the gym, looking for him. As I passed the trophy cases Grupp stepped out of the trainer's room. I must have been quite a sight, barefoot, dainty, tiptoeing along, but he did not smile or speak, just nodded once, staring, as if at someone he barely knew.

I opened the door that led to the vestibule. Outside I could see Coach Holden, standing near the steps that led to the track, staring at the field. Somebody else was also in the vestibule, stopped, momentarily, on his way up the stairs that led to the gym floor. He had his back to me, deliberately, I imagine. It didn't matter. I would have known that flat head anywhere.

"Nick," I said.

He jumped, turned to me, ghostly pale. "Keith. God almighty. It could have been anybody." He looked outside. "Who the hell's that?"

"A new coach."

"Like we need another one. He keeps looking at me."

"He probably thinks he should know you. He just got here."

"Will they throw me out if they find me?"

"Who?"

"I don't know. Grupp. Any of them."

"I don't think so."

But I wasn't sure. There was a rumor that none of the guys who painted the chapel was ever to return to campus again, that they would be treated as trespassers if they did.

"Nobody's seen me yet," he said.

"I'm not talking."

"I know." He grinned his sheepish grin. He was wearing what I took to be a straw golf hat, perched back on his head, an old T-shirt and some sloppy jeans, spattered with—of all things—paint; he had his hands jammed into his pockets. No wonder Holden kept looking at him. "I don't know what the hell I'm doing here," he said.

"Same old place."

"You don't want to come back until you can't."

We laughed. I was glad he could joke about it.

"So how's it going for you?" he said. "First string this year?"

"I don't know about that. I'm better than I was."

"That's a big line to crack."

It was an odd thing for him to know. The line was almost completely new. It made me think he'd been following the team, might have been out to watch practice before.

"I'll be going to Hargrove," Nick said.

"Well. You'll see me or you won't."

"Did you see the chapel, Keith?" he said. Abruptly his tone had changed, throat tightened. "After it had been painted."

His face was red, mouth dry, eyes staring at me.

"I saw it," I said.

"You saw the worst in me."

"Not just you."

"It was me."

"They drove you to it."

"Don't kid yourself. Nobody made me. It was my idea. And those other guys just did a little. But I went crazy, once I started. That was me in there. All of it."

A door slammed in the hallway behind me; we both started.

"Christ," Nick said. "I'm all jumpy. I'm going up

here." He looked up the stairs. "Nobody comes up here in the summer."

There was a lot I wanted to tell Nick—that I understood how he had felt, why he had done what he had—but somehow, as if it would endanger my wonderful football career, I was afraid of being seen with him, especially alone, upstairs.

"Listen, Nick. I've got to see this guy."

"It's okay. I just want to get out of this hallway."

"Then I've got practice."

"Don't worry about it. I didn't figure to run into you anyway."

"I want to talk to you. I really do."

"Sure." He had already started up the stairs, glancing nervously back at the door. "It's no big deal. Go."

"Okay." I shrugged.

"I got to get out of here." He was walking again, and I started toward the door. "Anyway. Keith." I stopped, looked at him. He was giving me that grin again, shy, half-embarrassed. "You kill those bastards," he said.

I grinned back, nodded. He went on, disappeared around the top of the stairs.

Mr. Holden was still standing out at the steps, staring down the field. I walked outside, felt the chill breeze of the early morning, before the fog had lifted.

"Mr. Holden," I said. "You wanted to see me."

"Yes." I seemed to have interrupted him at some reverie. He turned to me sharply, his face all red, wearing a scowl, though any expression on that face was bound to be a little comic. He was eating one of those damn apples, his mouth all moist, flecked with little chunks of the fruit.

"Mistah," he said. He always made the most of his New England accent. "If you have anything to say to me, you can say it to my face."

As he stared at me, his eyes were dark, cheeks stuffed with apple: a mad squirrel.

"I don't understand."

He raised his face, tightened his jaw. "If a man has something to say, to another man, that he wants the other man to hear." He frowned, stared, as if he were in the midst of a profound truth. "If it is important enough to say at all, he should say it to his face."

"Yes."

"It's one of the most important things a man can learn. In becoming . . ." He blinked. "A man."

I nodded. The chill was starting to get to me. I folded my arms across my chest.

"You can say it to my face," he said.

He spoke the words as if he would stake his life on them.

"All right," I said.

He was staring at me fiercely, his mouth pursed tight. Was I supposed to say something then? I had no idea what it was.

He turned away from me, back to the field. "That's all I evah say."

"Mr. Holden . . ."

He shook his head vigorously, still facing away. "I've had a long experience of coaching. Dealing with boys. Believe me. I've come across every situation." He shook his head again. "That's all I evah say."

He took a large crunch out of the apple. End of conversation. I gave a great shiver—it really seemed cold out there—turned and walked back into the gym.

Like everybody, probably more than most, I joked with friends about coaches, teachers. I tried to think back to some phrase I might have dropped, but I couldn't come up with a thing. He hadn't given me much of a hint. It seemed eerie, cold, quiet, as I walked back through the hallway to suit up.

Everything was that way then. Grupp stared at me as if he barely knew me. Wiggins hadn't reported to practice. Nick Kaiser was sneaking around the gym. My father was in the hospital with ulcers that bled. And while I stood shivering in my shorts on the steps of the gym, a man I barely knew was chewing an apple and telling me to say something to his face. He didn't mention what. The whole world had stopped making sense.

161

Starting ahead of me at inside tackle that year was a senior named Baumgardner. He was extremely fair, with light blond hair, ashen skin, but cheeks as fat and rosy—once he was sweating—as a German barmaid's. Already, at the ripe old age of eighteen, he was starting to lose some hair, so he combed it straight across, covering his temples; he had a jaw like a steam shovel and small sad worried eyes. He was squat, an inch shorter than I, and chubby, with a thick wedge of fat around his midsection. His legs were smooth and pale. He had a small flat butt. His round spectacles, as he slouched around the school, were always sliding halfway down his nose. He looked as little like a football player as anyone on the team.

But his uncle was the head coach at a small local college, and the kid knew football inside and out. When he blocked he was quick and hard, never more than a couple of feet off the ground, and his blocks stuck: those legs kept moving. On a pass he dropped back low, stayed in a crouch, and just about when you were on him he stood straight like a piston and rammed your face with his helmet. He wasn't above a little dirty stuff on the side, would swing a bony elbow for the side of your jaw, fall with his knee aimed at a tender spot. As small and beady as his eyes were, they never missed a thing, and when he beat you—I had plenty of experience of that—there was a little smile to them.

I had no hope of beating him out. I wouldn't have minded if he'd broken a leg. What I did hope was that I could substitute for him some, maybe get in on defense.

That Friday, before our first away scrimmage, Grupp was going over the lineup. He walked through a huddle of linemen, intoning names, slapping shoulders. He loved the ceremony of it all. "Krause at outside tackle. Baumgardner at the inside."

"I won't be there," Baumgardner said.

"What?" Grupp looked up belligerently, as if the kid had called him a name.

"I can't be there. You remember. My sister's wedding."

"What sister's wedding?"

"The only sister he's got," somebody said. "Thank God."

"Two months ago," Baumgardner said. "I called you. The day she set the date."

"That's right," Grupp said. "I completely forgot."

"I wonder when the baby's due," somebody said.

Grupp was in a bind. Preseason scrimmages were supposed to be informal, just a chance to work on things, but like every high school football coach he had the heart of a twelve-year-old kid, and threw a fit if he lost even the coin toss before a game. If he had remembered sooner he probably would have worked his lineup around, had a senior ready at inside tackle, but as it was there was no time for that.

"I guess it's going to be Dan Keith." He looked stunned, as if that were the most astonishing fact in football history. Slowly he searched the crowd until he found me. "I guess it's going to be you."

"Okay." My heart was hammering, the adrenaline already starting to pour. They could have started the scrimmage right then as far as I was concerned.

"You better practice there now. Switch jerseys."

The first team wore blue that year, the second gold, so every time somebody got demoted he had to strip and take some smelly second-stringer's jersey. The first-string jerseys, of course, smelled like roses.

"Enjoy it while you can," Baumgardner said, handing it over. "It's the last you'll see of it this year."

Through my mind was passing the list of famous athletes who had gotten their start through a lucky break. . . .

"Kiss your sister for me," I said.

"If you only knew what you're asking," he said. The kid could take a joke, no question.

"Well," somebody said. "Baumgardner won't get a workout on Saturday."

"But his sister will," another kid said.

The scrimmage was at Jefferson, a massive suburban high school like a General Motors plant. The place had money: their lily-white practice uniforms were softer than our game uniforms, and had been laundered for the occasion. A scrimmage was not a game, of course; the coaches were out on the field, analyzing every play, no official score was kept, and there was only a scattered crowd. But it was a big day for me, the first time I'd started with varsity players, and my chance, I thought, to show what I could do. I must have been the most worked-up kid on the field.

You don't normally think of a football player finding a groove, like a golfer with his swing or a pitcher whose curve ball is catching the corner, but that afternoon I couldn't miss. The kid over me was lean and quick, but every block I threw locked into his thighs like a vise: we took three steps and over we went. It was incredible how easy it was, after all the time I'd waited. I'd had rougher days on a JV field. The rest of the team, unfortunately, was getting clobbered; we got nowhere on offense. But that didn't really matter to me. I was a varsity player that afternoon, and knew it.

Jefferson had taken films of the game from a tower, and sent them over to us the next week. We spent an afternoon sititng in the locker room going over them. Grupp ranted and screamed about all the mistakes we'd made, how pitiful we looked, getting more and more worked up. I wasn't much listening, just watching myself on the screen, as I knew everybody was. Suddenly his voice boomed, "Look at that beautiful block by Baumgardner!"

"I wasn't there," a voice said weakly.

"His shoulder's into the man right away. He keeps his head up. Drives straight ahead with his legs."

The voice was a little louder. "It wasn't me."

"If the rest of you suckers had blocked like that . . ."

"I was at the wedding!" Baumgardner shouted.

"What?"

"My sister's wedding!" He was leaning against the side wall, shaking his head. "Jesus," he mutttered. "What a mind."

"That's right. You weren't even at the game. What's

this, then?" There was a long silence. "That's Dan Keith in there."

I couldn't see Grupp in the dark, but I could imagine his expression, the same gaping mouth as when he had discovered Baumgardner wouldn't be at the scrimmage in the first place.

"Look at that block," he said quietly.

Grupp with that projector was like a kid with a new toy; he kept running the same frames over and over. You could see it clearly, the perfect block I'd been throwing all afternoon. They all sat there and watched. On the hard cement floor, in the darkness, I saw myself on the flickering screen, again and again, in the moment I'd always dreamed of.

Chapter 12

HER VOICE AT the other end was a soft whisper. I pictured her stretched out in a chair, legs slung over the armrest, as she fooled with the cord. "What time?"

"I don't know. Eight-thirty."

There was a pause as she thought for a moment. "Sure," she said. "I'd love to."

I didn't even hear the words. I was waiting for the next part. I'd love to but an Italian count is flying over Friday from Milan. Just to spend the evening. In a whole year of calling Sara—not *every* week; I had some pride—I'd gotten only one date, to a party where so many people had asked her to dance that I'd barely seen her. What I couldn't understand was how she kept track of it all. She must have had a social secretary.

But that evening the sentence stopped. No qualifiers.

"Really?" I said.

"I might be a minute or two late. But I'd love to go."

I barely participated in the rest of the phone call. Something must have come from my mouth. After we'd hung up I fought off an impulse to call back. Sara? Dan. Did you just talk to me? If I'd had any idea she was going to accept I'd have suggested dinner at a posh restaurant. As it was, I'd just asked her to a crummy movie. I didn't even know which one. I'd have to comb the theater pages for one that started at the right time.

My mother had been in the kitchen cleaning up, pots

clattering, utensils flying around, and after a while I walked out there. She was getting things ready for the next day—she always insisted on fixing my lunch, though at sixteen I probably could have managed—since she liked to get to the hospital early. She was making careful slices from a homemade loaf of bread.

"I've got a date for Friday night," I said. "I wasn't thinking. I won't be able to get to the hospital."

Naturally, since I'd gotten what I wanted, I felt guilty.

"You go every other night," she said. "You can have a night off." As if she ever missed a visit.

"I just feel funny about it. I wasn't really thinking."

"He'll be glad you're going out. He'd much rather you'd go out than come down there."

Now she was cutting slices of turkey, razor thin, that she piled on the bread. Everything had to be just so. It always made me nervous to be around my mother in the kitchen.

"And I can have the car okay?" Must be some hitch.

"Of course you can have the car. It'll just sit here."

When Friday came, though, I insisted that we have dinner early and that I go to the hospital to visit my father for a few minutes before the date. I knew Friday evenings were desolate there, with just a small weekend staff.

The air had been cleared by a hard burst of rain that morning; when I walked out of the house it seemed more like an evening earlier in the summer, warm, but not heavy and sticky. The Nova sat out front on the street, where I'd spent the late afternoon washing it. It shone a bright white, but dented around the back and needing paint. It might have looked better if I'd left the dirt on.

I walked out on the street with my jacket slung over my shoulder. Some kids were playing wiffle ball; one, about twelve, scrawny, wearing a dirty T-shirt, stood by the front bumper. "You leaving?" he said.

"In a minute. I thought I'd watch some of your game."

His face collapsed in an angry frown. "The car's our home-run line."

Terribly sorry, old boy. I'll change my plans.

I shook my head. "You'll just have to make the adjustment."

It wasn't two minutes before a terrific argument erupted, everybody rushing in at the batter, shouting, jumping, wildly gesticulating. The whole thing—the soft summer evening, which like no other kind of evening seems to bring back memories, the kids in their T-shirts, with their dirty faces, angry high-pitched shouts—filled me with regret. I seemed just then to have so much I wanted, a good shot at the football team, a date with a girl I'd dreamed about for years, but at that moment I'd have given it all up to go back to the time I was wanting it, when I was the age of those kids and having the same arguments they were, and my father would have walked out carrying his newspaper and said quietly that if we didn't shut the hell up we'd have to take the game elsewhere. It was as if, when you had what you wanted, the other thing had to be, too, that when you finally went out with the girl you were in love with you had to stop at the hospital and see your father first.

Through the gate behind me I heard the pat-pat of the stubby little paws, the jingle of the leash, and I turned to see Rachel coming with the dog. Her evening walk seemed often to take that path, and if I was outside—sometimes, actually, I made a point of it—we talked for a while.

She was not a chubby little freckle-faced kid anymore, but as tall as I was and rather thin. She wore her reddish hair long and in a wave at her shoulders, had glasses with light tan frames that looked rather pretty on her. But I rarely saw her at the parties and dances I managed to get to. People in our crowd seemed never to lose the reputation they had once had. Rachel, in everyone's mind, was still the grumpy little girl who was never happy, who stood to the side most of the evening and frowned, found a reason to complain even when you did ask her to dance and never danced close.

I had a feeling she was not that way anymore. She

didn't care so much about pretty things. She would have laughed at that little girl who was never happy.

"Don't we look nice tonight?" She walked up beside me with a delighted smile.

"Don't we." I smiled back.

"Dressed for a young lady?"

"Naturally."

"Do I know her?"

"Sara Warren."

"Ah." Just the trace of a frown crossed her face. "She's darling."

I laughed. "Meaning what?"

"Just what I said. You have exquisite taste. You'll be the envy of young men wherever you go."

I got the same kind of reaction from Sara when I mentioned Rachel. "She's a brain," Sara said, weariness dripping from her voice. "The class genius. We all just wish we could do a tenth as well as her."

That was the kind of thing one girl said about another to get across the point that she was not really attractive, or desirable. Like saying she was darling.

"How's your father?" Rachel said.

"He's all right." That was what I said to everyone. I wasn't really sure. "We're hoping he'll be home soon."

"I sent some flowers."

"They were pretty. He was glad to get them."

So many of his patients had sent flowers that they had to be shipped out to rooms all over the hall.

"I was wondering if I should go down and see him."

Her face trembled a moment, and she looked away. She was not suggesting she do a favor. She was asking for one.

"I don't know, Rachel. They're trying to keep it to mostly family."

"Only if he wanted company. I wouldn't want to bother him."

"They say that what he needs now is rest."

"Maybe I'll drop in when he gets home."

She was biting her lip, looking toward the ground. I had always laughed at the way she felt about my father, but now it seemed touching, not just a little girl's crush. That was all I needed, though, for her to act that way on the one evening I was shortening my visit.

"I'm going down for a few minutes now," I said. "I'll say hello for you."

"Do, Dan. Give him my best."

The hospital my father was in for his ulcers was also in Oakland, but down on Forbes, further toward town. It was newer than the other, with bright hallways, linoleum on the floors and stripes painted different colors to lead you where you were going. His room was air-conditioned, and even when the door was open seemed hushed from the noise of the place.

Most of the times I went in he had an intravenous in his arm, glucose for nourishment, or a transfusion for the blood he was losing. For a while he hadn't been eating anything, just drinking milk and doses of an antacid. Now he was on a soft bland diet, colorless blobs barely recognizable as food. Always he looked pale and thin, almost gray, as he lay on the slight incline of the bed. His lips were flecked with little dots of antacid, which seemed to cling to everything.

Somehow, though, he seemed more cheerful during that stay in the hospital, or relaxed. He must really have needed the rest.

"You didn't have to come down tonight," he said when I walked in. "Lord."

"It was on the way."

"Or at least you could have brought the girl."

"I'm keeping this girl to myself."

"Actually, there's a cute little nurse in here tonight. I'll call her in and have her take your pulse."

My father always made an elaborate ritual of introducing me to the nurses, as if he expected me to make a date on my way out of the hospital. Somehow—did doctors have some special arrangement?—he seemed to get the most beautiful ones available.

"I saw Rachel Hardy," I said. "She says hello."

"That's who you should be going out with." Here we go again.

"I'm telling you, Dad. You ought to see this girl. She's beautiful."

"And she's an heiress. But Rachel Hardy is right there. Night after night. For a walk in the moonlight."

"The bulldog would probably have to come. You wouldn't be saying this if you'd seen Sara."

"I have nothing against Sara. I'm just saying. You've never had enough appreciation for what's in your own backyard."

We looked at television for a while—he had a channel changer in bed, and liked to fool around with it—but couldn't find anything but game shows. "What horseshit," he said. At eight a ball game came on, and he started to watch that. "I'll watch until the Pirates are four runs behind," he said. "After that I can't stand it."

"Forget what I said about Rachel," he said when I was leaving. "You go out with whoever you want. I'm glad you've found somebody you like."

"Half the guys in the city like her," I said.

II

There were no kids pl_____ ball in Sara's neighborhood, on that r__ _ that w__ _ among trees and past the stately hous_ __ou mig_ __have expected an aging billionaire out o__ ___f the lawns, playing fetch with a purebred Irish se___r. The Nova made a terrific racket sliding down Sara's driveway—I'd forgotten it was gravel—and skidded to a halt before the front door. My usual impressive entrance.

As I got out of the car a massive white German shepherd came bounding around the side of the house with easy loping strides, utterly effortless. Usually he was kept in a pen out back. He seemed interested to see me, stopped and stood alertly beside the walkway to the front door. He was a beautiful animal, his pelt sleek and thick. I took a step around the car, and he moved eagerly onto the walkway.

From upstairs a window flew crashing open and a voice emerged. "Tramp!" A harsh command. "Tramp! Stay!"

The dog sat immediately where he was, his head high, chest heaving. His eys were riveted on me.

"Dan?"

"Yes."

"I'm Mrs. Warren, Dan. Sara's mother. Very glad to meet you." The voice was pleasantly hoarse, as after a third whiskey sour.

"I'm glad to meet you." Especially under these relaxed and pleasant circumstances.

"He really *can* be very friendly. He's actually just a puppy." Her voice was descending into a lower register. "A wittle baby."

The dog snapped to attention. Was that some kind of command word? Wittle baby?

"Sit, Tramp! Sit!" The woman could be stern, no doubt about it. Reluctantly the dog settled onto its haunches.

"I think it would be better, Dan, if you just stayed where you are. Sara will be out in a minute."

"All right."

"Just stay still, I think. Don't make any sudden movements."

"Thank you," I said. Thank you for not letting your dog eat me.

Sara did come out of the door almost immediately, in a light blue dress roughly the color of her eyes, a white sweater across her shoulders. She stepped past the dog as if he weren't even there.

"I see you've met Tramp," she said. "And mother."

"Yes."

"They're both extremely dangerous.'"

Heading downtown from the east end, you drive alongside the Allegheny, and across the river is a high hillside of lights from businesses and homes that are reflected in the shimmering river rushing by with its swift current: the night is full of the lights on the hillside, and in the river, and the rush of cars that hurtle toward the towering lights of the city. We had the top down—Sara had requested that I leave it down—and the air was cool above our heads, but pleasant behind the windshield, the stars bright in the black sky. Sara slouched in the seat a little, resting her head against the seat back, and—sitting close to me, because the wind made it hard to hear—she talked, listened, leaned slightly against my shoulder.

"How's the football?" she said after a while. "Punts, tackles, first downs. I know it all."

I told her of the scrimmages the week before, the blocks I had thrown, the afternoon of watching films afterwards. I found myself excited in the telling—a little guiltily, because I didn't want to brag—but I must have wanted to tell someone. I knew I was glad for Sara to hear it.

"This all gets a little boring," I finally said.

"Not at all. But your coach got the point that it wasn't this Baumgardner in the movie. It was you."

"Oh yes."

"It sounds like you ought to be in there instead of Baumgardner."

"No. He's better."

"How could he be better than that?"

"I guess he couldn't be better than that. But he's better than me."

"Then you should be in there instead of somebody else."

"I never said I should start. I just want to play."

"I don't think you should sell yourself short. And don't apologize for wanting something. It's good to want something a lot. To work to get it."

I had been told that Sara, so charming and quietly elegant, was an incredibly fierce competitor on the tennis court, who especially hated to lose to boys, would have walked over anybody to make a point.

We parked in a garage across the street from the theater, down by the river; it was one of those high-rise labyrinths, with an elaborate system of floors and levels and ramps. We walked down the dim dingy stairway. As we crossed the street, as if we had been attending the theater together for years, Sara took my arm.

"This is outrageous," she laughed, once we had entered the lobby. "I feel like a teeny bopper. But I never got to eat. Could I have some popcorn?"

I grew indignant, blustered around about how we

could skip the movie, go have dinner somewhere, any-where—it was easy to be a big spender when you only had a date every six months—but she said no, no, pop-corn would be fine.

Sara did not rummage around in the box the way the rest of the world does, but shook a kernel or two at a time into her hand, chewed without a sound. I didn't take any when she offered it, because popcorn was a strange food for me: when I was alone at the movies, I found myself after the first few handfuls eating faster and faster, ignoring the movie; eventually I was lower-ing my head into it like a horse, loose kernels flying all over the place.

The movie was an international thriller, full of speedboats, sports cars, private jets, long lean elegant people, and punctuated by a jazz score: a whimsical bass, brushes on cymbals, a sudden startling shout from the brasses. It centered eventually on a jewel heist, a tall sleek woman in an evening gown who gained the attention of the guard by wrapping him in an elaborate kiss, then later drew a revolver from her purse and shot a neat hole into his forehead. The cli-max came when a man was lowered through a skylight by a rope tied to his feet, twirling slowly, in order to grab an expensive diamond. I believe he was wearing a dinner jacket at the time.

Sara did not speak during the movie, never looked at me. She was not the kind of person who had to keep making comments to show she was enjoying herself. When it ended she leaned back in her chair and sighed, blinked. "That was great."

"You liked it."

"I *loved* it. I love it when the crooks get away."

As we walked through the lobby she took my arm again. "Movies like that leave me all charged up," she said.

Outside the evening was balmy. The street was lined by tall buildings all alight. A couple of blocks down it ran into an intersection where traffic was snarled: above the intersection was a huge marquee on which red and blue borders ran in opposite directions and words raced sliding by. People milled along the side-

174

walks, got clogged at the intersection, lingered at bus stops. Cars jockeyed for position. A streetcar came swaying and sliding, sparks flying, down its tracks. "Come on," Sara said, spotting an opening and taking off across the street: hands tugging at the sleeves of her sweater, her small shapely calves moving in quick little steps, blond hair bright in the city lights. She was with me! I thought, and took off after her.

"Could I see your key chain?" she said—it was a gift from my mother, had all kinds of charms on it—and I handed it to her as we entered the parking garage. People were noticing us, staring at her, as we walked through the lobby. That was fine with me.

She stood with me for a while in the long line to the cash register, fingering the keys. "I don't think you've ever seen me like this," she said. "In this kind of mood."

"Really?"

"I get all excited. Mischievous." She squeezed my arm. "I *loved* the movie, Dan."

"Great."

"I'll wait for you here." She moved over into the crowd.

When I had reached the register, finally paid, I heard a voice behind me—"Dan"—and turned to see her standing in the elevator. With just the fingers of one hand she gave me a little wave as the doors closed.

In her other hand she had been holding up the keys.

Suddenly people were looking at me in another way, grinning broadly as they stood around the lobby. They all seemed to be in on it. Big joke. I walked toward the doors slowly, as if I expected them to open again, then stepped casually into a doorway marked STAIRS, started racing up. I had no idea what I was doing. The cement stairway was narrow and dingy, a single dirty bulb at each landing.

I jumped out at the second level, saw no one, the third, no one. But then I had realized I had no memory of where I had parked the car. A drunk was sprawled on a landing of the stairway, drooling, asleep. At the fifth level I jumped out on a couple engaged in a long kiss; they didn't even notice me. My footsteps slapped and echoed in the stairway: I was sweating, panting. All the floors looked alike, rows of cars gleaming under the lights, no one around. Finally I popped out on the roof—I knew we hadn't parked there—and an attendant trained a flashlight on me, "Yeah, what is it?" I headed back down.

For a while I leaned, gasping, against a wall, decided for some reason that I had parked on the fourth level, went down there and walked up and down among the rows of cars. Somehow, whatever else I was feeling, I wasn't surprised, as if this were a perfectly normal occurrence on one of my dates. I could picture myself catching a streetcar home, hiking sheepishly over to Sara's the next morning to pick up the car. It would be hard to explain to my mother. "I don't understand, Dan. She took the car?" I heard a horn honking, a car racing on the rough surface of the central ramp that ran like a corkscrew down the middle of the garage. It was Sara, in the Nova, with the top down. I shouted, she waved, and I took off after her, stumbling onto the ramp. "Hey," a voice shouted. "Get offa there. There's cars on there," but now that I had her in my sights I wasn't stopping, even if I had to run the length of the parkway. I figured I had a good shot at catching her at a stoplight downtown. My feet slipped on the rough surface of the ramp, and I kept banging into the wall, running around and around. She was waiting for me at the bottom, standing out beside the car, short of the check-out booth.

"I forgot about the ticket," she said.

For some reason—I normally didn't show much feeling—speechless, I slammed my fist on the trunk, as if that made some statement.

"I'm sorry!" Her face had brightened into a big smile at my show of temper, and she buried it in my chest, clutched at my lapels. "Sorry, sorry. I told you, movies like that always get me going."

Her forehead rested against my pounding heart; my mouth was in her hair, that was so soft, smelled wonderful. "It's all right," I said.

"That ain't good for the car, hitting it like that," the attendant said when I paid.

"That's right, Dan," Sara said.

"How come I didn't see you at one of the floors?" I said as we were riding home, her head resting on the seat back. "I stopped at every one."

"I hid behind a car until you were gone. You hardly looked."

"I didn't think you were hiding."

"It was the floor where that couple was kissing."

I had invited her to go somewhere afterwards, maybe get something to eat—one of my big problems on dates was that I never knew what you did after the movies—but she said no. "I've had such a busy day. And all that popcorn." When we drove down the driveway, Tramp immediately galloped up beside my door. "You'd better stay in the car," Sara said.

"That's all right." I would have battled a saber-tooth tiger to walk her to the house.

"No." She opened her door. "He doesn't obey me as well as he does mother. He's jealous. Raised me from a child."

It wasn't until later that I remembered Sara's mother had called the dog a puppy.

"And it's late," Sara said.

I was feeling the same sinking sensation as when I had seen the elevator doors close.

I tried to laugh. "I'm not afriad of a dog."

"Dan." She was already out of the car, leaned in at her side. Her eyes were watching me. "You know we're lovers."

"What?" Must have heard her wrong.

"'That was a lovely evening, I had a wonderful time." She was wearing a soft smile. "You know we're lovers."

"We . . ."

"You know that. I just wanted you to know I knew."

"I never said . . ."

"You don't have to say."

"I don't understand."

"I know. It's all right." She was stepping back.

I moved across the seat. My heart ached. "Let me come in."

"No."

"Just for a minute."

"Not tonight." She reached out: with her fingertips she touched my cheek. "Leave it at this. For tonight. It's enough. We're lovers."

She turned and, lightly, ran into the house.

I sat out in the car awhile. That neighborhood was utterly silent. Only a single light was on in Sara's house, up on the second floor. Crickets were chirping in the grass. Far off, if you listened closely, you could hear the rush of the city.

Our date had been like the phone calls: not much had happened, but I was left exhilarated. Sara was skilled at getting to the door, as skilled as, out on the tennis court, she was at parrying a hard serve. That is not to say that her words meant nothing, though God knows what they did mean, to her. I doubt that I understood much of what was going on at the time. In a way, though, I think I was getting what I wanted, that just then what I wanted was breathlessly to be chasing a girl who was out of my reach, who would never quite be in my reach, and who never—as she eluded me— did what I expected.

I stared at Tramp, who was still panting patiently beside the car. Probably that dumb son of a bitch didn't even bite.

Chapter 13

TOWARD THE END of preseason we had a scrimmage on the upper practice field, the same one, in front of the infirmary, that I had looked out on with Nick Kaiser. I doubt that I ever played in a game as rough as those scrimmages. There were so many tough linemen that year, all of us slugging it out day after day as if the last one left standing, dazed, bloody, would be the winner. There wasn't one of us who would have admitted that, if it came down to a brawl, he might not be the one who was left.

I was playing defensive guard that morning, over the center in the unbalanced line, the other co-captain, a kid named Baker. In the shower he looked fat, rolls of flab hanging on his sides like saddlebags, but there was all kinds of muscle under that blubber—his thighs were like a couple of old tree stumps—and he was surprisingly quick: within that massive bag of flab a classy little sprinter was fighting desperately to get out. On defense he was a terror; about the best thing you could do was try to bounce off hard as he barreled past, a matchstick hitting a locomotive, but that was his first year playing center on offense, and anyway the center is always at a disadvantage, since he has to snap the ball before he throws a block. If I cracked him with the snap I could lift him up a little, hold him off, like trying to support a bridge collapsing. That morning they were working on dives, and I was doing okay; they weren't getting through unmolested.

Baker's father was out there, my father's doctor. I didn't know what kind of doctor he was that he could take time off to watch a football practice, but there he was; I knew him because he often stopped in to see my father at the hospital. He was a tall man, white-haired, dignified, except for a slightly awkward manner he had about him, like an old country practitioner; he had big horsy teeth. He was standing back there talking to Grupp, and they were both looking straight at me and Baker, Grupp wearing one of his fat grins, as if he just loved to watch his boys beat themselves bloody in the trenches. You didn't see him slamming the old clipboard when there were parents around.

Of course I was hitting for Grupp's benefit. It was a perfect chance. They were running dives, and he was standing beside Baker's father: he would have to notice how I did. But I wasn't hitting only to impress Grupp, I don't think even mainly for him. I knew Dr. Baker saw my father every day. Above all things at that point I wanted my father to see me play. He had seen me my freshman year, when I kept backing off, scared to death. But he hadn't been able to see at the JV games; he'd only heard me talk about the games, about Wiggins, night after night. I knew he wouldn't be seeing me anytime soon. He had only my word for it that I wasn't the same kid he'd watched my freshman year. Now I had a witness.

After a while Grupp stepped forward and said something to the Rose, who was on one knee in a bunch of players on the sidelines; he got up and, with that awkward dainty trot of his, came in for me. I was going to join the rest of the subs, take his place, but before I could, Grupp called me back.

"Dan," he said. "You know Dr. Baker."

"Yes, sir."

"I had to pull you out of there," Grupp said. "I didn't want to get Baker beat up in front of his father."

"You're supposed to show a little respect," Dr. Baker said.

"That's the team captain in there," Grupp said.

Both men were wearing wide grins, as if they shared some private joke. I'd never seen Grupp like that. He whacked my butt with his clipboard. "Way to crack in there, Dan." He stepped forward, over among the rest of the team, as if better to see the scrimmage.

"You looked good in there, son," Dr. Baker said. "Mixing with the best. If I do say so myself."

"Thank you." Flushed, sweating, I was proud: I admit it. That was what I wanted most in the world, praise from those men.

"I've just been talking with your father," he said.

I knew that tone, the change in his voice; it grew light, breezy, harsh just around the edges, as a solemn expression settled over his face. It was the way a certain kind of prosperous man approached an emotional subject: he bullied it, to distance himself. Perhaps it was the way men were in general. We stood off from the rest, watching a football scrimmage, he with his hands in his pockets, I holding my helmet and looking down at it, for all the world as if we were just going over the prospects for the coming season.

But through my mind many things were racing at once. Dr. Baker hadn't just come out there to watch a football scrimmage. Grupp hadn't called me over just on a whim. It wasn't by accident that we were standing apart from the rest of the team.

"His condition is serious," Dr. Baker said. "The bleeding is the problem. You may know we've been giving him massive transfusions. But you don't understand about this, Dan, because there's something you haven't known. I wouldn't tell it to just anyone. Not even necessarily a man's son. But I talked to your father this morning and he's decided you ought to know. He asked me if I'd have a chance to come out here and tell you."

In a way he didn't have to tell me. I already knew. I had seen my father, still a young man, undergoing eye operations that should have been routine, and suddenly growing older. I had seen him at the hospital looking pale, really sick and thin and weak. I had seen the transfusions, day after day, even heard a doctor mention the figure, fourteen pints. I had seen the looks on the faces of certain people—my mother, doctors who stopped in at his hospital room. Wiggins when he had spoken to me even a year before, Rachel Hardy when she saw me casually that summer—who all, no doubt, knew different things, but who all seemed to know the one thing, that my father was sicker than we were saying. There had been times that summer—after a visit to the hospital, for instance—when that knowledge about my father had been all around me, as if I could take it in, make it a part of myself, but I didn't do it. No, I seemed to be saying. I won't do that now. There will be a time for that.

So as I stood breathless, my heart hammering, and listened to Dr. Baker speak, it was not as if I were hearing sudden shocking news, but as if I understood that this was the time, this was the moment; from then on everything I did, said, heard, would include that new knowledge, and would all be different.

For a moment I looked with loathing on the deep green field spread in front of me, the trees clumped on the hill above it, the blue sky pale above that. An ache was in my throat as I looked out on that world, and knew the truth.

I wasn't hearing the particular words, the disease he named that was a form of cancer, his nervous explanation of exactly what it was. I was hearing what I knew they said to me. My father was going to die.

"I've known your father a long time," Dr. Baker went on. "I remember when he first opened his practice. They did a lot of X-ray treatment then, more than they'd ever think of doing now, and the equipment was imperfect. He thinks in a way that might be the whole problem, with his eyes, the disease he has. That faulty X-ray equipment. I suppose we'll never know."

"What'll I do?" I was staring at the scrimmage, that senseless desperate activity.

"Just what you're doing. There's nothing you can do. He just wanted you to know. I honestly don't think you should worry too much right now. Things are serious. I wouldn't make light of them to you. But I think there's been a turn for the better. Even just recently. I have a feeling that this time he's going to pull through."

This time. But there would be other times.

He laid a hand on my shoulder, left it a moment, then took it away, walked down to his car. I watched him, for some reason. He had an odd, awkward, shambling gait, not like a distinguished doctor at all.

I have wondered sometimes why I didn't break down when Dr. Baker talked to me, why I wasn't the kind of kid who cried, like Nick Kaiser sobbing unashamedly in front of his locker. Was it something about me, from all my life, or was it something I had only recently learned, at that school: to take disappointment and even deep sorrow like what they called a man? After a while I moved back into the crowd, into the team, and, as if to acknowledge that, Grupp put me back in the scrimmage. I didn't even complain, ask to be taken out, when, for the rest of the morning, I was bounced around like a blocking dummy.

I have always been one to bear strong emotion alone, to carry it off and mull over it, like the jungle animal who wanders into seclusion at the end of his life to die. I could have borne all my disappointments about football by myself. It was when I had to face others—my father, when I was a freshman and had played a terrible game; Nick Kaiser, when, a year later, I knew my dreams of playing varsity were about to go up in smoke—that my disappointments were hard for me.

My family was a quiet one. My father, perhaps, was the exception—with his shouts of laughter when he was reading, of joy and exuberance when we were out fishing—but for the most part, when the emotion was strong, we went off with it alone. My parents did their fighting with the door closed in their room, and I, when I was heavy with sorrow or disappointment, was allowed to go quietly to mine. I have heard of families where the home was a tapestry of emotion, shouts of joy and raging tears, slaps and punches and hugs of desperate adoration, but my house was not like that. I think of my mother's parents—who died when I was a boy—and the quiet house they had, comfortable because it was quiet; I can still remember my grandmother's funeral, when, at the end of the service, my grandfather was allowed to have a last time alone with her: he reddened, embarrassed, and spent only a moment at the coffin, walking away with his head bowed. What grieving he had, he would do alone.

When I got home from practice on the day I had seen Dr. Baker, my mother was in the kitchen, and as she turned to me, the hardness and strain in her face had softened, but the grief was still there, a darkness around her eyes. "Dan," she said, and in her voice was an acknowledgment: she knew I had been told. "Mom." I stepped to her and hugged her, an awkward hug, stiff, because our griefs could not melt together.

"Are you all right?" she said.

"I'm all right," I said. "Are you?"

"Yes. Better now than before."

We went out to the living room to talk. The lights were off, and we left them off, just the late afternoon sunlight filtering in through the Venetian blinds.

"There have been times I thought I would tell you," she said. "No matter what your father and I had decided. I thought you should know."

"Yes."

"But he didn't want you to have to carry that around. For however long it would be. It was so hard for him. Hard for us. He didn't want it to be hard for you."

My mother was not crying, but her eyes seemed weary, vulnerable, ready to weep.

"How long has it been?" I said.

"Six years. Since we've known. The doctors at first thought it would be only two to four years. Then those years passed, pretty calmly. It's only this past year that things have gotten serious. And only this summer, with the ulcers, the bleeding, that it's been critical."

Stunned—I couldn't believe it had been that long—I thought back. It went back so far, to well before the time I had started at Arnold, to the days when that big man, burly, barely graying, had come out into the street to throw the ball around with me. For all those years it had been one world for me, another for him and for my mother. A vast distance seemed to separate those worlds.

"At first he didn't even tell me," she said. "That first

184

weekend he knew. It seems an eternity ago. He was so preoccupied. Staring off into space. He would heave these great sighs. He was just a young man. I knew something was wrong, wanted to ask him. Finally he said."

She was looking down into her lap, at her hands.

"It's so hard for me to imagine," I said. "How it's been all this time. For you."

"In so much time," she shook her head, "so many different things happen. The first thing your father thought of was providing for us. He opened trust funds, one for me and one for you. He went out right away and talked about getting you into Arnold. He wasn't sure how long he had, asked them to promise that if he didn't . . . have the time, they would arrange tuition help for you. He paid off the mortgage on this house. Worked so hard."

"He should have thought more about himself."

"Those were the things he was worried about. It was what he wanted to do. But after that beginning, the initial shock, things honestly weren't so bad. The two years passed, the four years. We had come to the point where we were just enjoying what we had, the time we were given. Little things, that you could take for granted otherwise. A trip to the beach could be a precious thing. It's only recently"—her eyes closed a moment—"that it's gotten difficult again. But we've had good months, Dan. Good years."

"I felt like, kind of a traitor. For not knowing. As if I've gotten away with something."

"It may be that we've handled it wrong. Who knows? It's been the great secret. Friends have heard things. Patients. I don't know how something like that gets out, but it does. The lies I've told. Sometimes I think it shouldn't be a secret. We keep it from people because it will be hard for them, or the whole thing will be embarrassing, but sometimes I think what is hard, what is embarrassing, is just that it is a secret. You hold on to it, won't let anybody see. But maybe it wouldn't *be* hard if everybody saw. If it were all out in the open."

She looked up. "It will be easier for me, Dan. Now that you know."

She was right. I hadn't known the particulars, but I had known something. For a few months, anyway, that knowledge had lived in our house, while we all—averting our eyes—did a kind of dance around it.

"I'd do anything to make it easier for you," I said.

"I know. But don't take that on yourself. You have plenty you have to live with."

Saying changes things, but it can seem to change them more than it really does. My mother and I would remain the people we were—we wouldn't handle our grief in some new open way—but I think that after that talk we at least understood better how we were. I saw ahead of me that day a role I would be taking as a man in that house, but a part of me was still a boy, would remain a boy, and the man that I was to become was the kind who thinks that in his silence, his refusal to show things outwardly, he is a bulwark of strength. He protects others from difficult things by bearing them silently himself, and acting for all the world as if they do not exist. It is not—I am convinced now—the best way for a man to be. But it is the way men often thought they should be then, when men were supposed to be strong, and certain words were just not said, and death, we thought, was best handled by keeping it a secret.

On the way to my father's room that evening, the hospital corridors were hushed, nurses hurrying by on their rubber-soled shoes, an occasional orderly wheeling a cart. I caught the strong familiar scent of hospital alcohol, heard the quiet urgent calls for doctors over the speakers. "Dr. Keith, Dr. Keith," I had often heard as a boy, but this was another time.

"Do you want me to come?" my mother had said as I left the house.

"I don't know."

"It might be easier if we were all there."

I hesitated at the door. "I think I'd rather go alone. Tonight."

I was afraid for anyone else to be there. Afraid, actually, of going at all. I wanted terribly to see him. But I didn't know how it would be.

My father still seemed weak and tired as he lay against the bed, his hair disheveled, but it was all right now: I didn't have to fight it. And it seemed to me—had seemed throughout that stay, but that night more than ever—that he was more at ease than before. He turned slowly and brightened as I walked in. "Danny." I could tell he had been waiting to see me.

"Hi, Dad."

There was an ache in my chest as I stood by the bed. I tried to smile back. Probably, at that point, I would have said nothing, just acted as if it were another visit.

But he brought it up. "Dr. Baker said you looked like quite a man out there today. Cracking heads with the best."

Even a day before, those words would have thrilled me, but now I barely heard them, just nodded. "I saw him," I said. I looked down toward the bed.

My father reached slowly to touch my hand, resting beside him. "It's hard on you, Dan."

Surprising me—I hadn't felt them coming—tears poured from my eyes.

"I'm sorry it's hard on you," he said.

I put my head down and wept, tried to choke back the tears. All my life, whenever I have cried—even at that moment—it has seemed a defeat, and I have been ashamed.

My father's hand tightened. "It will be easier."

"Never."

"It *will* be easier, in time. It's much easier for me now than it was."

"I'll be all right, Dad."

"I know you will."

"I mean, I *will* be all right. I want you to know. To know now. I'll do okay."

I didn't know where it was coming from, the crazy speech I was starting to say.

"I know," he said.

"You sent me to that school."

187

Wearily he gazed at me, shifting slightly on the pillow, frowning, puzzled, "I sent you . . ."

"To make something of myself."

"No, Dan."

"You gave me the opportunity. I didn't appreciate it at first. I hated the place. All that work. I couldn't do anything. Papers, tests. I couldn't play football. Answer in class. I couldn't even wait on the tables. I got pushed around. But I can do it now."

"I know you can."

"Do the homework, pass the tests."

"I know."

"And I can play football. Beat those guys. I'll be on the team. One of the best."

My voice broke, and I felt myself gasp: loudly, I started to sob. I put my head on my hands, on his chest, lay against the rough hospital gown, sobbing. My body shook, with great shudders. I felt his hand move, rest on top of my head. He let me cry.

"You don't have to, Dan," he said after a while. "You don't understand. I never sent you to that school to be anything but what you are. Sometimes I wish I hadn't, with all the struggle you've had. But believe me, Dan, you don't have to do a thing for me. I know what you are. What you'll always be, no matter what happens. You're my son."

But I couldn't hear him. I didn't believe. His hand on my head as I lay there sobbing was his blessing, if only I had known.

II

Dr. Baker was right. My father had been improving, even on the day Baker had come out to practice; the ulcers were healing, and soon he had graduated to a solid diet, though he still had to drink, constantly it seemed, doses of milk and the antacid. On the evenings I visited I picked up a couple milkshakes on my way down, and as often as not he would be sitting in the chair waiting for me when I got there; we sat and drank them and talked. He began to gain back some weight and color. They kept him in the hospital much longer than if he had just been an ulcer patient. By the end of his stay he was stronger, walking around the halls, and would go down occasionally and sit in the coffee shop. In September—the first full week of school for me—he was allowed to come home.

"I've got to be careful what I eat," he said. "And I need to get plenty of rest. But the ulcers seem to be all closed up. The bleeding's stopped. They say I can go back to the office when I'm ready."

"You'll do that?"

"Why not? I'll be careful about things. It's better than sitting around the house and stewing. I think I'll be happier if I'm doing something."

We were sitting in my parents' bedroom, where there was an easy chair with a plush footstool; he had himself set up with books and a thermos of milk. He was reading the American authors from the days of his youth, on weekends would send me to the university bookstore with a list to hunt for paperbacks. He was different even from the man he had been at the beginning of the summer, thinner, and grayer, and less vigorous, though as that different man he looked fairly well.

"So tell me about the game," he said. "What are the odds?"

We were gearing up again for the first game of the season.

"Nobody knows. Hargrove's already played a game, and they won big. That's not a real good sign, though people are managing to ignore it. Everybody at Arnold's saying we'll kill them."

"Naturally."

"I do think we're going to be good."

"What about Dan Keith?"

"I can't tell. A couple of weeks ago I would have said I was a sure thing. But there are so many linemen, and a lot of them are about the same. It just depends on how many he wants to play."

I didn't tell my father all that people were saying. At that point it was just talk. Our line was stronger and deeper than it had been before, and though part of the

189

backfield was young—Shealy at quarterback and Grunfeld at halfback were starting for the first time—it was talented, and spearheaded by Pollett, the last year he would be eligible against public schools. It was a solid team, the best, certainly, since I'd been at Arnold. Everybody was saying that if we were ever going to win the league, that would be the year.

It was the first time I'd suited up for a varsity game expecting to play. On the bus going over, in the heavy silence that always preceded a game, my heart was fluttering, and I felt myself start to sweat. As it always seemed to be for that game, the night was terribly humid. Under the lights, especially between defensive plays, you could see the linemen's chests heaving, their faces dripping with sweat.

On the bench I sat between the Rose and, of all people, Sennett. Out of nowhere he had become a deeply serious athlete that season. Instead of grinning sarcastically and sneering, he nodded solemnly when he saw me at practice, slapped me on the butt and grunted words of encouragement when I made a good play. He walked around campus with a meditative frown on his face. Late in the season, unfortunately, he was to suffer a relapse, lobbing a cherry bomb into an empty room in a visiting team's dormitory and getting bounced off the squad for good.

Every time Grupp turned even slightly from the field the three of us jumped. On defense he was using the substitutes we'd expected, Giles and Bert Foley; he was alternating Krause and Baker, and there were only four interior linemen. Late in the second quarter he turned and scanned the bench, looking for somebody. Rosy, Sennett, and I strained forward.

For a moment I swear he looked straight at me.

"Ryczek!" he shouted. "Harry Ryczek!"

"Jesus Christ," Sennett muttered.

"I don't believe it," Rosy said.

At the other end of the bench the big kid stood—six-three, stooped at the shoulders, baby-faced—pulled on his helmet and ran to stand beside Grupp.

"A fucking sophomore," Sennett said. "And he's putting him in here."

I just sat and stared. Ryczek was the new scholar-ship kid, raw-boned and strong and with all kinds of potential, but in practice he was gun-shy, hung back and waited for you to charge. He dogged his sprints, grimacing in agony. I'd walked all over him in one-on-ones.

"They give the kid a scholarship," Sennett said. "Then they got to play him. They're paying all that money."

I still wasn't talking, just watching, breathless, as Ryczek lumbered into the game. Whatever I had said to my father, however casual I had sounded, I'd been sure I was going to play in that game, but as I watched Ryczek going in, Grupp's back turning to us once and for all, I know I'd been wrong. He'd never use more linemen than that.

"There goes the old ball game," Rosy said. He wasn't talking about the game on the field.

Pollett played magnificently, scoring all three of our touchdowns, including one in the third quarter that he broke long, slapping his way past two tacklers and outrunning a third. But Hargrove was a powerhouse that year, losing only one game all season, and in the end beat us rather handily, 33–20. We were in the game until the fourth quarter, though, so there were no wholesale substitutions. As he did sometimes with sen-iors, Grupp put in Sennett at the end.

My father was asleep when I got home—he was keeping early hours—but I explained what I could of the game to my mother. When I saw him the next morning he was sitting at the breakfast table over the sports pages.

"Sounds like quite a game," he said. "From all it says here."

"Until the end," I said. "Anyway, I had a good seat."

"Your mother told me. I know you're disappointed."

"What the hell."

"Don't make light of it."

"I'm not. That's the thing. I don't know what to make of it."

More than anything I was just bewildered. By that

time, of course, football wasn't everything to me. My father was home, looking better than he had, and I had a superstition that I shouldn't wish for more than that, that it was ungrateful to want anything more. In a way, in the midst of all that was happening, I was numb to my old dreams about football. But I knew I was good. I had worked damn hard. And it would have meant a great deal to me, especially just then when my father was sick—there was no use denying it—to have played in that game.

Monday morning my father let me take the car to school, and I got there early, lingering in the hallway outside Grupp's classroom. Probably I shouldn't have. He took a loss hard, would have been doing well to have recovered by the time of the next game. I knew he wouldn't be in any mood to talk, but I wanted to see him. It was as if, again and again, I saw that scene from the bench, him scanning the team, staring for what seemed a long moment at me, then calling for Ryczek. I had to know.

No one else was around the science wing. The lights were off. There were lockers there—my locker was there—and I stood in front of it, trying to act as if I were just getting my books. Finally I heard an awkward fumbling at the door, and Grupp pushed his way in, carrying a portable projector and a large round canister of film. That was Friday night's game. He would spend the whole day going over it with his classes, lecturing on it, getting madder and madder, until, by the time practice started, he would be trembling on the verge of homicidal fury.

He barely noticed me. "Hello, Keith." His voice was hoarse and weak. He looked as if he hadn't slept in days.

"Hello." I was trying to seem casual, as if I just happened to be in the hallway. Fat chance. "Mr. Grupp." I took a deep breath. "Do you think I'll be playing varsity football this year?"

For a brief moment, wearily, his eyes closed. "I don't know, Keith. I haven't exactly been pondering the question all weekend."

"I know." It was all I could do to stand there and face him.

"I've got eight more games to try to win. A whole season to consider."

I nodded, staring toward the floor.

"I haven't felt I could depend on you," he said.

I looked up, my heart pounding. Just a small patch of light came in from the window above the door, shone on his face.

"In the Jefferson scrimmage," he said, "maybe that was unfair. Throwing you in there on a couple of days' notice with no experience at all. But that was the way things turned out. And our offense got mauled that day."

"But in the films . . ."

"I know, I know. You threw a good block. And I gave you credit for it. But I talked to the backfield, and most of the day, they said, they weren't getting much support. The defense was coming in over you."

There it was. I had played a superb game in that scrimmage, hadn't missed a block all day—there were even films of it—and he was saying it wasn't so.

I tried to make my voice firm. "I felt I played a great game that day."

He made a little sound—just letting out air—like spitting. "I see. Well. Of course you're welcome to your opinion." He was picking up the projector again. "I hope you'll allow me the right to mine. It's the feeling of the coaching staff . . . I'm not saying all year. But it's our opinion right now. Until we see something more. You're not the mature kind of player we need for the varsity."

"There are different things you could do," Wiggins said. "You could quit."

We were standing down on the field before practice. I had told him about my conversation with Grupp. He was wearing the same sweatshirt he always wore, that never seemed to be dirty—apparently he didn't sweat like the rest of us—and the same expression on his face, intent, serious, but empty of emotion.

"I've thought of that," I said.

"I hope you're not expecting me to make some big pitch for you to stay."

"No." I knew better.

"Ed Krause was in the same position last year. You may remember. He didn't exactly quit. He might as well have."

Krause, our mammoth outside tackle, had been so disgusted when he hadn't played varsity the year before that he had just stood around in the JV games, watched everyone else block, and pretty soon—despite the fact that the mere sight of him started the opposing line's teeth chattering—Wiggins hadn't played him at all, letting a six-foot-five-inch tackle sit on the JV bench. "I don't start a line for cosmetic purposes," Wiggins had said.

"He wasted a year," Wiggins said. "He didn't think the JVs properly used his talents, so he didn't play anywhere. I wouldn't pretend that made any great difference in his life. But I think it was stupid. Football is football. If you play it for the sake of a jacket on your back, that's what you get. Or you don't. But I think there's something more. That you can find it as easily on a JV field, or even in one-on-ones in practice, as on the varsity."

"There's such a thing as succeeding," I said.

"There are kinds of success," he said.

I could have tried to explain what I was playing for, all the varsity meant to me. He wouldn't have made light of it. But I think he would have said the same thing, that I was playing for the wrong reasons.

"It's up to you," he said.

I did play JV football, the Rose, and I, and a bunch of the juniors. We had quite a season, lost only one game, and after we were resigned to it had quite a time. "Don't feel bad," Tim Deitz would say, as we shook hands with our vanquished opponents after the game. "You really lost to a varsity team." Starting about halfway through the season, we did play a little varsity. It was strange. Grupp didn't just throw us in at the end of a game. He used us in key situations, but then didn't leave us in. The varsity had a good season too, lost only one after Hargrove, but that was to Asbury, so once again they came up short in the league.

For the first time I attended the Fall Sports Banquet, a big father-son dinner at the end of November. My father was still working, though it bothered me, in a way, that he was. He would come home exhausted, walk terribly slowly from out by the garage into the house. Everything seemed worse, his hands shaking, the hoarseness to his voice, weakness at his neck. At the banquet he didn't eat any of the roast beef they served—his stomach was acting up again—just sat with his hands folded in front of him, chin on his chest. The other fathers were eating heartily, talking loudly—they all seemed to have had a few before they came—and he and I seemed a little out of it, down at the end of the table, where we sat beside Rosy and his father, a quiet balding man who ate about half his food and then lit up a cigar.

After dinner one team after another was introduced, football last. Grupp spoke glowingly of the JV squad, how much he was looking forward to having us on the varsity—what the hell, we'd been around all year—but when he started to read the names forgot to say anything about standing up. All the other teams had stood. Around the banquet hall the other players were all looking at me, since I had been the first name on the list, the team captain.

"Get up," my father said.

"I don't know," I said. "Maybe this is better. We don't want to stand for him."

"That's right," Rosy said.

"Who said you were standing for him?" my father said.

"It's embarrassing," Rosy said.

"Then be embarrassed for a minute," my father said.

"They should have let Wiggins read the names," I said.

"We'll stand next year," Rosy said. "When we're on the varsity."

There was an awkward silence, and I looked away;

without thinking, Rosy and Mr. Malcolm had both looked, reddening, at my father.

He didn't even seem to notice. "After all these years," he said. "I finally came out to see you guys get some recognition. Now you won't even stand."

"He's right," Mr. Malcolm said. "We came to see you."

The other team members were still glancing around, looking toward us.

"Whatever you may have wanted to do," my father said, "be proud of what you've done."

So about the time Grupp was getting to the bottom of the list, we stood, Rosy and me first, then the rest of the team, one by one. As if because we had decided to stand, there was a burst of applause, and we were all—as if we held some secret—irrepressibly beaming. At times in the past it had seemed we were the scrubs, what was left after the varsity had been picked, but by that time we knew we were more than that. We had been through a lot. We were a team, and while everyone was really there to honor that year's varsity, they were on their way out, and a new year stood before us.

When we finally sat down, first my father, then Rosy's, leaned to shake our hands.

My father was beaming. "I used to watch these kids play, when . . . Hell." He shook his head. "They couldn't even hold a football."

Chapter 14

THAT CHRISTMAS VACATION I had spent a lot of time with the Rose; his girlfriend had gone with her family on a skiing trip to Colorado, and he didn't have much to do. We drove around a lot, went bowling and shot pool at some places downtown. On a Wednesday evening—New Year's Eve was the next night—we were taking in a movie.

My father had stayed home from the office that week, the first work he'd missed since he'd been in the hospital the summer before. I would hardly have said he looked any worse at that point; by that time he just always looked ill, drawn and weary, but that was the first week he hadn't felt up to the office. On Wednesday evening he called Dr. Baker, asked if he might come to the house and look him over. I stopped by his room just as I heard the doctor arriving downstairs. "I'll see you, Dad," I said. "I'm going out to a movie."

"All right, Dan." He was lying in bed, propped up by pillows, holding a book, though he didn't seem to be reading it, just stared off absently around the room. You might have thought he was pondering something, thinking some problem through to the end. He smiled at me. "Have a good time."

I'd stopped in my room, was heading down the stairs when I heard the doctor speak. He couldn't have been with my father more than a few moments. "I hate just to come over here and rush you off to the hospital,

Ben. But I can't help thinking that's where you ought to be."

Of all the moments in my father's illness, that one in my memory is the most poignant, those two doctors talking together in that room, knowing what they knew.

I stopped on the stairs. My mother had stepped out of the room and was standing in the hallway.

I spoke quietly. "I won't go."

"No," she said. "Go ahead."

"I wouldn't feel right. I wouldn't enjoy it."

"But what could you do? What good would it do to stay around here?"

"I could go to the hospital."

"And stand around while I fill out a bunch of forms? There's no reason to do that. He'll just want to rest when he gets there anyway."

I stood motionless on that step, as if taking the next one would decide me. Down at the front door, the Rose was standing with his hands in his pockets, a pained awkward expression on his face. He shrugged.

"Go," my mother said.

It wasn't just at that moment that I had to decide; there had been a long series of moments, that stretched back for months. When I had first found out about my father I hadn't wanted to leave him at all, even step out of the hospital room to stretch my legs, but of course I did. I didn't see how I could go home and sleep, how I could get up the next morning and do something so trivial as going to football practice, or to school, but I did. Soon I developed a superstition: that I could leave him for essential things, but not for anything frivolous, anything I would enjoy. But as he improved, came home from the hospital, went back to work, I gradually began to do even those things. With each one there was a moment of panic—is this the time I shouldn't leave?—but as such moments accumulated they had less and less impact. I began to grow accustomed to them.

The further I got from that talk with Dr. Baker, the less reality it had. There were times I could almost imagine it had not happened, that I was back in those days early in the summer before I had known. Odd fictions had developed in my mind, that possibly there had been some mistake, it wasn't what the doctors said, that doctors everywhere were wrong about the nature of the disease, that my father's would be the one case that was the exception to the rule: he would continue to improve, grow stronger, would finally be well. I began to think that perhaps if you treated a man as if he were dying, he would die, that all of your obtrusive hovering around would only remind him that he was ill, that the best thing might be just to carry on as if nothing were wrong. Acting that way, I sometimes convinced myself that nothing was wrong.

The truth was hard, and I did everything, it seems, not to face it.

"Go ahead," my mother said from the hallway.

There was a gentle stubbornness in her, harder to handle than real anger. "All right. But I'm going to call when I get down there. I'll want to see that everything's okay."

"You can call. Just don't spend the whole evening thinking about it."

My Uncle Billy, her brother, who had stayed with us as usual over the holidays, was sitting in the living room reading the paper. "Have a good time, Dan," he said. "We'll take care of things."

On the way home from the movies—I'd gotten through to Uncle Billy at the hospital; he said things were going fine—the Rose was driving. "How about coming over to my place for dinner tomorrow night?" he said. "Before Litchfield's party."

"I don't know."

"Look. You know how my parents are. It's bad enough for any party, but New Year's Eve, my God. They'll put me through the wringer. Who's going to be there, who'll be chaperoning, what'll everybody be drinking. If you're at the table they won't say a thing."

"I'm not at all that sure I'm going."

"Not going? New Year's Eve?"

"With my father in the hospital."

"Oh." He'd already forgotten; obviously he wouldn't

199

have had it on his mind all the time. "Well. If you do, it'd really help me out."

"I'll see."

My mother was waiting for me when I got home. "Dr. Baker called an ambulance to get him down there. That kind of scared me, but they said it was just easier, for admitting and everything. He got settled just fine. I know it will be good for him to have the rest."

"I'll go down tomorrow evening."

"You've got a party."

"It's gigantic. Nobody'll even know if I'm there."

"I think we should go on with what we would normally do." My mother felt as I did, had been at it much longer. "He's in there for a rest, not for us to sit around worrying."

"But I want to see him."

"You can go down in the afternoon. Uncle Billy will take me in the morning. That'll spread our visits out. We can go back in the evening if it seems we should."

"Rosy invited me to dinner."

"That'll work out well then. I can have something at the hospital and spend the dinner hour with your father."

Sometimes when I was at loose ends I took the car out for a spin—it was still something of a novelty for me—and that was what I did the next morning, driving through Schenley Park, getting out a couple times to walk. The morning was a pale gray, bitter cold, though not snowing; somehow it was bleaker for all that, the trees bare and black, jagged, the pond murky and afloat with dead leaves. The wind stung my face until it was no longer pleasant to be out. I got home about the same time as my mother.

She did not seem worried. "Your father just doesn't think he's up to a visit this afternoon. He wants to see you. But he'd rather you'd come tomorrow, when he'll feel more like it."

A couple of days later, the whole thing would seem monstrous, as if events had conspired to keep me from seeing him. Really it was just one coincidence after another.

"I'll go tonight. I don't have to go to this party."

"He wouldn't think of it. That you'd miss a party to sit around a hospital room. He made a point of saying that. He'll see you in the morning."

"I could just stop in for a minute."

"There's no need. To break up your whole evening like that."

It may be that my mother was thinking as I was, that if we just wouldn't treat it as something serious, somehow it wouldn't be. I could have stopped in, on the way over, or in the middle of the party. The hospital was only a few minutes away. It would have been easy enough.

Henry Litchfield had been with me at the Academy since ninth grade, though I had never known him well. His house was in a suburb about ten miles from town, south, down the river. From the front, well back from the street, it looked like many another brick dwelling, with a wide picture window and closely manicured lawn, but inside it was vast, elaborate, and ran way back; at an earlier party, looking for a bathroom upstairs, I had actually gotten lost, opening doors, wandering for minutes from room to room, up and down small stairways, without any idea where I was. For the most part, the parties stayed in the basement, where there was a game room with pool and Ping-Pong tables, a large open room with a bar for (supposedly) soft drinks, and, spectacularly, a spacious swimming pool, that in the winter was sheltered by a fiberglass roof and heated.

What made it everybody's favorite place for a party, though, was the supervision. Henry's father was not around, and his mother, crippled by polio, was in a wheelchair. I remember her from those earliest parties as a quiet woman, pale, wearing a bland smile. She would descend once every party, in the slow open elevator they had—while everyone jumped out of clinches, turned the music down, stamped out cigarettes, stashed beer cans—to say hello, wheeling slowly from person to person. Greeting me, she would grip my hand softly, seem not to take me in with her eyes.

Otherwise, the party was overseen by an odd assortment of servants—a groundskeeper, a young kid who kept up the game rooms and the pool, and the housekeeper. Mrs. Litchfield's nurse, a stern plain woman with a foreign accent, would be always hovering in the background. Except for the nurse, the help seemed close to our age, and after all it wasn't their house; so anything was okay, as long as they got their share of the beer, nothing in the house was damaged, and as long as—the cardinal rule of that household—Mrs. Litchfield was not disturbed.

"She's a Warren," the Rose told me, on our way over that night in his car.

"You mean Sara's family."

"She's Sara's aunt. I don't know that they're all that close. But they are related."

"Where's Henry's father?"

"God only knows. I've never even heard him mentioned. Henry's adopted anyway. I guess they're divorced."

I had invited Sara to the party, of course, but she had turned me down. All fall, though I continued my phone calls to her, I had hardly seen her. It may have been that what she said to me that night at her door meant something to her, and she felt she had said too much, or perhaps she was pointedly letting me know it had not meant anything, but she seemed distant on the phone, refused my invitations without making a big deal of how much she would really like to go. She began telling me specifically what she was busy with, as if to show me how much better it was than what I was offering. Often enough that fall it was a weekend trip to New Haven, apparently to see her friend in the blazer. All that didn't make me want to see her any less. I ached, in fact, to see her, just to ride beside her again down past the lights on the river, sit with her in a movie theater.

"I'm busy New Year's Eve," she had said to me. "I don't know just what we're doing. But I had heard about that party. Everybody's going. Probably we will stop in for a few minutes." No mention of seeing me there.

By the time Rosy and I got there the place was already jammed. In the open room downstairs people stood around talking in groups—dancing seemed suddenly to be passé, though the lights were dimmed and music played—while from the pool came muffled shouts and splashes, from the game room the clatter of Ping-Pong. A gang of kids from Kingston, our close rival school, sat sullenly in one corner, drinking beer in long draughts, talking little, smoking, eyeing the crowd. One, a short chubby kid with a baby face, was smoking cigars.

I wished I hadn't come. Away from them, I thought I enjoyed those parties, but really it was just the idea I enjoyed, the luxurious house, the lovely girls; when I was actually there I stood around glumly with nothing to do. That night, too, I was uneasy at the thought that I should have been elsewhere. My thoughts went back to my father. I drifted from group to group, trying not to look isolated. I shot a couple games of pool. Normally I might have drunk some beer, but that night I didn't want to do anything I would feel guilty for. I didn't see Sara anywhere. Midway through the evening, suddenly anxious, I felt I had to get in touch at the hospital.

I didn't like being upstairs—if somebody found you, it was as if you'd been caught with a bomb—but I knew I couldn't have heard well enough downstairs to make a call. Lightly I stepped across the marble floor of the hallway to the study where I knew there was a phone. From the basement the uproar was muffled, hollow.

While I was rummaging at the desk I heard a voice behind me. "What do you want, kid?"

"Oh." I jumped. "Mrs. Litchfield. I was looking for a phone book." Slowly, the wheelchair squeaking, she moved toward the desk. Her face was pallid, worn; her hair hung straight, brownish, limp. She wore a rumpled house dress. One leg was tucked oddly under the other. "I'm Dan Keith," I said, as if that explained everything.

"A *phone* book?" She smiled coyly, as if embarrassed to be there with me. She still had not raised her eyes. "What do you want with a phone book?" It seemed terribly still in the small room.

"I need to call my father. He's in the hospital." As soon as I'd said that, I wished I hadn't; I could have said anything. "I just wanted to check up."

"Oh God." She seemed shocked. She touched her glasses—tan fragile frames—knocked them askew, fumbled them off. "I'm so sorry, dear. I hope it's nothing serious."

"Oh no. No. I just thought I'd call."

"Which hospital?"

"Forbes."

"Jesus Christ, Jesus *Christ*. You don't need a phone, you don't need a *phone* book to call Forbes Hospital. Haven't I been in and out of there for years?"

I stood frozen at the desk, watching her. Her head was sagging, eyes nearly shut. She waved vaguely at me with her hand. "Pick up the phone. Pick up the phone." She reached behind her on the chair, produced a glass, drank from it. Suddenly she seemed annoyed. "Dial, kid."

I stepped to the phone, lifted the receiver.

"Six six four," she said.

I waited. I knew that wasn't a Pittsburgh exchange.

"Dial. Six six four."

I didn't know what to do. Her face was buried in her hands. "Six six four," I said.

"Oh God. God. I know that number as well as my own."

"Six six four," I said.

"What are you doing here?" The voice was harsh; I hadn't thought I'd ever be glad to see that nurse, but I was then. I didn't know who she meant that question for. She turned to me. "The guests are supposed to stay downstairs."

Mrs. Litchfield had snapped as if to attention. Suddenly her tone, too, was sharp. "Greta. I need this drink freshened."

"The party is to stay downstairs," the nurse said. "Henry's guests are supposed to know that."

"If I could just make this one call," I said.

"Did you hear me, Greta?"

204

"There's a phone downstairs," the nurse said.

"If I could just make this one call," I said.

"Did you *hear* me, Greta?"

"Of course I heard you. The whole house probably heard you." She looked at me angrily. "Make it then. And get downstairs. Don't come up here again." She began to wheel Mrs. Litchfield out.

"We'll freshen this drink," Mrs. Litchfield said.

I could have called information, but by that time I was too shaken even to think of that; I called home. "It's just as well you didn't get the number," my mother said. "I think he's probably asleep. We had a nice dinner. He said to have a good time, wished us all a Happy New Year. He'll see you in the morning."

Downstairs the party had grown more raucous. At the pool table they were playing a kind of hockey game, using the wrong ends of the cues for sticks. The Ping-Pong players were standing way back, slamming every shot. The stereo was up, vibrating the woodwork. The Kingston crowd had dispersed. Some had taken to the pool, where they were lunging and splashing like porpoises, dunking each other. Others climbed gingerly up the rafters, swinging off into the water; they shouted drunkenly, slamming onto their backs, bellies. Beer cans floated in the shallow end.

Out in the hallway a new element had arrived, the Ivy League and their dates. They had on dress clothes, much nicer than what everyone else was wearing. The men wore tired smiles, their hair rumpled, faces flushed, eyes glazed, as if they had done nothing since getting into town but go from one party to another. They were drinking something from paper cups, and it wasn't beer; they must have brought it with them. They seemed to be having an intense but sporting conversation, about sculling, or polo ponies, the kinds of things they really got worked up about, while all around them grimy adolescents were swilling beer and playing Ping-Pong like a street fight. It wasn't a big crowd, just five or six guys with their dates, but the man with the miniature chin was there, working that cigarette holder of his, and beside him, holding his arm while he barely noticed, was Sara.

I stood across the room and watched for a while. She was wearing a long white dress, as if they'd just been to a dinner dance, and it was cut low, showing her milky white skin, the top of her small bosom. She held one of the paper cups and now and then drank from it. Her eyes drifted around the room, and finally saw me. She gave me a little wave, just with her fingers, the same way she had waved that night from the elevator. I smiled at her. But then she turned back to her crowd, to that conversation, away from me.

At midnight all hell broke loose. People had gathered in couples, waiting for the big moment. Noisemakers were passed out, beer cans raised. At the stroke of the hour a firecracker detonated out at the swimming pool, people started singing, embracing, the lights went off, and after that it was wild, everyone bumping around and embracing indiscriminately. It was pretty nice, I had to admit, staggering around in the dark, girls fastening to my lips like leeches. I could barely tell one from another. There was one, of course, who I wanted to kiss more than any other. I bumped around among all the bodies, seeking her, imagining how it would be—a gentle squeeze of affection, a few whispered words. I had seen her just before things began, running her fingers through her date's hair—he didn't even seem to have a good hold on her, the fool—but after the lights went out I couldn't find her again. She seemed to have disappeared.

Eventually the crowd began to thin out, wander upstairs, either growing unruly or just breaking up. Those who remained were drinking seriously, standing around the bar with what was left of the beer. The Kingston kids began to drift in from the swimming pool, still wearing their bathing suits. I didn't see the Rose, figured he must have gone up.

But when I got upstairs the party was not dispersing. People were standing around the edges of the marble hallway, silent, holding their coats. Somehow, saying goodby to Mrs. Litchfield, a regular feature of those parties, had turned that night into a solemn ceremony. Under the massive glittering chandelier everyone seemed suddenly sober. Their eyes stared. At the top of the stairway Sara was standing beside the wheel-chair, her hand on Mrs. Litchfield's shoulder. I didn't see her date anywhere.

"It was a lovely party, Aunt Helen," Sara said. "A wonderful party. Everyone enjoyed it so much."

Mrs. Litchfield's eyes were nearly closed, but her head was up as if she were staring around the room. She beamed. "I'm glad."

"You were so nice to have us."

"Oh, it's Henry who has you. He does all the work." She looked suddenly perplexed. "Where is Henry?"

"I think he's downstairs. Some of his friends are still downstairs."

"But I want him to have you, whenever we can. To have big lovely parties. I enjoyed them so much when I was a girl."

"I know."

"And I was beautiful then. Beautiful like all of you."

Those were sad words, as she spoke them, but the expressions I saw as I gazed around the room were not of sorrow, but of fear, as if all their gaiety could come to that.

"You're beautiful still." Sara always had the right words.

Mrs. Litchfield's eyes opened. In all the times we had met, she had never remembered my name, shown any particular sign of recognizing me, but now she saw me beside her chair, and remembered. "How is your father? How is your father, dear?"

"He's fine. Thank you."

"His father's had to be taken to the hospital. We're all so sorry."

I reddened, looked down. I knew she was ill, pathetic, but I didn't like all those eyes on me, in that ludicrous scene. I didn't like her talking about my father. I wished I weren't among all those people who didn't know him, who had spent the whole night drinking and celebrating and thought Mrs. Litchfield was still just babbling incoherently. For a moment it seemed I had left my dying father for that shallow world. It was like my first days at Arnold: I felt I had left the world where I belonged for one that was not my own.

"We're all so sorry," she said again, and I realized she was pulling me toward the wheelchair in a gesture of sympathy. For a long awkward moment I looked down at her as she stared up at me, then leaned; it seemed the easiest thing to do. She took my head in her hands and kissed my lips.

There was a gasp, as if from everyone at once. I had caught myself awkwardly on the arms of the wheelchair. Her hands were strong, held me tight. I heard laughter, muttering. Her lips were soft; they opened as she kissed me. I had never before been kissed in quite that way. There was something knowing, almost lewd, about it. Her grip relaxed. I stood. Her smile was radiant as she gazed up at me.

There seemed to be an endless pause.

"I guess we need to be going," Sara finally said.

"It's New Year's Eve," Mrs. Litchfield said. "It's so early."

But the crowd needed no more excuse than that; they moved toward the door as if panicked. Mrs. Litchfield was holding my hand. I turned to Sara. Her gaze at me was open, sad, unapologetic. However she felt about me, it seemed to say, the family came first.

"I've got to go," I said.

Outside the crowd was practically in a stampede. People shouted, laughed. Car motors started, horns honked. I was trembling until I could hardly walk, but the cold air braced me and I made it to the car.

The Rose winced, shook his head. "How did she ever know about your father?" he said.

"Let's not talk about it."

"If only you hadn't come up those stairs."

"If only I hadn't come to this fucking party at all."

We didn't say much more on the way home. By the time we got to my street snow was beginning to fall. In the houses all the lights were out. I went straight up to bed.

What happened after that seems now to have followed like the last step in an airtight argument, as inevitable as the sunrise. It is hard to remember how I felt at the time: bleary, bewildered. I was a man defenseless in a fight, so shocked he can't even raise a hand to protect himself, incredulous: he can't believe there will be another blow.

I awoke the next morning tense, as if already hurried. Light poured in the windows. My eyes ached. Far off in the house the phone was ringing, ringing. I waited for somebody to get it, but nobody did. Finally I made it there myself.

"Dan. It's your Uncle Bill. I think you'd better get down to the hospital."

That was why no one else had answered the phone. No one else was there.

The streets as I drove to Oakland were slick with a thin film of snow. I slid crazily down Fifth Avenue, wheels spinning, but it didn't matter, because the day was deserted. People were sleeping it off, or just awakening, lying back in bed, relieved, as they remembered it was a holiday. The wind gusted. I had the whole four lanes to myself.

When I pulled up at the hospital, Uncle Billy was waiting for me, bareheaded, an overcoat bundled up around his neck. His face was thin, wrinkled, always a little sad, as if his eyes cringed at the whipping wind.

"I'm sorry, son," he said. "I couldn't tell you over the phone. He didn't know us when we got here. He died before I called."

The little knot of dread that for months I had carried in my stomach, the brief breathless premonitions of disaster every time I had left my father had been right. This had been the time when I should not have left him. The other times were all just pointing toward it.

The thin film of snow that lay on the ground was just a beginning. Not like a blizzard, but just dropping silently from the sky in large wet flakes, snow fell all day, blanketing the earth. People stayed in, anyway, eating holiday dinners—special dishes to bring luck for the new year—watched football on television, and sat drowsily beside their fires. At our house people were in and out all afternoon, friends, neighbors, patients, and nearly everyone brought something. Some of them stayed for dinner, I think six in all, but we still had leftovers enough for a couple weeks.

But earlier in the day, before people had begun to come, I had had a few minutes with my mother, up in her room. In the rush of things, the confusion of all that had to be done, we were both, I think, a little numb.

"I wish I could have been there," I said.

"I know. But you have to realize. It wouldn't have made any difference."

"Just to have been there."

"I can feel the same way. I went when they called, but I could have gone earlier, on my own. Or I could have spent the night at the hospital. It occurred to me. I knew how serious things were."

A resident had called from the hospital early in the morning—the phone had rung just once, hadn't awakened me—and she and Uncle Billy had hurried down. But when they got there, as Uncle Billy had told me, my father hadn't known them.

"It was as if I didn't care," I said.

"Of course you cared."

"I didn't show I cared"

"You showed for months."

"But he didn't know."

"He knew. Oh, Dan. Of course he knew."

"I never . . ."—it was the thing that bothered me most; words had always stuck in my throat—"said anything."

"What could you have said?"

That was the thing: I never knew what to say.

"The things you had to say can't be spoken," my mother said. "There are no words. But he knew how you felt."

"I wish I could have been there . . . for you."

"Dan." She touched my shoulders; we held each other. "I would have gotten you if I'd needed that. I was all right. Uncle Billy was there."

"I just wish I hadn't gone to the party. Been sleeping when that phone call came. I could have been around."

What I have always remembered from the days of my father's dying is that I was absent. We had that brief moment Wednesday evening, but I didn't know—did he?—that we were saying good-by. I remember words, scenes, from those two days, and it seems they were warnings, calling me back to him, but I wouldn't hear. To this day I feel myself an accomplice. I was part of the plot. I let them keep me from my father at his death.

On that first morning we were to spend at the funeral home, I left my mother and Uncle Billy at the front door, saw some friends as I drove into the parking lot and nodded to them as I got out of the car and hurried to get away. But one of them shouted after me, walked over to my car and turned off the engine, then, without a word, came over and handed me the keys. It wasn't until then that I realized how out of it I was, though I could tell by their eyes that they knew. They kept close to me as we walked to the door. Scores of people came, that day and the next, speaking words and reaching out to me as they could. It is striking, as I look back on it all, how little I actually remember. A few people were noticeable by their absence. Rachel Hardy, at an odd hour when no one would be there, came and left her name in the book alone.

The funeral home was like a large old quiet residence, and outside the room where we received people was a long hallway with a door at the end. I was looking down that empty hallway on the second afternoon, in the daze that I was in that whole time, when the door opened and Sara entered. As soon as she stepped through the door she saw me. I had a crazy impulse—though she was probably the person I most wanted to see—to step away. But I couldn't; she knew I had seen her. She walked quietly up the hall. I tried to smile—strange, that I thought I had to smile in that place—but she did not; her face was just intent, perhaps a trifle pale, and she was not trying to wear sympathy or grief, just looking openly and seriously at me. Of all the things I loved about Sara, I think I most loved her open serious gaze. I wasn't to see or even to call her again for months. I couldn't face her. But as she stood before me that afternoon in the funeral home she reached up to touch my shoulders—"Dan," she said, "I'm so sorry"—and she leaned forward, slowly, and kissed me.

Part Five

Chapter 15

SENIORS AT ARNOLD didn't have to be anywhere during their free periods, and that year I had two of them at the end of the day. It was hard to work then, the afternoon coming to an end, a dining hall lunch gurgling around in my stomach. That Thursday, the second week in October, I was sitting alone under a tree out in front of the library, my tie loosened, books scattered all around me. We'd had some crisp fall weather, but that week there was a brief Indian summer, so the afternoon was mild. That Saturday, in fact, for the biggest football game of our lives, it was to be for one day blistering hot, like the hottest August afternoons in preseason.

The bell in the clocktower struck its four gongs, and all over campus, as if they'd been standing there waiting for a starting gun, doors flew open and people began to stream out. From the library, behind me, Bert Foley and Rosy came lumbering along. They'd been hanging around together all week, since Foley—in his fifth year—was now eligible for the games, and he and Rosy were on the same side of the defensive line. He was a blond, brawny good-looking kid with a rear end as big as all outdoors. He had a reputation as the leading carouser on the team and made no bones about his attitude toward training rules, flagrantly lighting up a Camel in his car on the way home from practice. It was miraculous he never got caught. With fingers like a stevedore's, he didn't just smoke a cigarette, he pun-

215

ished it, squeezing it into almost nothing by the time he was through. His exploits around the beer keg were legendary. On Mondays he sat around in the commons room all through his free periods, holding his head and sweating it out.

"Off your ass," he said to me. "Time for the pep rally."

"Pep rallies are for shit," I said.

"They're for shit like you," he said. "You got to get introduced."

"They won't miss me."

"Don't you want to be famous?" Foley was grinning, holding his hands out as if to acknowledge applause. "Like me?"

The two of them were standing a few feet away from me, all 400-plus pounds. Hate to be double-teamed by that.

"Come on, Dan," Rosy said. "For God's sake."

"I was really thinking of not coming," I said. "Those things make me nervous."

"Like hell," Foley said. "You eat it up with a spoon."

"What if nobody came?" Rosy said. "Jesus Christ."

He was wearing the expression of disgust he often wore those days. Quit being such a pain in the ass, it said. He didn't want to have to act as if the pep rally were some wonderful thing. He just wanted me to do what everyone else was doing. For months he had been trying to get me to do what everyone else was doing.

"He's just modest," Foley said. "Too shy."

"This is no fucking time for modesty," Rosy said.

"It's okay," Foley said. "He's coming." He squatted down, poked a thick finger, like a rifle barrel, in my chest. "If he won't walk, we'll carry his ass over there ourselves."

There wasn't much to say. I could have handled Rosy, who—however mad he got—wouldn't have insisted, but Foley had a wild streak, was just as likely to throw me over a shoulder and do a war dance on the way over. I figured I'd just as soon go under my own steam.

"All right," I said. "Dammit. But I'm not making any speeches."

"Nobody wants to hear you talk," Foley said.

After our opening loss at Hargrove we had done all right. We'd taken a sloppy game in the rain 6–0, at a little steel town named Hillsdale, won a hotstopper against Compton in our home opener, 13–12, then, unaccountably, tied 7–7 against a mediocre team at Edgeworth. But a week before everything had changed. We had opened against the league, so the fifth-year players who up to then had been ineligible were allowed to play. Foley for one; a long bony awkward tight end named Kasunich; Cortese, a squat fierce middle linebacker; most notably of all, of course, Pollett. We had probably been a little better up to then than people had expected, but with his breakaway threat Pollett would have turned even a mediocre team into a contender. In our first league game we had rolled over Canfield, 34–7. That Saturday we were playing Asbury, champion of the league three years running.

In front of the dorm where the rally was, somebody was banging a bass drum, and people were hurrying from all over campus. It was a big deal for underclassmen, if for no other reason than that it got them out of study hall, which could be like a steam bath at the end of a hot afternoon. I remembered myself as a freshman rushing to the pep rallies, pushing to get to the front of the crowd. I had seen the players in uniform on the field, but now would be able to recognize them in their unguarded moments around campus. Unshaven—linemen liked to go a few days without shaving, so they'd look tough—their ties loosened, collars unbuttoned, as if no collars could have restrained those massive necks, they heard their names announced as if with surprise, stepped forward, wearing little smiles, to loud applause. Cheering with everyone else, I stood in awe of them. They had what I wanted.

If they had been around my senior year, I could have put any one of them on his ass.

The crowd in front of the dorm—over 200 people—was cheering, clapping, stomping their feet.

From a little space up front, the cheerleaders led a few cheers, then dragged out Pollett to do the introductions. Red-faced, wearing a look of pained sincerity, he spoke at first so you could hardly hear.

"They turned me away one year." He winced, as if in pain at the memory. "They turned me away two years. They turned me away three years." A long silent pause. "They're not going to turn me away again."

The crowd broke into wild applause. Like rugged athletes the world over, Pollett spoke in halting phrases, as if his brains had been scrambled by too many hard shots. His audience edged forward, hanging on his every word. Bear with us here, folks. It's not easy being a moron.

"I'd like to bring out a few of the guys who are going to go through Asbury like a knife through butter."

Everybody roared with delight at this apt metaphor.

"Let's let these guys know we're behind them!" a cheerleader shouted.

It was the same people who had been introduced two or three times before. When Pollett came to me— "Our inside tackle, now a guard on defense, he's a tank in there"—I had the reaction I always did: heart pounding, face flushed, I stumbled to the front amid the applause, hands that grabbed and shoved me forward; I tried to smile, but managed only a contorted grimace. Ryczek, on the line beside me, slapped my back, but not too hard, since it looked as if a solid whack would send me sprawling. With the whole school standing in front of me, a host of faces, I stared off vaguely toward the sky, some high trees behind the library.

Someone watching might have thought I was bored, mocking it all, as if I didn't care. But that wasn't the case. It was more as if it meant so much to me that I couldn't give in to it. Or as if, despite all I knew I could do, I still didn't think I belonged up there. It was as if you had pulled that fat little freshman from three years before out of the crowd and told him he had to quit idolizing people, that he wasn't part of the gaping crowd anymore—that he was now one of the heroes.

When a place spent a couple years telling somebody he was worthless, it ran the risk that it might convince him.

There was one other thing. In practice now Cortese, Kasunich, and Foley had been working into the drills, and when I turned back from the line, glanced toward the backfield, Pollett was standing there—bowlegged, slabbed with muscle, swaybacked—that hero of my youth. It wasn't just that it seemed odd playing beside those guys. I had come up through the ranks with other players, and we had worked into a team. The new guys made us better. People even spoke about us being favored in the league. But it didn't seem my team, somehow. I didn't think I liked it as much.

II

The first thing I saw on the day of the Asbury game was Bert Foley hefting a sledgehammer, winking in the sunlight, taking dead aim, as he stood on the hood of a car. I'd driven out in the old Nova a couple of hours early that day, just to be in on all the hoopla, since it was Homecoming. The whole campus was decorated, crepe paper in the trees, elaborate displays in front of the dorms, even a few floats flanking the home stands down on the track. The old car Foley was standing on was part of the celebration, fifty cents and you got three cracks with the sledgehammer. Since Foley was a big celebrity and had such a fat ass, he was getting the first cracks for free. He had no business doing it—what with the flying glass, scraps of metal, he could have hurt himself—but Foley did what he wanted. Grunting, sneering, his face nearly purple, he took three slugs at the roof—"Damn. Shit. Son of a bitch"—hardly making a dent, then tossed the hammer away in disgust and jumped off the hood, shaking the earth for miles around. In front of a few timid-looking females he stepped over to me, slapped my belly with the back of his hand.

"I hope that cocksucker Kotar goes down easier than that," he said.

Kotar was Asbury's answer to Pollett. In a way it was hard to see what he had. He was a big lunk, built more like a tackle than a fullback, but he wasn't too quick and didn't have any moves. For three years I'd seen Asbury push us around, and nothing much seemed to happen. They'd go on long scoring drives where they never seemed a threat, it looked as if we could stop them anytime, then they'd stumble and groan along and score. But on the first series of downs that day I got an idea what it was that carried them. Kotar was coming off tackle, and we absolutely had him stopped; Deitz at end was holding off his man, Rogan was up quickly from his linebacker spot, and I'd caught the guard off balance and knocked him down. We all hit Kotar at pretty much the same time, though by a split second I was in there first: I cracked him at the gut with a terrific shot. Just as I did, a fist like a blackjack hit me above the eyes; I saw stars, felt myself crumble under all those knees and cleats. That was what he had, an uncanny knack; anytime you hit him, no matter where, you ran into something bony, heavy, hard: a knee, an elbow, a fist, his head. You could almost stop him—though by just lunging and falling down Kotar had picked up a couple yards—but he punished you for it. Everyone I talked to after the game said the same thing. We didn't know how he did it.

I wasn't the only one hitting at the beginning of that game. The whole team was up, chattering, jittering between plays. On every down you'd hear digging, snorting, groaning, slugging, as if the whole game depended on that one play. We had a massive front four that day. With Ryczek at tackle beside me, Rosy and Bert Foley on the other side, I was the smallest guy there. Asbury kept coming at you; they never ran a fancy play, but were always on top of you, like a fighter with no technique or knockout punch who just keeps wading in, wears you down, too stupid to notice you're kicking the shit out of him too.

Rosy and Foley were having their problems, sinking to both knees and gasping between plays, but it was the two of them who finally stopped Kotar, cracking

220

together with a hit that would have split anyone else in half. When Foley stood up he had a mouse under his eye, but it was fourth and two; Asbury had to punt. I knew Grupp was going crazy. That was the first time in three years they hadn't scored on their first possession.

The pressure on Pollett that day must have been terrific. There he was before the first snap, so bowlegged you'd think he could hardly walk, vaguely reaching out toward Rogan's back to space himself, settling into his stance like an arthritic old man. He knew every eye in the place was on him and expecting some miracle, expecting that he'd dive into the middle of the Asbury line like a bowling ball hitting the pocket and knock the whole team down. Asbury was really up, and no kind of footwork gets you away from five or six tacklers; Pollett would be tearing toward the outside when one guy would slice in low, a couple of others pounce while he was stumbling.

On our first two series we made the sticks, though not by much. But from about our forty, on second down, he broke through a big hole up the middle and came one-on-one with a single linebacker: the kid was diving in low, closing the hole, but Pollett shot out a forearm as he cut and that linebacker bit the dust like a gored bull. For a moment, watching that, as if transfixed, the whole defense seemed to go flatfooted, and Pollett was gone. For the first time in four years we had drawn first blood.

That was why Grupp was so enraged when Asbury finally scored. "You guys should have been cocky out there," he shouted in the locker room at half-time. "Swelling with pride. You should have spit on anybody who even mentioned the word touchdown. You were league champions out there."

It was just a slip-up toward the half. Everybody was tired, not ganging up as they should, so Kotar got off what were, for him, a couple of long runs, and just before the gun they bulled it over to tie it up.

Grupp in the locker room was sweating, pacing, frantic. "Now we've got to do it all over again." I think he had really expected to be holding the league trophy by then. He kept running a hand through his hair.

Words popped out of his mouth at random. "Shealy, you've been relying on Pollett too much. You've got a whole team out there. You've got to vary the attack. I want to see Grunfeld carry the ball. I want some passes to Kasunich." Nobody mentioned it was Grupp who called in most of the plays from the bench. He had been overworking Pollett, as if his masterpiece of recruiting had to be the thing to win it all.

The breaks seemed to go against us. We did start to vary the attack, pitch to Grunfeld and pass to Kasunich, but we fumbled once on the fourteen, had a nearly perfect pass intercepted, and Asbury, rolling along behind Kotar like a crusty old tank that never quite stops, took it over after a long drive toward the end of the third quarter. It was into the fourth quarter before we tied it up, on a play that wasn't exactly characteristic. Pollett started wide on third and long, his classic move, but right about at the corner slipped the ball on a reverse to Rogan. He was a marvelous blocker, but hardly ever touched the ball, so Asbury had been ignoring him all day. He was into the secondary before they'd even turned around. With eight minutes to go we were all tied up, fourteen apiece.

By then both teams were shot, and we traded punts on a couple of series, nobody getting anywhere. With about three minutes left we got the ball around midfield, and to no one's particular surprise, we tried a second-down pass to Kasunich. He had gone striding as usual out into the flat, the picture of determination, fists all balled up, legs stiff as a pair of stilts, then stumbled, stooped, and slowly pivoted. We might as well have interrupted the game for a special announcement that the next play would be a short pass to Kasunich. As usual, Shealy lofted it pretty high, and Kasunich went up well, took it gracefully in one hand, slapped it on the way down into the other. Unfortunately he never reached the ground, because just then, from behind, a linebacker hit him a terrific shot.

The sight and sound were awful, Kasunich draped with the small of his back over that kid's shoulder, the single short-vowel sound choking out of his throat, *Aaaa*. It looked like a runaway tractor uprooting a young pine. The ball, of course, popped into the air, like something Kasunich had swallowed the wrong way and that the linebacker, courteously, was helping him cough up. You might have thought offhand it would be up for grabs, except the play developed so obviously that the whole secondary converged on Kasunich as he went for the ball. He was so tall there was room for everybody to get in a good whack, and he went down in a terrible flailing of arms and legs. An Asbury half-back just barely tipped the ball, batting it up again.

From out of nowhere Pollett came into view. If you hadn't seen Kasunich get hit you might have thought the whole thing was planned, the ball floating gently into Pollett's hands, though the fact was that he had just been heading over that way to block, usually a futile pursuit, since Kasunich never ran anywhere. The next week, in fact, we put that play in, a short sideline pass to Kasunich, a delay and lateral to Pollett trailing. Grupp kept grinning while he watched them practice, calling it the play that had given him the league.

He may have been a little premature in that. But you could forgive his enthusiasm as he watched Pollett glide into the end zone without even being touched, Rogan taking out the last defender with a perfect rolling block. We held Asbury on their last series with the ball. Once the gun had sounded the whole school poured out of the stands to surround Grupp, and his boys—Cortese, Kasunich, Shealy, Pollett—battled back through the crowd to carry him off the field. You couldn't begrudge him his celebration. He'd waited a long time.

He wasn't the only one, of course. A lot of us had.

III

The Homecoming Dance was the most elaborate of the year. There was a band in the large hall—like a low-ceilinged recreation room—beneath the chapel, and combos in the commons rooms of a couple of dorms. Every year somebody cooked up a theme, and that year it was an evening in Las Vegas, with the main hall decorated like a nightclub. They even persuaded some poor sophomore to dress in a feathered costume and do a sort of strip. The commons rooms were made to look like casinos, with poker, roulette, dice, the works. Out on the quad, if you stood around, you could hear the echoes of music from all three places, see couples strolling from one of them to another.

Often enough it was bitter cold by the time of Homecoming, but that night, after the blistering hot day of the game, the evening was breezy and pleasant.

Except casually, if we met somewhere, I hadn't spoken to Sara since the afternoon I had seen her at the funeral home. We hadn't talked much that day; she had spoken to my mother, and signed the book, come over just to squeeze my hand, and left. If anything could have made me break down that day, it would have been the moment when she kissed me: as she held me I felt the tears spring to my eyes. All the times I had wanted to kiss her, the hours I had dreamed of it, and now she was kissing me, because my father was dead. I was touched that she would do it, a little ashamed under the circumstances at how much it meant to me; I wondered what she meant by it. It seemed to me that if I saw her again that moment would stand between us; we would have to say something, and I didn't see how I could. I felt the words would stick in my throat. So I never called her.

A few days before the dance I had been out on the front street watching the kids play ball—I wasn't exactly there by coincidence; it was the third night I had gone out to wait—when Rachel came walking through with the dog, and after the usual small talk I said, "I was wondering if you'd like to go to the Homecoming Dance."

She broke into a broad smile. "Why, Dan."

"What's so funny?" I was embarrassed.

"It's not funny. It's just . . . All these years. How long have we known each other? Eleven years. It's taken you eleven years to ask me for a date."

"I knew I'd get around to it."

"I was beginning to wonder."

"So what about it? Are we going?"

"I wouldn't pass up the opportunity. There's no telling how long you might wait again."

In a way Rachel looked older than she was; on the night of the dance, in a lavender dress, her reddish hair sweeping down across her shoulders, she looked ready to be stepping out with a young business executive, not a high school kid. Often enough when I saw her in the evening, she was still in her school uniform, pallid and serious, as if she were always deep in thought, but that night she looked radiant. She was lovely. She wasn't even wearing her glasses.

"You need some help down the steps?" I said, when I picked her up. "Can you see?"

"I wear contacts."

"I've never seen you wear them."

"I wear them all day at school. My eyes get tired. I don't feel I need to wear them to walk the dog."

"I thought you were just doing that to see me."

"From now on I'll wear them."

The band in the main hall was the kind that you saw everywhere those days, two electric guitars, an electric bass, a set of drums. They wore matching jackets and ties, haircuts that hung straight in bangs all over their heads. The drummer—in contradiction to lessons he had been taking for years—held both sticks the same way, as if he were shaking hands with them, and mostly just pounded out a rhythm with both at once. The boys sang with mock British accents the songs of southern black rhythm-and-blues artists, at climactic moments shook their heads like pompoms. All this in imitation of a well-known group of the day. The shrill scream of the guitars was deafening.

"What do you think?" I said to Rachel between numbers.

"About like all the others," she said.

"Do you like to dance?" I said.

"I *love* to dance."

I was stunned. "I thought you were a brain. An intellectual."

"I take an evening off now and then."

"But this music is so uninventive. So repetitive."
Now I was the intellectual.

"I didn't say I liked to put my feet up and listen to it. I said I liked to dance to it."

"Give me the ballads of the fifties anyday." I was speaking a little glumly.

"Dan. If you don't like to dance, you don't like to dance."

"I don't think I have the build for it."

"People with various builds seem to be dancing. But it's all right. You should do what you want."

"Maybe we could go to one of the other places."

Everywhere I went that night, people, even guys I didn't know, were shaking my hand, slapping my back, grinning. "Good game, Dan. Great game." There was an air of excitement at the dance that it had never had before. Asbury hadn't lost a league football game in three years.

"I had no idea you were such a hero out here," Rachel said, as we were walking to one of the dorms.

"I didn't either."

"What's this game everybody's talking about?"

"Rachel. This is the Homecoming Dance. Today was the Homecoming Game. Football. It's a very big thing out here."

"I like to dance. At football I draw the line."

"Well. Anyway. That's what it's all about."

"What did you do that was so wonderful?"

"I played. Blocked and tackled."

"How many points did you score?"

"You don't score points when you block and tackle."

"Then what's the big deal?"

"It's hard to explain. You can't score unless you block. They score if you don't tackle. Everybody contributes."

She was looking at me, nodding, with a vague interest, as if I were explaining the culture of the cave man.

"Forget it," I said.

My team was on the verge of winning a league title—the climax of my football career—and there I was at the Homecoming Dance with probably the one girl from Ellsworth who knew absolutely nothing about it. Typical of my entire life.

226

She slapped my back. "Good game," she said.

Over at Collins dorm they had guys dressed up in tuxedos running various games of chance, and they gave you a stack of chips for the asking. We played blackjack for a while, and Rachel nearly cleaned the place out. She would stick with an eight or nine showing, and when the dealer had dealt himself out would turn over a three or four. The one time he called her bluff she had a king under there. She seemed to hesitate with every decision, shaking her head, tapping her chin, but that was the thing: she *always* hesitated.

"Remind me never to play cards with you," I said.

"This guy can't figure it out. This is the way my father plays."

After their break the Collins band came back, and it turned out to be a group of middle-aged Italian men. The leader kept flashing his romantic eyes while he played a violin, and a couple of his sidemen actually played accordions. If only we'd had a checkered tablecloth and a couple of plates of spaghetti. I couldn't wait to find out where the dorm had scraped these guys up. Las Vegas indeed.

But they played a kind of music I could dance to, and we stayed awhile. As I had suspected, Rachel was no longer the grumpy little girl who refused to dance close. As she held her body against mine, she was slightly taller than I. Her hair was soft and tickled against my face. The faint perfume she wore smelled a little like honeysuckle. As we moved together I could feel her firm breasts touching my chest.

"This is the kind of dancing I like to do," I said.

"You have the build for it," she said.

After a couple numbers the bandleader stepped forward. He spoke in a hoarse whisper. "Ladies and gentlemen. I don't want you to think we're just a bunch of old men who can only play romantic ballads. We were young once. We called it swing. What do you call it?" He flashed a knowing smile. "The twist. The frug. The watusi."

"Oh my God," I said.

"Don't panic," Rachel said.

"I was having such a nice time."

227

"I can teach you. I'm a superb teacher."

"Let's go for a walk."

"Dan. You coward."

"We'll come back. I promise. Or we'll even go to the main hall. You can teach me all you want. But first let's go for a walk. I was feeling so peaceful."

Peaceful wasn't quite the word. More like romantic. Or turned on.

"How such an abject coward can play football," Rachel said, "is beyond me."

The night was perfect, stars out, a light breeze blowing. It seemed more like April than mid-October. A number of couples were out strolling. Officially such behavior was discouraged—we were just supposed to walk from one dance site to another—but there we all were. Rachel and I went over to a side road of the campus, down the hill past the infirmary and some faculty houses. Partway down, I put my arm around her, and without looking at me—though her face seemed to grow serious—she snuggled slightly closer.

Near the bottom of the hill, beside a little clump of pines, I slowed us down, and stopped, and pulled Rachel around to face me, and kissed her.

That was the thing about me. When I was deeply in love, as with Sara, I couldn't so much as touch a girl, but when I didn't care, when it was just old Rachel Hardy from around the neighborhood, I could sweep her into my arms and kiss her. Nothing to it.

She let me kiss her, smiled a little, blushing, looking down. I kissed her again, and she looked up at me, straight into my eyes. For a moment I had the feeling I was a math equation she was trying to solve. She hesitated, then leaned forward, kissed my cheek.

"Dan," she said. "I do . . . care for you."

"I like you, Rachel. I really do. I always have." I was totally sincere in these statements. It was as if, after all those years, I had just made a remarkable discovery.

"We've been good friends." For a moment her face seemed to tremble.

"*Great* friends." I squeezed her hard.

"But I don't think we should be kissing."

She didn't mean it, I was sure. Had to put up a little resistance.

"We haven't known each other long enough?" I said. "You don't kiss until the twelfth year?"

"Long enough. Maybe not well enough."

"Rachel. We used to do everything together."

"You even kissed me once." She smiled, but weakly, her mouth tight.

"And you slapped me. You're not going to slap me again?"

"No. I could kiss you. We could stand down here and kiss and kiss. It would be nice."

"Great."

"But I don't really like to kiss . . . just for the kissing. I want to be a person first."

"You *are* a person." I had no idea what the hell she was talking about.

"A friend. A good friend. Somebody you can confide in."

"You're my friend. We're friends. My God. Eleven years."

"All these nights I see you on the street. We never talk about anything but the weather."

"I know. I try to think about things to talk about. Really, I rack my brains. I'll think of something good, I swear."

"There are things we've never talked about."

"You name it. I'll talk about it."

"I didn't want to bring it up. It didn't seem my place. I kept thinking you'd bring it up. Then so much time had passed."

Rachel was staring down at my chest, fooling with my lapels. I was so far gone in thoughts of hugging and kissing that I still had no idea what she meant.

"All right, all right," I said. "Just say what it is."

"You know what it is."

"I don't."

But I was beginning to have an inkling. Her face was so serious.

"If you'd just think for a minute. Since last winter, seeing each other all those times. We've never said a word."

My heart started to pound, so hard I could feel it up in my throat. I felt the blood rush to my face. I didn't know if I could get the words out.

"I can't believe you're saying this," I said.

"There's so much I'd like to say."

I felt my arms drop from around her, but Rachel still held my shoulders with her hands.

"What kind of time is this. . . ." I said.

"I know, I know. It's a crazy time to bring it up. But it seems so strange. All these months, you've never said a word. And then you're down here kissing me."

"I don't want to talk about it."

"I've seen that. You're all closed up."

"I don't talk about it to anybody."

"I think you should."

"It's none of your business." I pulled away from her. "Let's go."

"Dan." She grabbed my shoulders again. "It is none of my business. But I loved your father. He was a special person to me. Even when I was a little girl, and went to his office, it wasn't like I was some little thing my parents were dragging along. He saw *me*. He talked to *me*. He made his patients feel they were really there. Particular people. Not just illnesses without a name. All his patients loved him, you could see it. He came out in the waiting room and they all beamed. It was wonderful what he was to people."

I couldn't stand it, remembering those days.

"I've wanted to say this to you for so long," Rachel said. "I feel so much better for saying it. If we were friends, if we were really friends, we could talk about things this way. We could help each other. Then we would really be close, it would be fine to hug and kiss. . . ."

Of all the words I've ever spoken, I think I most regret what I said next to Rachel, in pain, and embarrassment, and shame at not being able to face what she was facing.

"There are certain things I won't do just to get a kiss," I said.

She slapped me. Her hands had been resting on my shoulders and her right hand slapped me, then she pulled back, and put her fist to her mouth, and bit her knuckle. "Oh, Dan."

But it was all right with me. It hurt, and I liked that it hurt, and that it was a good end to things.

"We're going home," I said.

I walked up the hill to the car, and she walked a couple of steps behind me the whole way. As we drove home, she sat at the other end of the seat, not sobbing, but her eyes were moist and red. I ached so badly—a pain in my chest—that I felt I would burst. That was weeping too, I suppose, if I had let it be, but I didn't.

"I'm sorry I slapped you," she said when we got to her house. "And for the things I said. I'm sorry I hurt you."

"I'm sorry too," I said. I think I really was.

I started to open my door, but she said, "No. I'll let myself in." She got no argument from me.

At that moment I hoped I never saw her again.

They were both lost to me at that point, the girl I loved, and the girl I just liked, the friend of my childhood, from around the neighborhood. Lost to me, I've said, but if anything it was I who was lost, shutting off, as if systematically, one part of my life after another. I didn't realize that then. It seemed to me then that much in my life was far off, inaccessible. I didn't understand that I was the one who was putting it there.

Chapter 16

GRUPP CAME TO practice smiling every day the next week. I'd hardly ever seen him smile at practice, unless it was just the last thing to do before strangling somebody, but that week he was content. On Monday he even arrived at the field chewing his cigar, gesturing grandly with it as he lectured us. I have heard a football maxim that wise old coaches work the team hard after a victory, easily after a defeat; naturally Grupp did just the opposite. Since that was the biggest victory of his career, he worked us that week hardly at all, no one-on-ones or tackling drills, wind sprints only once. Mostly we just ran mock scrimmages, the JVs holding dummies. Apparently he thought the season was all wrapped up.

The opponent that weekend was our arch rival, Kingston. It was an odd rivalry in a way, since they weren't in the league, but they were the closest private school we played and the series went back a long way. Kingston was known to be second-rate. If you flunked out of Arnold, or couldn't get admitted in the first place, you knew where you could go. All the sleazy rumors that existed about private schools were circulated at Arnold about Kingston. It was said that the teachers were all fairies, drunkards, incompetents; the students openly defied them in the classroom, even challenged them with their fists. Scores between students were also settled with fists, wild brawls, broken-bottle fights. Students smoked illicitly in their rooms, had late beer parties following lights out. At school dances, girls from nearby boarding schools were secreted off into the woods and molested, despite the saltpeter that the administration imported by the truckload and laced all the food with. It was said that, what with the long isolated winters in the Pennsylvania countryside, the guys were all half-queer, groped each other in the showers, had frequent circle jerks.

Still, we were told, the only thing they were really interested in, the only subject they ever talked about, was beating Arnold. At the beginning of the season, every member of the football team was assigned an opponent from Arnold whom he was to concentrate personally on demolishing. They held weekly anti-Arnold pep rallies. Every other contest was just a tune-up for the Arnold game. The whole school was on hand for it, home or away.

It was a wonderful set of rumors. I had no idea where they came from. Maybe a student committee had been appointed at Arnold to think them up.

Early that fall I'd heard that Nick Kaiser, after a bad year at public school, was repeating his junior year at Kingston.

II

Tuesday that week, I was relaxing in Collins—Bill Menhardt let me use his room for free periods—when a kid named Lietzke stepped in. I had always felt sorry for him. He had a crew cut, a soft pinkish baby face, and wore an incredible expression, with huge wide pop eyes, eyebrows about three inches up on his forehead, as if he'd just seen a corpse, or fallen out a third-story window. He looked that way all the time. His hands were constantly damp and trembling. Either he looked ridiculous from being so nervous or he felt nervous because he looked so ridiculous: it was hard to say which.

Naturally he'd be a nut for football, aching to make the team, and he went out, so help me, for quarterback. Nobody could believe it. I had been there for his first drills. Our signals at the line began with a state followed by a number—Pennsylvania was an audible switching to a pass, Ohio to a run; any other state meant nothing—and the first time Lietzke got under center he yelled, "Canada, thirty-one." All the coaches started screaming, "Canada, Canada, that's not a state. Start again." Lietzke kept crouching there, hands under the center, looking around; finally he just stepped away.

Grupp came trotting up. "It's okay, Lietzke," he said. "What's the matter?"

"I can't think of one," Lietzke said.

One day between sessions at preseason I was sitting around in the locker room when I heard some thumping around from down the hall, terrible screams. "What the hell's that?" I said. "They're spraying deodorant up Lietzke's ass again," somebody said. "Man, I bet that stings," another guy said.

So I was lying that morning on a bed in Menhardt's room, looking through some magazines he had, when Lietzke strolled in, as if that were the most natural thing in the world. He sat lightly on the edge of the other bed, as if he weren't really doing it.

"Hi, Dan." He always tried to make his voice sound low, down from its high tenor. "How was it out there on Saturday?"

I tried to be nice to the kid. I think he had always looked up to me, ever since I had been JV captain the year before. But the fact of the matter was he drove me nuts.

"Listen, Lietzke," I said. "You're not supposed to be here."

"I signed out of study hall. I had to get a book. Nobody cares. Just tell me what it was like out there."

Sadly I put down the magazine. "How do you mean?"

"What's it like in a varsity game? A big one, for a championship. How's it different from JV?"

I could see the light in his eyes, that was familiar enough to me. Somehow it just made me angry. I de-

234

cided to tell him the truth. I knew he'd never believe it.

"It's just the same," I said. "It's exactly the same thing. They're bigger and faster and better but so are you. The plays are more complicated, but you still just do your two or three things."

"There's got to be some difference."

"The crowd's bigger but that's all bullshit. When did you ever look at a crowd? It's really just the same thing. The same old game. You and the poor bastard over you."

"I'd have given anything to be out there on Saturday."

I was actually getting a little worked up. In a way I pitied him, hoping for something that would never be.

"You're not listening, Lietzke." I had raised my voice a little. "I said it was the same thing. The same game. It doesn't matter where you play it. And Wiggins is twice the coach Grupp is. You're more of a player after one game with him than if Grupp coached you all your life."

"You're just saying that to make me feel better. Jamison's the man next year." He was the JV quarterback ahead of Lietzke. "If it wasn't him they'd get somebody else. I know the way it's going to be."

That was the thing about Lietzke. He seemed to know the truth. He just didn't do anything about it.

"Maybe you're right," I said. I paused, as if it had just struck me. "Jamison might have it all sewed up. He's got all those moves. All that confidence." He was the cockiest kid I'd ever met. "Why don't you make a change? Start working out, put on some weight. Tell Grupp you want to switch to guard. There are places on this team. There's nobody backing up the line, nothing for next year. You'd make a good guard with a little weight."

"No." He looked straight at me. It was the first time I'd ever seen him sure of himself. "It wouldn't be the same. All my life I've wanted to be a quarterback. I'm not giving up now."

I wanted to say, You want to be one, you want to be one. But you're not. My God, man, look in the mirror.

235

Do you look like a quarterback? But I didn't say it. I just said, "What the hell. You never know."

He stood up to go. "Listen, Dan. I was watching you the other day. I watched you a lot. You look great out there. The best on the team."

"Thanks." That made me feel wonderful, after all I'd said. "Look Lietzke. Don't worry about it." I tried for the nicest thing I could think of to say. "Jamison might get hurt."

"I guess he might."

A few minutes after Lietzke walked out I heard Pollett's voice. I had always hated the sound of it; high-pitched, slurred, it got caught on long words and just managed to choke them out, like a dog bringing up something he shouldn't have swallowed.

"Lietzke," he was saying, from down the hall. "What kind of underwear do you have on?"

"Aw, Ron." Immediately Lietzke started to talk fast, the way he did when he was nervous. "I just signed out of study hall. I got to get back."

"Don't get excited, Lietzke," Pollett said. I could hear his footsteps shuffling down the hall. "I was just asking."

"What is it, Lietzke? Fruit of the Loom? Jockey?" It was Ryczek talking, the tackle who played beside me. "We sure could use some Fruit of the Loom."

"Did your mother buy it for you?" Pollett said.

"Please, you guys. I should have been back by now."

"Don't be in such a hurry, Lietzke. You really could help us out."

The perverts over in Collins had started what they called an underwear tree. Where they got an idea like that I'll never know. It was a big dorm thing, as if it showed what a wonderful communal spirit they all had. A big branch had fallen down out back, and they'd set it up in an empty room to decorate with underpants. When some poor unsuspecting slob wandered through, they'd jump him and rip them off; supposedly there was all kinds of technique to that. Then they'd hang them in the tree with the name and the date. Apparently they got a big thrill out of it.

The Collins underwear tree. On its way to becoming a school tradition.

"You want to go quietly, Lietzke?" Ryczek said.

There was something sickening about the whole thing. It was bad enough when it was the whole dorm, a bunch of kids jumping an outsider, all kinds of cheering and a big procession when they'd stripped him, but this was personal, brutal, just the three of them struggling in that hallway on a Tuesday morning. Lietzke did try to run, then wrestled with them when they caught him, but he was being quiet about it, grunting and puffing as if he were keeping his teeth clenched. He didn't want anybody to hear. There was a lot of thrashing around, some muffled cries, a loud rip, and the struggle stopped. A long silent pause. Suddenly I heard Lietzke's voice, sharp, assertive, for the first time, breaking the quiet like a pistol shot. "You stop that!" That brought me out of bed; I looked through the open door.

"Take it easy, Lietzke," Pollett said. "I was just looking. You got nice balls."

"Nice balls, Lietzke," Ryczek said.

The two of them stood, big hulking forms, hovering over Lietzke on the floor.

Another time I might just have turned away. There wasn't much I could do with two guys their size, especially Pollett, who with his reputation couldn't back down to anybody. But the sight of Lietzke on the floor unnerved me. He looked so young. His body was smooth and white as a baby's. Red-faced, he was struggling to cover himself.

I stepped into the hallway. "You guys enjoying yourselves?" I said.

Pollett and Ryczek looked up at me. Apparently they'd had no idea anyone else was in the hall. That made it a whole different scene, with somebody watching.

"Just adding to the collection," Pollett said. "What are you wearing?"

"One way to find out," I said .

Pollett was blushing a little, but trying to act serious,

matter-of-fact, as if he were running a session of the student council or something. Ryczek was grinning, looking more embarrassed.

"Just having a little fun," he said.

"It takes an asshole to have fun like that," I said.

They were staring at me, trying to see to what extent we were all joking.

"Or in your case," I said, "two assholes."

Pollett took a little step forward. Ryczek was trying to smile. "Come on, Dan." We knew each other pretty well, since we played beside each other on the line. "You don't have to be like that."

"It's the way everything is around here," I said. "Everything's at somebody's expense. You guys want to have fun so you get together and give Lietzke shit. Or it could have been somebody else. Everybody gets together and gives some poor kid shit. It's a big time."

"But not you," Pollett said.

"It's not my idea of a big time."

"We weren't hurting the kid," Pollett said.

"It's all right, Dan," Lietzke said. His face couldn't have been redder. Beads of sweat stood out on his brow. "It was all in fun."

It was incredible when you thought about it, though it hardly surprised me—Lietzke was on their side.

"It wouldn't hurt you to be in on a little of it," Pollett said.

"Oh?" I stared at him.

His face had hardened; his voice had taken on a belligerent tone.

"You don't do *anything* with the team. Around school, or down at the gym. You don't screw around with us. You didn't come over at the dance when we were celebrating. And in practice, even the games, you're not really a part of it. Guys have said things to me."

"I haven't heard any complaints."

"You're good at what you do, I'm not saying that."

"I watch my three yards."

It was what Wiggins had told us, time and again: if every lineman took care of his three yards of turf, nobody would ever get through.

"Sometimes it doesn't hurt to help out with somebody else's," Pollett said.

It was hard to believe. I had come out to speak for Lietzke, and Pollett was making it sound like a plot to undermine the whole football team. But there was truth to what he said. I knew that I did just occupy my three yards of turf, obsessed with what was going on there. To some extent I didn't care what was going on around me. It was as if I were burying myself, digging a trench to occupy alone. I didn't see it as some big moral issue, the way he was making it sound. But as I heard him speak I was struck by how lonely it sounded, struggling away out there on my own while all around me a team was working together.

What he said hurt me, and I couldn't speak to it.

"It's not good for the team," Pollett said. "The way you are."

"If this is the team"—those two big lugs standing there, Lietzke at the feet on the floor—"I don't want to be good for it."

"That's a hell of a thing to decide now." Pollett was scowling, his face dark. "Why'd you want to play in the first place."

I had often wondered the same thing myself. I answered with the first words that came to mind.

"It was the only team there was," I said.

III

The day of the Kingston game, a Saturday, the field was terrible. It had started to rain Friday morning, not a storm, just dark skies and a slow steady pelting. To stay dry, on Friday afternoon, ludicrously, we dressed in our game uniforms and stocking feet, and ran through plays up on the gym floor, sliding and skidding all over the place. That was better preparation than we knew.

The rain just didn't stop. Saturday, if anything, it was darker, rain still plopping out of the sky. The coaches even considered postponing the game, but we were right in the middle of a league race, and anyway, football games aren't supposed to be postponed for anything short of a tornado.

You knew in the locker room things weren't right. It was stuffy with all the windows closed, gloomy. Everybody pulled on their pads without a word. Maybe we weren't talking because of the weather, the way you're naturally a little testy when every time you step out the door rain falls on your head in buckets, or maybe because of the field, knowing that every time we got hit we'd be stumbling. Nobody on that team had entirely forgotten Nick Kaiser's broken leg.

It may have been, though, that we had all just figured out the party was over. We'd spent most of the week celebrating our league championship, which was still two games away. We hadn't done anything harder in practice than a dummy drill. And now we were about to walk out on that field and face our closest rival, who, since they had no league to belong to, spent the whole year pointing toward us.

Early in the first quarter we called a pass—we called a lot of short passes that day, since the runners couldn't get any footing—and I was glad to come back on a pass block where I could catch my balance. The rain was still pouring down, the sky gray as slate, and every time you stood straight out of your stance water poured in a cold stream off your helmet and down your neck. The kid over me wasn't much taller, but he had a torso like a beer keg, his forearms and hands all swatched in muddy pads, a cage over his face. I expected him to come in low, to the inside but instead, as soon as I stepped back, he leaped at me as if he'd been waiting all day for the chance and shot out the heel of his fist at my eyes. I was wearing special athletic glasses at that point, a substitute for the contacts my mother had wanted me to have, and I had a good view of the approaching blow. The helmet dug down on my forehead as his fist drove past my face mask, his hand smashing into the crosspiece of my glasses, then my nose, blood spurting. I staggered back a couple of steps and sat down. There was a terrific rush going over: the whole defensive line was on our quarterback before he even raised his arm.

That was the way the whole game went. We stood there watching and they came at us. I don't remember how they scored. I can't imagine how anyone could have scored on a field like that. People said the next week that it had been a typical Kingston game, close all the way, a six-point victory, but that was ridiculous. No team was ever beaten worse than we were that day. There was a huge crowd of people on the Kingston side, wearing ponchos and holding long sheets of transparent plastic over their heads, and when the game was over they broke onto the field, mobbing their team and dancing around in the mud. We could hardly make our way through. One by one we straggled up to the gym.

When I finally made it up the steps I saw a lone figure outside the gym, pacing, waiting to speak to me. Nick was soaking wet, his hair black and hanging down into his eyes, but he looked good, a lot bigger and sturdier than he had been a year before. His eyes were serious, watching me, in case I seemed all broken up. I wasn't, but I wasn't happy. I hadn't been beaten up like that on a football field in years.

"I saw you out there, Keith," Nick said. "You looked good."

"Come off it, Nick. I was terrible."

"That kid's tough. Dillon, who was over you."

"He sure as hell is. But I've been better than that."

"We were up and you were down."

Nick was keeping it matter-of-fact, trying not to gloat, though he couldn't have minded coming out to that campus and seeing Arnold get beaten.

"How's Kingston?" I said. "I'd heard you were going there."

He shrugged. There was a certain tension to his face. He was, after all, up there, not down at the celebration.

"You want to know the truth?" he said.

"Sure."

"You won't believe it. It's another Arnold."

I had to smile, after all the Kingston rumors I'd heard.

"That bad?" I said.

"Maybe worse." He shook his head, grinned a little. "I never miss. If I die and go to heaven, I swear to God there'll be seniors there. And I'll be a new kid."

Chapter 17

MONDAY AFTERNOON, AFTER we got suited up for the meeting—a message on the chalkboard had said, "Full Pads, Meeting at 3:30"—we must have sat on the locker room benches for five minutes in utter silence. Guys would clear their throats, move their spikes a little on the floor. Everybody was just staring straight ahead. Finally we heard the door open, turned to see Grupp enter, got one look at his face and looked back at the floor again. His eyes had seemed transfixed, the color in his face moving past red and on toward purple; his mustache had been bristling like the quills of a porcupine. He started pacing. Up the room and down the room, up the room and down, his rubber soles squeaking. The clipboard behind his back, eyes fixed on the ground, his belly before him like a great boulder. When finally he spoke, his voice was a hoarse whisper, the last words from a deathbed.

"We didn't block." Squeak squeak squeak. "We didn't tackle." Squeak squeak. "We didn't run with the ball." Squeak. "We didn't catch it. We didn't do a single thing that a football team is supposed to do." He stopped in the middle of the floor, grew thoughtful. "You know, after watching that game, I wouldn't have been in the least surprised, I mean it wouldn't have shocked me a bit, if one of you had come to the locker room and asked the correct technique for putting on a jockstrap."

That was the trouble with Grupp's speeches. When

he was at his most serious, white hot with anger, it was all you could do to keep from rolling around on the floor in hysterics.

"Maybe I should assign a special coach to that. We could have drills every day before practice. Walk through it a couple of times before you went full-speed."

It seemed about time for a full-scale explosion, but he held it back, started to pace again.

"I was hoping this would be the proudest time of my life. I thought I might be able to enjoy it a little. Last Monday Ray Brannon, the Kingston coach, gave me a call, and offered his congratulations, he said I must be feeling pretty good. I had to admit, I felt pretty good. He said it must be pretty satisfying after all these years and I said yes, it had been a long time. He was worried he'd get embarrassed on Saturday, blown right off the field, them being just three and two and not even in our league, and I said no, I knew those Kingston kids, they weren't going to let an Arnold team embarrass them. I knew it would be a good game.

"Well, it wasn't a good game. It wasn't a good game. It was the saddest excuse for a football game I ever saw. But I was right about one thing. He wasn't embarrassed. When I think of that bunch of misfits, flunkies, reform school dropouts." That did it: he spun, flung the clipboard across the room, a rising line drive; it hit the top of an end locker, bounced off the ceiling, clattered, its papers fluttering, to the floor. "It's like getting beaten by your idiot kid brother." He ran a hand through his hair as if to tear it out. "I thought you were champions. I treated you like champions. I thought last week your game was in shape, I could keep you finely tuned, razor-sharp. But I can see I was wrong. I've still got to drive you like a bunch of mules. Today we start all over again. Four laps on the track before practice. Fifteen wind sprints after, fifty yards. One-on-ones. Tackling drills. And Tuesday, Wednesday, and Thursday we scrimmage, full-speed, no dummies, game conditions. We might not win another game all year, but it won't be because we didn't practice."

Grupp was a great bullshitter. He was just as likely

to say that one afternoon and send us out the next day in shirts and shorts. But that time he meant it. Every day that week, in full equipment, we ran a mile before practice, Foley, the Rose, and me bringing up the rear while he made some sarcastic remark ("Every day I lose ten minutes of practice waiting for my tackles to finish their last lap."). We beat ourselves silly in basic drills. And the scrimmages were killers, varsity against varsity, no time-outs. It was preseason all over again. By Saturday half of us belonged in the infirmary—I ached, laced with bruises—and that day we were scheduled to ride a bus to Cleveland and play Rollins, our third league opponent.

It turned out to be all right. Rollins was strong in some sports, wrestling especially, and track, but in football they couldn't execute. They ran their offense in slow motion and fumbled about every third play. At first they were tough on defense, but after a while, when they realized they were going to keep handing us the ball, they started to get discouraged. It was just the kind of game we needed, a hard workout, but one where we looked good. We won, 34–6. Late in the fourth quarter our back-up quarterback, Jamison, hurt his shoulder and had to be taken out, but by the time we were heading home we had heard nothing was broken.

The big Greyhound got back to the gym just about the time a reddish sunset was settling over the field.

"Tonight we celebrate," Rosy said to me.

"I don't know. I'm tired."

"After that game? Christ." He shook his head. "You be there."

"You think a lot of people will show up?"

"Leggett's parties are like an orgy. Everybody comes." He shook with laughter at this ancient witticism. "And his parents are out of town."

For a while I'd avoided parties, as if disaster inevitably trailed them, but it would have taken a hermit to miss that one. I was still thinking about what Pollett had said to me.

"All right," I said. "I got to get cleaned up. But I'll be there."

I'd never been to Leggett's house, though I'd heard
about it. It was the same suburb as Arnold, not far
from campus. From the road you saw nothing more of
the place than the pine trees that fronted it. You drove
through stone gates and slightly uphill along a long
winding drive that also was overhung, darkened, by
trees. The house itself, massive, looked down on a vast
expanse of lawn. In the cold clear moonlight it was
quite a sight, headlights sliding along on the road far
below. Inside it was plush, with thick carpets, heavy
furnishings, and a large wing of the house allotted to
Stephen. With his parents gone, we had the run of the
place.

Most of the football team was there, some other seniors and juniors, girls from the girls' schools, even the
usual contingent from Kingston, out on some kind of
free weekend. Tensions had somewhat diminished with
them since they'd beaten us. They didn't sit off in a
corner all evening looking like a street gang from the
slums. They mingled more.

The girls, also, were getting around. There had been
a time—my freshman year, say—when parties included
only boys from the East End and an exclusive suburb
or two. Now you weren't surprised to see guys from
little mill communities all over the city. I didn't like it.
They could play on our fields, study in our libraries,
sleep in our dorms, but I wished they'd keep their
hands off our women. I was having enough trouble
with competition from Anglo-Saxons without opening
up the field to the whole continent.

I'd noticed something of that at the Homecoming
Dance, but things were starting to look serious. I put
the question casually to Shealy, our quarterback.

"Sara Warren. That little blond. Did she come here
with Pollett?"

"Looks like it. Kretchmer took her to the Homecoming Dance." Another country heard from. "But she

seemed to take a shine to Pollett. I guess he saw an opening."

"God."

"He's got all the moves."

It should have been incongruous. She was so delicate, petite, with gentle gestures, elegant ways, while he had those hands that could crush a coconut the way the rest of us crack a peanut, and a fixed moronic expression on his face. But she seemed different that night, knowing, with a heightened color, more animation, while he was suddenly as suave as a nightclub bouncer. Somehow they were almost right for each other, brought everything together, the lion lying down (pardon the expression) with the lamb.

I'd run into Shealy early in the evening, at a buffet table that looked like Sunday brunch at the country club. "You must be feeling pretty good," I said. "After a day like that."

"There wasn't much to it."

"It was almost like a football game."

"Don't get me wrong. I'll take it anytime. I'd like it next week."

Of all the stars, he looked least like an athlete; he was short, seemed slight (until you saw him stripped, muscles rippling, hard as a rock) and had a friendly pug-nosed face. He acted least like a star too, studied a lot, was quiet. You might see him around campus with anyone. He had a girlfriend off at college somewhere, so he didn't participate much in social events. We'd talked some before. I'd always remembered that though we weren't terribly close, I'd seen him off to one side at my father's funeral.

"What do you hear about Jamison?" I asked him.

"A shoulder separation. He won't be around next week. But he's okay."

Together we had wandered off to a couple chairs in the living room. We were in a corner, the party milling all around us.

"You ever think we'd get this far?" I said. "One game to go."

"If we beat Asbury. I never thought we'd do that. They'd always been way stronger than the rest of the league. They were a little down this year. And we played over our heads."

"I guess."

"Then the next week we stank. You never know what's going to happen."

Around us the crowd was socializing, drinking beer, smoking, eating. Music blared through speakers all over the house. A crowd of jocks were sitting on a long couch across the room, Sara perched on Pollett's thigh. He nodded to me once, in a show of patriarchal approval, and Sara, blushing a little—the way old friends do when they haven't seen each other in a while, embarrassed that they haven't been in touch—gave me a little wave. The lights were dim. A haze of smoke hung toward the ceiling.

It was what I had always dreamed of, attending a party like that after a big victory. I had imagined girls falling all over me. It didn't seem to be happening, but by that time I knew it wouldn't. For some reason I felt almost content, as if I could give up the struggle: its whole premise had been false. That can be a beginning, when you finally give up on something.

I was in a pensive mood with Shealy.

"You ever stop to think," I said, "now that it's about over, why you wanted to play football? What you wanted it to do?"

He frowned, puzzled. He seemed honestly not to know what I meant. "I'd always played ball."

"But didn't you want anything from it? Fame and glory. Beautiful women."

He laughed.

"It got you into Arnold," I said.

"They don't tell you that."

"What?"

"That you're coming to play football." He spoke sharply. I seemed to have hit a touchy subject. "They have scholarships anybody can apply for. They contact certain kids to let them know. They might talk to you a lot. But they never come out and say they're signing you up to play football."

"I didn't know that."

"I always resented it, to tell you the truth. As soon

248

as I got here kids were calling it a football scholarship. I hadn't seen it that way. I thought they wanted me, not a football player."

"I'm sure they did."

He shrugged, softened a little. "I'd always played ball, always loved it. Even in grade school, I could tackle better, beat the other kids wide. And I loved a pass play. Seeing it develop, laying the ball in there. The first time I did that, I can still remember, I knew I was a quarterback."

I was astonished. I'd talked football with guys before, guys from the old JV team, and there were things we all liked as we got better at them, but there was always that understanding, that most of it had been a pain, there was something driving us to do it. I'd never heard anyone say he played just because he liked the game.

"It's the same with Pollett," he said. "We played on the same sandlots, the same youth league. Eleven, twelve years old, he had all the same moves he has now. He wasn't even big then. It was unbelievable. He was born to play football."

"Huh."

"Then you come over here and somebody's trying to take advantage of it. Don't get me wrong. I'm grateful to Arnold. It's meant a lot to me, to my family. Something we could never have had any other way. But just for the football, I'd have rather played in public school. Or on a sandlot somewhere."

Shealy was usually such a mild guy. There was almost bitterness in the way he spoke.

"It's funny," I said. "I always resented scholarship kids. I thought if they hadn't been here I'd have played more. I wished the school hadn't brought them in."

"I can see that. But it wasn't our fault. Of course we'd take the opportunity. But you get the feeling somebody's using you. I'm not saying anybody really is. I wouldn't know who."

Across the room, the jocks had somewhat dispersed. Gradually Sara had draped herself across Pollett. He was smiling dreamily, like a baby when you tickle him.

I watched as if from miles away. After a while they wandered out.

"I didn't know football was natural for anybody," I said. "I mean real football, not the stuff kids play. For me it was the most unnatural thing in the world. Almost torture, at first."

"So why'd you play?"

"I thought I had to. I got here that first year and it was all anybody said, do something for your school. Like you weren't welcome if you didn't. I looked around. I was big. I'd always thought I wanted to be a football player. So I went out."

"And you made the team. What you set out to do. You did what you wanted. That's something."

"It didn't make me happy."

"How's that?"

I was gazing around the room, at people laughing, chattering, swilling beer. They looked happy enough. Happier, anyway, than I was. In that moment it seemed simple. You didn't have to be a football player. You didn't have to be anything.

"I think I was doing it for my father," I said.

Shealy nodded.

"I've thought about it a lot. All this year, when I've had what I wanted, but I didn't have it. It must have been that. I wanted it for him. It's kind of ridiculous. I don't think it meant shit to him. But I kept telling myself it would. Like I was using him for an excuse. So this year was too late."

"Yeah."

"I've never gotten over last year. I thought I should have played."

"You should have."

"You think so?"

"I never thought about it much. But I've got a reason for saying that. It's something I've thought about telling you. I was going to tell you sometime."

"Oh?"

"You're not going to like it."

Shealy sat forward in his chair. His face had clouded; he wasn't looking at me. He rubbed one hand with the other.

"We had these meetings last year," he said. "Still have them. The coaches, some of the starters. Me, Cortese, Pollett. Last year Baker. We'd talk about different things, strong points, weak points, who should play. The players never had any say in that, but it came up. Last year you were a question mark. Grupp never wants to use all he has. It was between you and Ryczek. Wiggins thought you were good enough. He thought you should play, get experience, make some mistakes. But they never listened to Wiggins much."

"I can imagine."

"One day Holden spoke up. You remember Holden."

"Yeah."

"He said you weren't ready to play varsity ball. You weren't mature enough."

I could hear him saying it, "vahsity boll." I pictured him on that strange morning in front of the gym, with his bug eyes, lips flecked with fruit.

"What the hell did he mean by that?"

"Nobody knew. He'd never said anything about the linemen. Wiggins kept asking him what he meant, and he wouldn't get specific, just kept repeating the same thing. 'That's all I need to say.' Wiggins finally walked out. I'd never seen him so mad. But Holden had had that famous coaching career. Grupp was always nervous around him. That was the kind of thing Holden would say, like he had a sixth sense, and Grupp wouldn't question. He said we'd go with Ryczek."

"But I could beat Ryczek. I still can. We're even, at least."

"I know."

"Holden said something to me one day." I was trying to remember exactly. "Some crazy thing."

"Pollett had talked to Holden before the meeting. He said he'd heard you talking about him. Saying things behind his back. About his drinking."

"That's ridiculous. I didn't even figure that out for months."

Shealy shrugged, "Pollett and Ryczek were friends."

I stared at him. "Jesus Christ." Until that moment, I'd had no idea what he was telling me.

"It sounds bad. It sounds even worse to me as I'm telling it. If I'd known, if I'd had any idea what it meant to you, I'd have said something."

"Sure."

All the days, weeks, months, I'd spent working at football, thinking about it, slinging weights in the basement, running sprints in the schoolyard, all that wasted because one overgrown simpleton wanted his friend to play. My father had never known I was good enough. Maybe that wouldn't have meant much to him, but it would have meant something to me. It would have made all the difference in the world. Maybe if he'd known I could play I would have been proud of it.

"I always thought I'd tell you sometime," Shealy said. "But I didn't know how much it meant."

"Yeah. I'm glad you did tell me. It's something I should know."

"It is."

"I think . . ." I hardly knew what I was saying, "I think I'll go for a walk."

I rose slowly, stepped toward the hallway. As if just awakened from a long sleep, I felt oddly removed from all that was going on. The lights were dim. From massive speakers in the living room, in a nearby den, guitars screamed, a drum pounded, voices shouted. Bodies were sprawled on the stairs, curled in chairs, they leaned against the walls. People chattered, gestured, but I heard no words, saw faces staring, frowning, wrinkling in laughter. They leaned back, sucking at beer cans. One guy, cross-legged in the middle of the floor, drank beer from a fishbowl. Their mouths nipped at cigarettes, gulped in smoke.

I'm not sure at first I would even have said I was looking for someone, as I stepped through the den and walked past the buffet in the dining room. I felt strange. My muscles were crawling, all but twitching, under my skin, and I stifled an impulse to shout, run, knock things over. At the same time it was all I could do not to go off in a corner somewhere and lie down. I kept walking, up a short back stairway to a game room, then up some more stairs to the second floor.

The hallways were wide, thickly carpeted, dim. From behind the walls I heard occasional voices.

I don't know, either, what I thought I would do if I found him. He was five inches taller, twenty pounds heavier, quick as a cat, hard as diamonds, a brawler, streetfighter, mill worker's son: He would have killed me. I wasn't envisioning anything in particular, some desperate gesture, a knee to his groin before he demolished me. I just wanted to do something that would stop me from thinking. Toward the front of the house, as I stepped into a narrow side hallway, darkened, in a small den lighted only by a dim lamp, I saw them.

He lay on his back, on a short leather couch. Covering about two-thirds of him, she lay on top. They hadn't heard me. All their clothes were on, their hands tame. I don't know why what I saw was the one thing that could have stopped me. It was as if the small doorway, the lamp above their heads, formed a lighted picture for me to see. I leaned against the wall, my heart hammering. There was something so much beyond my experience in what she was doing, her mouth moving lightly over his face, nipping, kissing, tracing small lines with her tongue; slowly her mouth would open and settle in a long kiss over his. If he had been making the advance, some brutal sloppy pass, it would have been one thing; this was quite another. Pollett was pinned more helplessly than he had ever been on a football field.

A thought crossed my mind as if from nowhere: that poor dumb bastard. He's the whore.

I stepped away—the floor gave a loud crack; probably they heard me—hurried back through the wide hall, down the back stairs to the kitchen and out the door. It was cold, clear, out there, stars hanging off in the black sky. I stood in the doorway a minute, bracing against the air. My head started to clear. I walked to the driveway, out to the front of the house. A small crowd of guys were standing on the front lawn, smoking, drinking beer; one of them tossed a can down onto the field. They noticed my arrival, turned my way. "Hey," somebody shouted from the midst of them. "Keith. I'm talking to you. Arnold eats shit."

Ordinarily I would just have turned around and walked back; there were seven or eight of them, and I wasn't proud. But I was all worked up—I'd just been ready to fight Pollett, about equivalent to eight of anybody else—and took a few steps toward them. They spread out a little. One guy stepped from the midst of them. "Arnold sucks," he said. "Everybody there." In the light from an upstairs window I could make out the flat face, hair hanging almost into his eyes, the little circle of a mouth. Almost shyly, he grinned.

"Nick," I said. I grinned back.

"Arnold eats shit," he said.

"Sure. Maybe it does."

"Oh fuck," somebody said behind him. "Come on, kid."

"You're going to fight me, Keith," Nick said. His eyes were hazy, cheeks flushed, that silly grin on his face.

"No, Nick. I'm not going to fight you."

"You are. That's what it's all about. That's what we're here for. Arnold and Kingston."

"No."

"You came over here."

"I didn't know it was you."

"Isn't that sweet," somebody said.

"We'll just fart around," Nick said. He started to dance like a boxer, bouncing up and down, flicked out a jab that smacked against my cheek. "Just for the hell of it."

Somehow, seeing Nick had calmed me down, that flat funny face—it had all just drained out of me for a few seconds—but that slap, the crowd behind him, were getting me started again, with that anger that had nothing to do with him.

"Listen, Nick," I said. "I don't feel much like farting around."

"Good. Then we'll really fight."

"No."

"Jesus, Keith." Nick grabbed me by the lapels, stuck his face into mine. "You're a big fucking football star. A big Arnold football star. You're not going to let

254

yourself get pushed around by a kid like me. From Kingston."

"We were friends, Nick."

"Jesus Christ," somebody said behind him. "Kiss him, kid."

Nick pushed me away, jabbed again; it caught me flush on the nose, stung, my eyes watering. "Fight me, Keith."

I took off my jacket. "All right. But I swear to God, Nick. I'm not going to stop. If we do start fighting I'll kick the shit out of you."

"Great." He jabbed again, missed. "I won't let up either. See what you can do."

As a matter of fact, like everybody else at Kingston—it seemed to be their favorite occupation—Nick had a recent reputation for fighting, in Shadyside on Saturday nights, at parties. Just a couple of weeks before I'd heard a story about him sitting on some kid, punching his face with a fistful of gravel. Any other time I'd have been scared to death, even if I was way stronger, with forty pounds on him, but that night I wasn't even afraid. It was ridiculous. There was no reason for us to fight each other. We were two buck niggers in a dark alley on a Saturday night, slashing with razors; somebody should have told us: the enemy was elsewhere.

I rushed him, swung a wild right—what the hell, I didn't know anything about fighting; I just wanted to smash his head like a melon—but he sidestepped me easily, shot out a right that smacked against my cheek. I swung to face him. He wasn't bouncing around anymore, just up on the balls of his feet, his fists around chest level. His face had changed, was solemn, intent. I rushed again, trying to stick a shoulder in him, but he was too quick again, slipped away, then planted a foot and smashed an uppercut to my nose: it gushed blood, stung; my eyes watered; I swayed.

He stood back, watching. "You had enough, Keith?"

"Shit," somebody said. "He hasn't had enough."

I stepped after him slowly—those big rushes were no good—looking for something to grab. He backstepped, his eyes cold, hard. I lunged, grasping, and his left flew out, grazed my jaw. He pivoted into a right but I had his shirtfront when the fist smashed my eye—I staggered, saw stars—and I held on, grabbed for his hair and yanked. He yelped like a dog as his head snapped down and I got a lock on it from the front, stumbling. He grabbed my leg. We hit the ground.

Suddenly there he felt small, his torso slight, as if his spine would snap like a stick. I knew I had him if we didn't get up. By his hair again I snapped back his head, smashed my fist into his face, chest, pounding as if at all my frustrations, hatreds. He thrashed, defenseless; his leg was flung over my shoulder. I grabbed it and yanked. He screamed as if I'd snapped it off.

"Oh Keith. Keith. My God. That's my leg. My broken leg."

"You son of a bitch." My voice was hoarse, and as if far away. "I'll break it for you again."

The heel of a boot smashed just above my ribs, threw me to my side, crashing into Nick's leg. Again he screamed. I rolled, turned. It was Dillon, the big barrel of a kid who had been over me in the football game. He crouched like a linebacker above me.

"Lay off his leg."

"What's it to you?"

"The guy's my buddy. You knew it was broke."

"It was a fight, kid."

"It's going to be now. I'll bust your fucking ass."

I stood, backed up a little. Dillon moved toward me. Nick had been lying on his back, now sat up, his leg limp, twitching.

"Goddammit," he said. "Fight your own fights."

"He's mine now, Kaiser."

"The hell he is."

Dillon stared at him, eyes narrowing. "Who you think you're talking to?"

"It was my fight. It got out of hand. It's still my fight. Fuck off."

"Say one more thing, Kaiser, and it's going to be you."

"Jesus Christ." Nick started to get up, put weight on his leg, but winced, sat down again. "Keith's a friend of mine. I knew him before I knew any of you. We were messing around. He didn't mean anything." He was wrong about that. There was a moment there when I'd have snapped his leg in two. "Him and me got things to talk about."

"Goddammit."

"Find somebody else to kick around."

"Asshole." Dillon turned, shaking his head. He spit. "You start something, Kaiser, you ought to finish it." It must have been the old Protestant work ethic coming out in him. He stood there a moment, as if trying to decide, then walked away slowly, the rest of them followed, slouching, grumbling, looking back at us over their shoulders now and then. They were headed toward the field where the cars were parked.

"I'd have fought him, Nick," I said when they were gone.

"He'd have killed you. He's out of his fucking mind. Probably carries a razor on him. They're all crazy." He tried to push himself up again, winced. "Help me up, would you? I got to walk on this thing."

"You sure?"

"This happens all the time. When I work out. Getting ready for wrestling again. I just got to walk on it."

I pulled him up and he put weight on it, almost keeled over again, waited a minute, started to limp around. "Oh, God." At first he was almost bent double, then started doing better, grunting a little every time he stepped on it. "Let's walk down a ways." I picked up my jacket and we headed toward the road.

"We shouldn't have had that fight," he said after a while.

"Damn it, Nick." I was wiping the blood from my nose with a handkerchief. "I said that three times."

"I know. Sometimes I got to do something half-crazy, just to do it. Nothing personal, with you. It's just like fucking a girl. You fuck a girl yet, Keith?"

"Sure. Millions of times."

"There's this girl in Sharpsburg. She'll do it for anybody. We do it pretty much. Everybody gives her all this shit. But she's so nice. She practically cries if you stay afterwards to talk to her. It makes you sick, thinking of all the guys been in and out of there. But while you're with her, at least, you don't go to a fucked-up school, have all these fucked-up friends, a fucked-up leg. You ought to fuck her sometime, Keith."

"I'll make a point of it."

"I mean it. I'll take you down there sometime."

Actually, my mouth was watering. I wouldn't have minded meeting a girl I didn't have to chase.

We were about halfway to the road, and it was freezing, but Nick was going strong, limping along pretty fast, his face fierce and intent. "You're big shit out at Arnold," he said.

"Come off it."

"You are. Those guys knew you."

"Great. I guess I'm what passes for big shit. What I once thought was big shit."

"What we both thought. Hell. You look back on something like that, it's embarrassing. The way we looked up to those guys. Now here we are."

"Yeah."

"All the things that have happened since. You would never have believed it."

I had often thought of that, have often thought of it since, the incredible events of the past, what it is that the future must hold. You couldn't face it if you knew. I wondered if Nick knew about my father.

"I wish to God I'd never painted the chapel," he said.

We were almost to the road, stopped and looked at each other, he with that hurt in his eyes that had always been there, even when I first met him, that fierce thrusting jaw.

"I know why I did it, and I was pretty drunk anyway, and I hated that place, I still hate it. It'd be nice if I didn't, but I still do. But I wish I hadn't painted the chapel. There are things in your life and you look back on them and think, Jesus Christ, I'd give anything if that wasn't there. If that one thing could be wiped out."

I knew those things, my father's death of course but that was unfair—deaths had to be—but, if not that, at least the party I had gone to, my telling an alcoholic woman about my father's illness so she could slobber

258

all over it. I knew the words I'd spoken and wished I hadn't, others I hadn't spoken and would wish forever that I had.

"But it's there," Nick said. "You'll never wipe it away. You've got to live with it."

It didn't matter that I hadn't had my talk with Nick, about how I understood, I knew why he had painted the chapel; nothing I could have said would have made it better. That's what the years had taught us, that those things were, they wouldn't change, all our dreams of glory and the glory we achieved wouldn't change them.

I loved Nick. He was the one guy I knew—flat head, jutting jaw and all—who could face things and say them just as they were.

"So we'll live with it," I said.

Nick shrugged. "What the fuck," he said.

Chapter 18

SATURDAY NIGHT, AFTER I'd left Leggett's party, some guys had been fooling around with the massive radio in his living room and picked up an Ohio station. They had heard some football scores, including ours against Rollins, which they got a big kick out of. But they also heard another score, Asbury against Northrup, our last league opponent. By the time I got to Arnold on Monday, the news had spread all over the school. Northrup 27, Asbury 12. We were tied for the lead with one game to go.

Practice that last week was nasty. By then, of course, it was early November, but there was a spell of bad weather too. As we arrived at the field, the sky was a dull gray, a bitter wind whipping through the grass. Everyone wore extra jerseys and sweatshirts. Nobody stood around before practice, but jumped into drills, running pass patterns, chasing punts, anything to get the blood moving. Football was a mean game those days. The ball slapped your hands and left them buzzing. Getting spiked was like being slashed with a knife. A lineman's hands, forearms, stayed swollen, lumped with bruises. Throughout practice the sky grew darker until, by the end, it was almost black; runners were just shadows who lunged out of the backfield and popped you a moment before it seemed they should.

Wednesday we had the usual scrimmage. It had stormed that morning, and the ground was soaked; a couple times during practice a burst of cold rain came down. The coaches wore parkas, hunched in the hoods; players stood around with hands wrapped in their jerseys or stuffed in their pants. The scrimmage was short, mean, Pollett and Grunfeld blasting through holes we opened in the JV line. Our practice pants and jerseys got soaked with mud. Afterwards Grupp put the JVs into the Northrup offense. He was obviously feeling good about the scrimmage. Hoarsely he barked out the players to face them. "Tackles, Ryczek and Foley. Guards, Kretchmer and Malcolm."

"Kretchmer?"

I'd spoken without thinking, standing almost next to Grupp. Since the league games had started, there had been some extra linemen around; I hadn't been playing every minute. Grupp had said something to me about my defensive performance against Kingston—it had been terrible—but then he had started me against Rollins. In every game all year I'd started both ways.

"Kretchmer and Malcolm," he said, "playing at guard. Did you want to make out the lineup?"

"I could make out a better one than that."

I suppose a part of me thought I was joking—another of my jokes to muffle disappointment—but the words didn't come out that way. All that week I'd been meditating on what Shealy had told me at the party, as if there were something I'd do about it. Now in an odd moment I'd spoken up. Instead of stammering an apology, backing off, I was staring at Grupp, a few feet away. For years I'd swallowed whatever he had said. Suddenly I wasn't doing it anymore. I felt a swelling— fear? pride?—in my chest. It was as if I were being changed on the spot.

Grupp was staring at me bug-eyed. "What the hell are you talking about?"

"I can beat Kretchmer. It's not even a contest. I'll go one-on-one with him right now."

He took a couple steps at me. "What you think you can do one-on-one has nothing to do with it. What you even can do has nothing to do with it. I'm the coach, and I make out the lineup. If I want to start an eighth-grade team I'll do it. You got nothing to say about it."

"Sure. I know." There was a long pause as he tried to stare me down. "That doesn't make it right."

His nostrils flared, mouth sneered. For a minute I thought he was going to haul back and let me have it. His voice was a growl. "Take a shower, Keith."

The silence on that field was terrible. I walked through the players—who stared down, avoided my eyes—slopping through the mud, past the bleachers, toward the steps. The rest of the team looked as if they'd just seen a man condemned to the gallows, but I felt suddenly strong; if I'd taken a shot at the blocking sled I'd have snapped it in two. By the time I made the track I'd started to trot. I didn't know what was happening behind me. But Rosy told me later that Grupp had started to pace, still in that deadly silence, muttering, looking toward the ground. When I hit the steps he was staring at me, eyes flashing; if someone had handed him a rifle he'd have picked me off. He started to shout.

"Check the lineup card on Saturday, Keith. There might be a change on offense too. I go with the kids who are part of the team."

I was running by then, sprinting up the steps. When I got to the top I took off my helmet, spun, reared back, pegged it into the air, shouting (a wordless "Ah"): I can imagine that sight, the lone figure at the top of the steps, the helmet flying high in an arc, falling past the lights of the gym that shone bright against the darkening night sky.

"Turn it in, Keith." The voice was hoarse, shrill. Grupp had charged at me a few steps, his parka hood flying off. "Turn your uniform in. You won't be needing it anymore. I'll go with some kid who wants to play ball for me. . . ."

But I was running again, over the grass, through the high wide doorway of the gym, down the halls to the locker room. I ripped off my things and started throwing them, shoulder pads, hip pads, shoes, practice pants, mud and all. I opened my locker and tore it up, pitching things around. I knocked over a table. By the time I noticed someone at the door I was standing in the middle of the room, getting ready to tear the lockers off the walls. I stopped, I realized I had the shakes. It was Wiggins (Rosy told me that too, that he had started loping when I disappeared into the gym; Grupp was shouting, "Let him go. Let the little bastard go." But Wiggins kept running). Now Wiggins glanced around the room. "Fast work." He was holding my helmet.

"Yeah." I must have looked great, standing in the middle of the room in nothing but my shorts. By that time I was shaking so much I could hardly stand up. I walked over and sat on a bench.

Wiggins sat on the next one, about ten feet away. He put my helmet on the floor. "What happened?"

My head was in my hands. "I don't know. I couldn't take it anymore."

"Take what?"

"All his bullshit. Kretchmer starting on Saturday."

"That's not bullshit. It's going to happen. Especially now."

"I'm better than Kretchmer. I can murder the kid."

"That's true."

"I can beat every one of those guys starting. It's the same thing all over again. The same thing as last year. I should have played. I could hold my own with those guys. Beat them half the time."

"Not half the time."

"I could have helped the team. He should have played me. You would have played me."

"I'm a different coach."

"It would have meant so much." An ache like a sob choked in my throat. "My father . . ."

There was a pause. I had no end to that sentence.

"We don't play this game for fathers," Wiggins said.

That was all I needed just then, one of Wiggins's moralistic lectures about football.

"I hate the goddamned game," I said.

But his voice was quiet, softened, not his lecture voice.

"I thought you would understand, you more than anybody, after your father died. You can't play this game for a father. Either he's the kind who won't be satisfied or he's the kind that doesn't care. You're

263

working away trying to do something and he doesn't even notice. That's not what's important to him."

"He told me that once. I didn't have to play football."

"He didn't care what you were doing, I could see that when I met him. He just wanted to be there with you."

There was a long silence. We weren't looking at each other.

"But you didn't believe him," Wiggins said.

I nodded.

"You've got to get where you don't play for a father."

"For what then?"

"For the game."

"I'm so sick of that. Do this for the game. Do that for the game. Love the game. I hate the goddamned game."

"You're trying to use it."

"You sound like the rest of them. Love the game."

"I do not sound like them. You know I don't. And that's not what I said. It's not anything about football. It could have been something else. But it's what you're doing now."

"Maybe not."

"Maybe not. You got me there."

We sat again for a while in silence.

"I don't think you entirely chose the game," he said.

"I chose it. I went out that year. I was terrible at first. But I was going to show everybody. Coaches, teachers . . ."

"How many kids have I seen do that? And quit after two days. The game took hold of you. I saw it happen. You played as good a game on a JV field with twenty people watching as you've played anytime all year. You weren't showing anybody then. You were discovering yourself. All kinds of things. I know why people start to play this game. But that isn't why they keep it up."

"I liked playing for you."

"Because I made you play for yourself."

"That wasn't the only reason."

"It should have been." He had stood, talking to me, walked around the room, now was standing by the door. "You can't play for me. You can't play for Grupp, to show him he was wrong. You can't play to show anybody anything. They see what they want to see. Above all you can't play for your dead father. You'll break your heart playing for those things. You've got to play for the game. You've got to play for yourself."

I looked away from him, around that empty room. I hated his words. I didn't want to be alone out there. Who would play anything if not for someone?

"I'm glad this happened in a way." When the world ends, the mushroom clouds hovering all around us, Wiggins will be saying he's glad, in a way, that it happened. "It's something you had to go through. I'm going to try to get you back on the team. There's no guarantee. He's plenty mad." He shrugged. "But he does want to win on Saturday." He opened the door, walked out. It slammed shut behind him.

II

On Saturday everybody and his half-wit brother turned up. It was the first time in six years the Academy had had a crack at a league title in anything, and everyone was there, students, girlfriends, parents, younger brothers and sisters, grandparents, faculty, former faculty, administrators, alumni, trustees, friends of the school: jammed into the bleachers and stretched all up and down the sidelines, prosperous, ruddy-faced, wearing bright colors, breathing out steam, shouting for a winner. The game was in the morning, to give Northrup time to get back home. A dew almost like sleet lay on the grass, that all but crunched when you walked on it. A hard chill wind was gusting, but the air was clear, the sky a pale blue.

On Thursday, at Wiggins's suggestion, I had gone to see Grupp. I apologized for all I had said. I acknowledged that he had the responsibility for making out the lineup card, and that might include consider-

265

ations I had no idea of. I admitted that the kind of attitude I had shown was bad for team morale, and I apologized again. Grupp said he realized I hadn't meant what I'd said. He knew I had put in four hard years of work for the school, so he was going to let me keep my uniform for the last game. I thanked him. The whole time we spoke—in his empty science lab, with the lights off, as he was opening up for the day—there was an air of tension, as if two men who didn't really like each other were going through the motions of an apology for the benefit of an audience. But there was no audience. Thursday and Friday, in practice, I was still in the lineup on offense, but I didn't even get mentioned when we were practicing defense.

Northrup wore white uniform pants, jerseys a light bright green. Their offense was small, not a bruiser among them, but they jumped off the ball with one lunge, low to the ground. When their guards pulled or trapped they snaked right down the line past a row of digging spikes. On defense, too, they were lean, quick, rangy. In the middle they had monstrous guards, sophomore twin brothers, who didn't make any tackles, but clogged things up something awful, and their linebackers and halfbacks moved laterally like crabs, wrapped your ball carriers in perfect tackles. All through the league we'd had as good an attack from tackle to tackle as you could want, but those two oafs pretty much took it away from us.

Early in the first quarter Pollett broke one around left end, gunning past the linebackers and popping out of the safety's arms as if he had blasting caps in his thigh pads. That was one of those moments early in a game when it looks as if it won't even be a contest. The score was 7–0 before we even looked up. Northrup got their first points on a long drive in the second quarter, finishing up with a seven-yard keeper by the quarterback when our linebackers had gone for a fake the other way. We should have gone into the locker room like that, one touchdown apiece, but late in the half, on what looked like a simple end run, their halfback lofted a long cross-field pass that took everyone by surprise. The guy who caught it was all alone.

Grupp ranted and raved in the locker room, but no defense on earth would have diagnosed that play. Northrup had missed both extra points—their kicker was terrible—so when we came out for third quarter it was 12–7.

We began to realize in the second half that Northrup was mainly a defensive team. Those monsters in the middle took away the inside game. Their linebackers and secondary worked together like a Swiss watch; Shealy had two passes intercepted in the third quarter alone. Pollett was shiftier when he got up a head of steam anyway, but that was a frustrating afternoon for him. Time after time he'd get the ball, leaning a little to turn the corner, gliding along with his loose bow-legged stride, and wade into that waiting secondary, who was gathered and poised. He might spin, kick, straight-arm away from two tacklers, three, but it was like a swarm of dogs after a bear: sooner or later they'd get him cornered. That safety, in particular, wouldn't make another mistake after he'd had that one tackle broken. Just when it would seem Pollett had shaken loose, the safety would lunge in and slam shut on his legs like a steel trap. It was uncanny. Pollett would get up slowly, staring at the kid. It looked as if he'd met his match.

Late in the fourth quarter Shealy got hit a cheap shot after pitching out, and his knee went on him. The whole crowd grew silent, watching solemnly as the trainer had a couple of guys slowly lift him up and help him hobble around, but it was no use. He was all right, but he wouldn't be playing any more football that day. He couldn't have run two steps.

I didn't even remember what that meant—nobody did; we hadn't given a thought all week to Jamison's injury—until the new quarterback came running onto the field, his uniform as bright and clean as on the day it was made, that big cage of a face mask hanging from his helmet; he leaned forward a little as he stiffly ran and his butt stuck way out behind him. It was a good thing he had his helmet on, because one look at that face and Northrup would have known the game was over then and there. It hit me all at once. My God, no. Lietzke.

Everyone had already started to swear when Pollett stepped in front of us and hissed, "Shut up." We paled a little, stared at him. His jersey was oiled and damp, his face dirty, dark with anger. For a moment you had to admire the guy. Even after all the shots he'd taken, frustrations he'd had for four years, playing on a team that was nowhere near worthy of him, he hadn't given up. And he wasn't begging, like a cheerleader, pleading for one last drop of spirit. He was giving orders. "He can hand off," he said. "He can pitch out. You guys can still block. You'd better do it."

Lietzke, when he stepped up to the huddle, inspired a little less confidence. His mouth was dry, his face blood red. His hands trembled as he placed them gently on a couple of helmets in front of him. His eyebrows flipped around while he tried to call a play. Come on, Lietzke, I thought. Get it out. Say anything. "Strong right," he mumbled. "Twenty-nine sweep. On two." Brilliant.

The play where Shealy got hurt had given us a first down on our forty-three. Lietzke got the ball to Pollett going around left end for four yards. The next play he gave to Grunfeld off the strong side tackle for three. He tried the same play to the weak side, and Grunfield scratched and punched his way to a first down. We were all hitting savagely, trying to make up for what we didn't have. Lietzke hadn't done anything brilliant—Grupp, sending in the plays from the bench, was sticking with the basics—but at least he hadn't taken the snap and given it to a Northrup linebacker, the way he might have.

The next one Grupp sent in started off with Grunfield going right, blockers leading, but that was just a fake; after the quarterback had slipped the ball in and out of Grunfeld's gut, he was to spin and pitch to Pollett, who had already moved the other way. I was on the right side, and was to bump my man, get out behind the line of scrimmage, then change to the left, hoping to get there in time to pick off a half

I wasn't just supposed to watch my own three yards

on that play. My assignment, if I could, was to get downfield.

Things started off fine. Rogan led the blocking, Grunfield diving for the fake. He had a way of lunging over the ball that made you think he really had it. The fake must have been convincing. It even convinced Lietzke. He actually gave Grunfeld the ball.

Grunfeld was the most surprised man on the field. "Jesus Christ, Lietzke," he said—Rogan and several linemen have sworn to that—clutching at the ball and stumbling. He could have gone ahead and run, but nobody over there was blocking in earnest, thinking it was a fake. He started inside, moved to the outside, then, in desperation—the whole Northrup team was moving in on him, with no blocking in sight—pivoted and leaped, pegged it back to Pollett, who was way to the far side, about to turn the corner.

I don't know how it registered with me. If I'd stopped to think about it, I would have realized something was screwy. From my standpoint, the play was going too well. But I didn't have time to think. At some point I realized there were just three people left in the play. Pollett was taking it wide, heading out toward the sidelines, the safety was gliding to meet him, and I was barreling ahead on a straight line to the point where they would come together.

I know how it must seem. It seems I've told this long story about those years when I played football, and now, just to end it with a bang, I'm inventing a crazy spectacular play. But that's not the way it is. It may be that I exaggerated slightly elsewhere to liven things up (I realize this is a fine time to be admitting that), but it would be more accurate to say I just wrote all those other things to lead up to, try to understand, this one play, that I keep seeing again and again, as if it typifies my whole career. I see it happening slowly, a little from above, as if in a dream. That play *is* my football career: Pollett digging wide, seeing I was there; the safety gliding after him warily, knowing he would cut back; Pollett slowing about five feet short of the sidelines, faking outside, waiting for me to get there; the safety not even flinching at the fake; Pollett

269

cutting back inside, so the safety would be moving into my block. Pollett could use a blocker so well.

That moment. It is fixed in my mind as if the choice were still before me. When Pollett—who had run that famous reverse, a foot stepping into his own end zone, to break open the Hargrove game when Nick Kaiser and I were just breathless kids gawking from the sidelines; who perhaps was responsible for my not playing varsity for my father; who just days before I had seen kissing the girl I had been in love with for years—Pollett was carrying the ball. Just beyond him the crowd in the stands—students, girlfriends, teachers, trustees, that whole little society that three years before I had determined to please—stared intently. A safety stood poised who would dump Pollett if I didn't stop him, and what was involved was a championship for that school and that team and that coach about whom my feelings were so ambivalent. I like to think that for a few seconds there I was a free man, free of old loyalties, old encumbrances, free of my dreams, just alive on that piece of turf where everything was converging. The moment stands before me, waiting for me to act. What would I do?

I lowered my head and knocked the safety on his ass.

The crowd roared! Not for my block of course, but for the beautiful cut Pollett made stepping around us. I lay on my belly, watching the stands. The crowd had stood, all of them, shouting, waving their fists, every eye fixed on that fleet figure that raced down the sidelines. They were a little late; the play was already over. I stared.

Possibly somewhere in the stands was an old lineman who knew enough about football to have noticed my block, maybe even followed me out from the line of scrimmage. I knew there were guys on the bench who had seen it. My mother was in the stands, cheering because everyone else was ("Of course I saw it," she would say later, if I mentioned my block). Grupp was cheering, his heart about to burst, as he watched his boy take the ball in. Wiggins was cheering, not for the players exactly, but for the beauty of the play, the way it had all come together. A lot of people were cheering.

I lay there and watched. It was as if I were looking for the one in the stands who could have told me my block was good, that I was good for having thrown it, that my football career was a success, that I could be at ease; I raised up on my arms, straining, my eyes staring—I searched that crowd—but he wasn't there.

I WISH I could tell the rest of it. Not the celebration afterwards, when the Coke flowed like champagne and Grupp got dragged, sputtering, into the shower, Wiggins jumping in of his own accord; not the Fall Sports Banquet (which I attended alone, ignoring the athletic director's question of whom I had brought to "represent" me) where Pollett movingly and at agonizing length presented the championship trophy to Grupp; not the remaining days of the school year, filled also with their small successes; not even the day of graduation, when beside the Rose I marched with the rest of the seniors down the long hall to the gym, all of us resplendent in our white ducks and blue blazers, showered by the applause of the crowd, the last time—until about three weeks ago—that I ever set foot on that campus.

What I wish I could tell is beyond that, the way I tried to escape it all by moving on to a large university and wrapping myself in work as in a cocoon, until, as if by a miracle, I found myself reaching out to another human being. I wish I could tell about April and little Ben. Those seem to be other stories, belonging to other times. I'm not sure though. Sometimes I think it is all one story, that you pick it up here or pick it up there, tell it for a while, but it is all one story in the end.

I saw Rachel not long ago, on a trip home at Christmas time. We ran into each other in front of a bookstore on Murray Avenue. She told me she is an anthropology professor at a large university out west. I had heard that already, from my mother. Rachel smiled radiantly when she saw me, beamed at Ben, who just stared at her; when we parted she gave me a kiss square on the mouth. Just as well April wasn't along. April is jealous of all redheads. Rachel has grown her hair, in fact, and it hangs down her back to where it just about brushes her bottom. Her figure has blossomed a little from the time when she was eighteen. My father was right. I don't know how he knew. She is a ravishing beauty.

I still have dreams of playing football. Sometimes, in fact, it is just like the old days: I am lying on the couch, leafing through a magazine, and suddenly I am picturing the familiar scenes, myself as the ferocious middle linebacker, raging all over the field, taunting the opposition, cutting down ball carriers, batting away passes, or as one of the fabulous pulling guards, chugging wide ahead of a fleet running back and mowing down a helpless defender. April will look over at me— "Playing football again?"—and I will grin, sheepishly. But those aren't the dreams I'm thinking of. There are others, more complex, that take place at night and express, I suppose, a deeper part of myself.

In those dreams, the game in question is at night, away, at a field that is new to me but vaguely familiar, and the weather is inclement: a hard icy rain is pouring down, or it is so hot and humid that a fog is hovering over the field, or snow is gusting in a blizzard. My problem in the dream is always in getting ready. I am late getting to school, or I can't find my equipment bag, or I have the bag but my pads are missing.

Sometimes I am getting dressed with everyone else, but when they are ready and moving out of the room I notice that I have hardly begun. Always, whether dressing at home or at our opponent's gym, we are in the midst of an elaborate cagework, more like a trainer's room than a locker room; the lighting is bad, just one bare bulb, and the room is a mess, old equipment and first-aid materials lying around. The pads are ill-fitting, awkward; they won't tie or buckle correctly.

I do not seem uncomfortable with the people around me, but I don't know them.

Frequently I miss the bus—I have stepped out of the room for a minute, telling someone to be sure to wait for me, but when I come back everyone is gone—so I have to make my way as best I can, bumming a ride or hitchhiking. I am struggling along in the snow or rain, half-dressed in football equipment, trying to get to the game. When I finally do reach the field, standing outside a fence that surrounds it, the opposing team looks monstrous, lumpy in massive pads, but even that doesn't daunt me; I hurry along the fence, looking for a gate.

Often in those dreams my father shows up. Not in some crucial, logical way, as if he had some major role in the drama, but incidentally: he might pick me up hitchhiking, or he might be standing alone outside the fence where I am looking for a gate. It is wonderful to see him. I'm not sure of this, but it seems to me that during the dream I have some awareness that I am dreaming and that really my father is dead; still, he is very real in the dream, as if he might have changed, or I might find out something new about him, and I am glad at the chance.

He is standing relaxed, in old khaki pants and a rumpled shirt, maybe with his hands in his pockets, the way I remember him. He is gray, but not in the least thin or weak. He slouches a little, his shoulders sloped. It is nice to hear the sound of his voice, which I cannot remember when I'm awake. We talk for a while, joke about things, laugh. I don't know what it is we say, but it is an interlude in the dream; for a time I forget what I'm doing. I'm sure we never talk about football. For some reason, eventually I leave—even though I am so much enjoying our conversation—and began again my frantic search.

I've often wondered if he stays for the game. It's a crazy thought: the whole thing, after all, is a dream. But it does seem real, and I've often wondered if finally, in those dreams, I get a chance to play football for my father. I don't think I'll ever know. For one thing, as I've said, the game is always at night, so, as in that first varsity game I ever played—the one game, perhaps, when I was most content—the stands are all in a darkness, bright lights glaring down. But there is another reason that question will never be answered. For in those recurrent dreams I often see the teams on the field, the warm-up drills have sometimes taken place, the players gathered to line up for the kick—still I am racing around, searching for some trivial thing—but in those dreams of a frustrating search, a task I am never ready for, in those dreams of the night, my football dreams, the one thing that is always the same is that the game never begins.

About the Author

DAVID GUY was born and raised in Pittsburgh, Pennsylvania. He graduated from Duke University, where he studied writing and taught for six years. He is the author of an award-winning play, and reviews books for a monthly magazine. He lives in Durham, North Carolina, with his wife and son.

SIGNET VISTA Books by John Neufeld

☐ **EDGAR ALLAN by John Neufeld.** In this penetrating novel, John Neufeld examines the problems that arise when a white middle class family adopts a black child. (#Y6628—$1.25)

☐ **LISA, BRIGHT AND DARK by John Neufeld.** Lisa is slowly going mad but her symptoms, even an attempted suicide, fail to alert her parents or teachers to her illness. She finds compassion only from three girlfriends who band together to provide what they call "group therapy." (#AE1189—$1.75)

☐ **FOR ALL THE WRONG REASONS by John Neufeld.** From the bestselling author of *Lisa, Bright and Dark* comes a tender, taut novel about a teenager marriage that speaks of today. (#E9146—$1.75)

☐ **SUNDAY FATHER by John Neufeld.** The touching story of a young girl's painful adjustment to her parents' divorce. (#W7292—$1.50)

☐ **TWINK by John Neufeld.** The hopes, failures and courage of a young girl with cerebral palsy who could have been forgotten, and wasn't, and how love and touching and caring made the difference in the face of an almost overwhelming physical handicap. (#W9145—$1.50)

Buy them at your local

bookstore or use coupon

on next page for ordering.

Books from SIGNET VISTA

- [ ] **A BOAT TO NOWHERE by Maureen Crane Wartski**
  (W9678—$1.50)*
- [ ] **RUN, DON'T WALK by Harriet May Savitz.** (#AE1488—$1.75)
- [ ] **A FIVE-COLOR BUICK AND A BLUE-EYED CAT by Phyllis Anderson Wood.** (#Y9109—$1.25)
- [ ] **I THINK THIS IS WHERE I CAME IN by Phyllis Anderson Wood.** (#AW1482—$1.50)
- [ ] **I'VE MISSED A SUNSET OR THREE by Phyllis Anderson Wood.** (#Y7944—$1.25)
- [ ] **SONG OF THE SHAGGY CANARY by Phyllis Anderson Wood.** (#W9793—$1.50)
- [ ] **ADVENTURES IN DARKNESS by Derek Gill.** (#W7698—$1.50)
- [ ] **THE BETRAYAL OF BONNIE by Barbara Van Tuyl.** (#W8879—$1.50)
- [ ] **BONNIE AND THE HAUNTED FARM by Barbara Van Tuyl.** (#AE1184—$1.75)
- [ ] **A HORSE CALLED BONNIE by Pat Johnson and Barbara Van Tuyl.** (#Y7728—$1.25)
- [ ] **ELLEN GRAE AND LADY ELLEN by Vera and Bill Cleaver.** (#J7832—$1.95)
- [ ] **I WOULD RATHER BE A TURNIP by Vera and Bill Cleaver.** (#W9539—$1.50)
- [ ] **ME TOO by Vera and Bill Cleaver.** (#Y6519—$1.25)
- [ ] **GROVER by Vera and Bill Cleaver.** (#AE1313—$1.95)
- [ ] **THE WHYS AND WHEREFORES OF LITTABELLE LEE by Vera and Bill Cleaver.** (#Y7225—$1.25)
- [ ] **WHERE THE LILIES BLOOM by Vera and Bill Cleaver.** (#W8065—$1.50)

*Price slightly higher in Canada.
